A
LOVER'S
SIN

RAMSEY TESANO SAGA
III

ALTONYA WASHINGTON

A LOVER'S SIN

Copyright © 2012 by AlTonya Washington

ISBN: 9780982978160

Printed in USA by CreateSpace

To my awesome readers. This book and all those before it would not be possible without your support. It is the fuel that feeds my motivation.

FIRST PROLOGUE

Brooklyn, New York 1952~

"Lee me 'lone, Hump..." A groggy Aaron Tesano murmured when his brother nudged him awake. It was still in the early morning hours, still dark in the fifth floor walk-up they shared with their parents and younger siblings.

"I heard her, Ari. Let's go and see."

"She never yells..." Aaron, still groggy grumbled.

His little brother was right, Humphrey Tesano acknowledged even as frown lines bumped the black tendrils of hair that tumbled onto his broad forehead. Their mother was a lady as she often reminded them. According to Athena Tesano, *a lady never yells.*

Humphrey knew what he heard however. His mother *yelling* had pulled him from sleep.

"Close your eyes, Ari." Humphrey moved to the double bed he and his brother shared. He tucked in the homemade quilts around the little boy who had showed no signs of rising from the covers.

"Go back to sleep," Humphrey whispered.

"Mmm hmm…" Aaron nuzzled his head; matted with dark curls, deeper into his pillow.

"I won't have it, Liam!"

There it was again. The phrase clearly negated Athena's claim that a lady never yelled. Humphrey blinked, causing the hair just grazing his eyes to do battle with his long lashes when he blinked. He cast a quick look back at his sleeping brother and spared no additional time before making a hasty exit from the small room.

"The decision's been made, Thea!"

Humphrey was half way down the narrow dark corridor when his father's voice rang out. The man's bellow far outweighed his wife's angry yet higher pitched tone.

"Then why did you bother to tell me, Liam?!"

Humphrey made his way to the end of the hallway dotted with framed pictures of family and Christ. His toes felt chilled where they peeked out from the overlong cuffs of his blue and white striped pajamas.

Standing at the mouth of the hall, Humphrey realized why his parent's voices came through so clearly. They were in the dim, no-frills kitchen which sat right off the hall from his and Aaron's room. He wouldn't have to strain to listen in on their conversation.

Liam's and Athena's voices came through so clearly; in fact, that Humphrey could tell that his mother had been crying. Her voice wavered and shuddered as though she had been sobbing quite heavily.

"I'm telling you so you can start getting the house in order." Liam said, on his way to the icebox in the corner.

There, he pulled a block of aged sharp from one of the shelves inside.

"In order?!" Athena sounded incredulous and watched her husband through voluminous dark eyes. "Have you forgotten that I *am* getting things *in order*? *We* are expecting a baby, remember?" For emphasis, she smoothed both hands across her fully extended belly.

"In case you forgot, our own family will be growing in a few months." She said.

Liam cut a chunk from the cheese he'd selected. "I don't have the time to go back and forth on this with you, Thea."

"Apologies, husband, are you exhausted?" Athena's lovely olive-toned features were tight, belying the sudden sugary tone of her voice. "I suppose I'd tire too if I were just getting in at two-thirty in the morning from a night of fucking."

The knife hit the wooden counter space with a dull clatter. Liam straightened. "Mind yourself, woman."

"Mind *my*self?" Absently, she wiped her hands on the white apron at her waist. "Is that how you speak to your whores, Li? Do you tell those black bitches you run around with to mind themselves, Li?"

"Athena-"

"Obviously not if one of 'em's bold enough to expect your wife to care for *her* bastard!"

"He's mine too, Thea."

"And how do you propose we care for this one when we already have four and another on the way?" She moved to the counter and tapped five fingers to the surface.

"Thank God Humphrey's smart-thirteen and big enough to work. Just how do you plan on feeding this new addition? Or is your whore coming here to let him suckle at her tit?!"

"I've had enough of this, Athena!"

"Oh Liam my love…so have I- so have I. This makes…how many now? I'm beginning to lose track of all your Negress sluts!"

"That's enough!" Liam made a sudden rush forward and backhanded his wife's face.

Athena clutched the edge of the counter that was littered with a week's worth of copies of the *Wall Street Journal*. She curved both hands around the counter to keep from falling to her knees.

"Papa no!" Humphrey cried, rushing into the kitchen and to his mother. He held the woman tight against his lean, wiry body.

Liam blinked as though he were snapping from some daze. Sorrow pooled the obsidian depths of his long, probing stare. He raised a soothing hand to his wife and son while moving toward them.

"Get out!" Athena spat, thick black waves of hair had unraveled from the bun she wore. Her expression was pure venom. "Go back to your dirty black wenches and keep your cock out of me!" Bristling then, she pushed out of Humphrey's embrace and left the kitchen.

Alone with his father, Humphrey turned to pin the man with an unreadable look. Liam tilted his head as though trying to decipher its meaning. Unsuccessful, he left the kitchen moments later.

SECOND PROLOGUE

Sambava, Madagascar, 1989~

"Screw that," the young woman; who towered over the others, pulled them out of her path with the exertion of little energy. Bracing hands on either side of an elegantly carved door, she planted a boot square in the middle. Attacking it with a perfectly executed kick, she sent the white oak crashing in her wake.

"Jesus…" Santi Dumont breathed; her small oval face was a picture of awe in response to the vicious display of power.

Rain Su blinked, just as enthralled by the aggressive act. "Come on," she ordered her female companions with a nod. Together, they followed Maeva Leer into the soft-lit bedroom suite.

For a time, the girls were mesmerized by the sheer plushness of the room. They strolled the spacious area, taking in the ornate light fixtures. Beautifully embroidered throw pillows were strewn across the oversized suede sofas and loveseats situated throughout the aromatic suite. Extraordinary tapestries complimented the rugs over the oak hardwoods.

Unlike her associates, Maeva was left unimpressed by the lavish quality of her environment. The beautifully furnished, albeit disarrayed room held no affect for her. While the others surveyed the area, Maeva went in search of her sister.

"Hey look-" Lula Velez, cut herself short. She was about to marvel over a glassed in wall of wine goblets when she caught sight of a familiar shoe. Hurrying over to the pump, Lula was stooping to collect it when Maeva's full bodied voice roared from the remote bed area.

The other young women followed the wounded sound and were soon piling into the doorway. They were too stunned to move any further.

Evangela Leer was sprawled naked half in, half out of the massive bed that occupied almost the entire back wall of the room.

"What's wrong with her?" Maeva's dark eyes were focused on the bed where her sister lay.

Casper M'baye was already kneeling near the head of the bed. She was inspecting the nightstand and the uncorked vial she found there. After sniffing at the clear, plastic cylinder she raised it for her friends to see.

"They gave her something." Casper's mouth twisted into a grim line across her round face. She set aside the vial and then stood and carefully covered Evangela's prone form. "It's what they do now," she added sorrowfully.

"Looks like they recorded it too," Lula tapped a finger to the lens of the camera standing on a tripod in the corner.

Maeva made an indecipherable sound akin to animalistic rage and reached for the gun holstered at her hip.

Uneasy looks were traded between the other girls but words of caution were not instantly forthcoming. The young women knew that it was useless and quite possibly deadly to sway Maeva from whatever course of action she deemed fitting.

"We should get her back to her room," Casper's lone voice of courageous wisdom filled the air. "They might come back," she warned.

"Or send some of their friends to have a go," Saffron Manoa foreshadowed.

"They're dead." Maeva snarled. Un-holstering the .9mm, she checked the clip before returning the weapon to its leather sheath.

"Maeva...no..." Evangela's weak voice croaked as her sister was turning to stalk from the room.

Maeva's tall, broad frame and ruggedly lovely features appeared to soften at Evangela's words. At once, she changed directions going to settle to the bed where her sister rested.

It was an awkward sight to see one so imposing behave as meekly as Maeva did when she rested her big head on Evangela's delicate chest.

"They have to pay," she almost growled, nuzzling the top of her head beneath Evangela's chin.

"She's right," Santi agreed, moving toward the bed. "Somebody has to do something. It's bad enough that he gives us to them for reward, but now they're drugging us? Where will it end?"

Maeva growled again low in her chest, the words having stirred her tethered anger. "I'm going," she decided.

"No Mae," Evangela forced more strength into her voice.

"E-"

"We'll get them" Evangela told Santi before she could argue. "I promise you all that we'll get them, but not now. We aren't strong enough. Not yet."

"*I'm* strong enough." Maeva boasted, having pulled away from her sister to glare down into her face.

"He'd have them kill you and you know it." Evangela spat and then closed her eyes as a wave of dizziness enveloped her in its haze.

"I want all of them," she continued once the spell had passed. "The captain, his fucking brats, the doctors, that- that other one...the pervert... I want to bring down this whole fucking place but we aren't ready."

"E..." Casper licked her lips and glanced at the others. "What you're talking about it- it could take years. Decades even."

"Then it'll take years- it'll take decades. But, I won't half ass this and miss the chance to make them suffer." Evangela tried to sit up and accepted the boost from Maeva.

"But I can't do it alone." She said, once she was leaning back against her sister's unyielding form. She looked to Casper. "Years, huh? That's good. They'll have more to lose by then."

ONE

Paris, France~

Darby Ellis DeBurgh's vivid gaze was widened by fear
and apprehension as she observed the crazed atmosphere in
her midst. It was difficult to believe that the place had been
so serene; accentuated only by love and romance, moments
earlier.

She stood in the wide doorway of the café where
she and her husband had languished in desire and
contentment. The newlyweds; with whom the DeBurghs
had come to share in the celebration of robust futures,
would never be the same.

Darby was virtually unmindful of the bodies
rushing past her- in and out of the establishment. Police
canvased the area and took witness statements. A chilly
wind swept by and Darby wrapped herself tighter in the

drab gray blanket one of the emergency workers had draped across her shoulders upon their arrival. Darby felt her lashes settle downward as if they were weighted by some invisible force. She felt ready to collapse.

Thankfully, Kraven's arms prevented that as they enveloped Darby. He gathered her close, pulling her back against his broad frame. She took comfort in the refuge of his embrace. The scent of soap and outdoors clung to him, combining to form the evocative fragrance that he alone possessed.

"I'm getting you out of here," his voice thrummed through her like the pulse of a bass drum.

Darby dug deeply to find the strength to turn in Kraven's arms then. "How's Fernando?" She searched his striking green stare with her own, until he averted his gaze by focusing on her hands fisted against his chest.

"Contessa's riding with him in the ambulance to the hospital."

Darby pushed back tufts of the lush black hair that fell more heavily into Kraven's face when he bowed his head. "How is he?" She asked again, trying and failing to obtain eye contact with him.

A muscle flinched along Kraven's jaw, but he was otherwise unemotional. "Police will talk to us later about what-what happened."

"Kraven-"

"Lass please," he shook his head then and finally met her gaze with a look that proved his weariness. "Don't make me answer that." His affecting stare, shimmered with doubt.

Pressing her lips together in hopes of warding off more tears, Darby moved to her toes and hid her face against Kraven's neck.

***

A Lover's Sin

Seattle, Washington~

Quest Ramsey twirled his fingers between the ever-thickening mounds of onyx curls covering his little girl's head. Responding to her father's delicate touch, Quincee Ramsey gently nudged her head against Quest's palm. Mesmerized, Quest's hazy stare studied the twenty-month old's every movement. He uttered the softest laugh when she began to suckle her tongue and put herself to sleep.

Exercising the utmost care, Quest removed his hand; watched his daughter for another few moments, and then left the nursery.

Quest strolled the short corridor which connected the nursery to the master bedroom suite. There, he rested on the doorway to observe his wife unaware. His uncommon gray stare darkened with an enticing mix of possessiveness and desire as he studied Michaela fidgeting with the satin tassels of the petal pink teddy she wore.

Mick did a double take when she noticed her husband in the doorway. Forgetting the tassels, she moved to her knees and watched him from her position in the middle of their bed.

"She asleep?" Mick's query sounded hopeful.

Quest pushed off the doorjamb. "For the night-if we're lucky."

Mick let her eyes close as she pretended to swoon. "For the night...mmm," she dragged all ten fingers through her hair, adding more disarray to her already tousled curls. "What do we do with all that time?" She whispered.

"I got a few ideas," Quest gathered his wife close.

Mick splayed her hands across the chocolate-dipped expanse of his sleek chest. "Mmm...only a few?" She taunted, seconds before her mouth was taken in a throaty kiss.

      The couple tumbled back onto the center of the bed, kissing feverishly and savoring the closeness. Sadly, the bliss lasted for only a brief period before the phone rang from its perch on the night table beside the bed.

      "Dammit..." Mick almost growled the curse. "That's gonna wake her, mmm..." She cautioned just as a wave of sensation hit her when Quest circled a bare nipple with the tip of his nose.

      "I got it," Quest tugged Mick with him to the head of the bed. He barely lifted the receiver from its hook, before slamming it down without answering.

      Laughter filled the room in a soft melody. Kissing resumed until Michaela's cell vibrated loudly against the surface of the other night table.

      "Your turn," Quest grumbled, turning her toward the grinding phone.

      With his mouth charting an erotic course across her back, Mick found it hard to think of the phone let alone which button to push to silence the annoying grinding. She managed to grasp the mobile by the third vibration. Her intention was to reject the call until she saw the name on the faceplate. She sat up and offered her mobile to Quest.

      "It's Jasmine," she whispered, referring to Ramsey Group's Administrative Director Jasmine Hughes.

      The announcement gave Quest pause and he studied the phone Mick held out as if he were certain that his wife had mistaken the caller's identity. When Michaela gave the phone an impatient shake, Quest snapped to.

      "Jazz? What's up?" He reached over to brush aside Mick's hand when she moved to tie the tassels of her lingerie. "Mmm hmm," he replied into the phone in a clearly absent tone. "Right...wait-what?"

      Mick watched Quest leave the bed and she frowned when she noticed the look that had taken control of his face. She flinched when he barked a second 'what?' into the mobile's small receiver. Mick doubted she could have predicted his next move, had she been given a thousand clues.

In disbelief, Michaela watched her cool, unnervingly laid-back husband stumble into the armchair near the double doors leading to their private terrace. She scrambled from the bed and was kneeling before him seconds later.

"Quest? Baby?" Mick smoothed the back of her hand across his jaw.

Quest was holding the phone but had apparently lost interest or the ability to comprehend Jasmine's words. Mick could hear the woman calling out to him through the phone line. She pressed her hand against Quest's cheek while working to tug the phone from his grasp.

"Baby? Talk to me...Quest, dammit," she snapped and gave a final firm tug to the phone, managing to retrieve it from his hold.

"Jazz? Jazz!" Mick cried to cease the woman's speech. "What the hell happened?"

Michaela listened in silence for a few seconds before she sat flat on the floor next to the chair Quest occupied.

"Don't you want to know?" Tykira Ramsey asked her husband as they lounged on the pallet they shared with the twins.

The family had just finished the second in their super hero movie marathon. Unfortunately, Dinari and Dakari fell asleep halfway through the sequel. The boys were sprawled at opposite corners of the large quilt. Asleep, they had unintentionally left their parents to their own devices.

After long moments of delightful and naughty deeds, talk resumed and turned to the upcoming addition to the family.

"I just don't know if I want 'em to tell us whether it's a boy or girl yet," Quaysar Ramsey's dark, sinfully gorgeous features were relaxed in contentment as he sighed his opinion.

"So you *do* want to be surprised?" Ty almost laughed the words. Until then, it had been near to impossible to encourage a preference from the man.

Quay chuckled and moved his hand up and down Ty's back while he held her. "What surprises me is that it took us so long to get to this point."

Ty bit her lip and studied their interlocked fingers and the wedding bands gracing them. "A long time, but worth it, right?"

Quay's midnight stare was undeniably soft when he looked down at Ty. The love he felt for her shimmered as though alive in the depths of his gaze as he took in every nuance of her dark lovely face.

"Damn right," he murmured against her temple and then settled her to her back. "I never thought we'd get here," he said, rubbing a lock of her lengthy tresses between his fingers. "After a while, I made myself stop thinking about it," he smirked and triggered his right dimple. "At least, I *thought* I made myself stop thinking about it."

Ty's almond shaped eyes sparkled with the love she felt- had *always* felt for the man who held her tight.

Quay outlined her mouth with his thumb before flashing a devilish wink. "Gimme some," he beckoned a kiss.

Ty raised her head slightly yet eagerly and moaned when Quay had claimed her mouth.

The expectant parents were in the throes of an enjoyable kiss when the cordless on the coffee table began to ring. Quay had moved the heavy oak table next to where he and Ty relaxed at the base of an oversized lounge chair when the family gathered in the TV room for their movie night.

"You're closer," Ty said during the heated thrusting of her tongue against her husband's.

"Fuck it," Quay growled, happily content with his current endeavors.

"It's gonna wake the boys," Ty just managed to voice the warning before the kiss deepened.

That possibility got Quay's attention though and he reluctantly withdrew from his wife to reach for the phone. The lone dimple flashed in his cheek once again when he read the caller ID.

"Q, this better be damned good," he grunted the phrase to his twin while drawing Ty close again and settling back to the pallet.

Their lazy positioning lasted barely a few seconds more. Tykira sat up when she felt Quay tense beneath her. Quaysar sat up as well. His expression had gone cold with something Ty couldn't describe. She tilted her head inquisitively when he clicked off the phone without as much as a goodbye to his brother.

"Quay?" She rubbed her hand across his thigh. "Baby, what's wrong? What'd Quest want? Quay?" Tentatively, she reached up to cup his face between her palms.

Instead of replying, Quay pulled Ty into a crushing embrace that almost stopped her breath.

Taurus wouldn't let Nile by once he'd opened her passenger side door to the Mercedes Crossover. They were parked outside Carlos and Dena's home.

"You don't have to do this," he said and gave her a little shake. "You know I understand if you want to try getting through to Darby again."

"No," Nile tucked a lock of hair behind her ear and shook her head. "Kraven said she wasn't in any shape to talk so..."

"Hey..." Taurus pulled his wife close when she shuddered and her eyes filled with water for the fifth time since they'd gotten the news. "Let me take you home. I can come back-"

"No Taurus, no," She shook her head again and smiled weakly at the feel of his mouth brushing her temple. She swallowed down the sob in her throat and lifted her dark eyes to his striking champagne colored ones. "They're my family too and I don't want you to do this alone."

Taurus seemed convinced by the strength in her voice. He dropped a sweet kiss to Nile's mouth and then tugged her hand into the crook of his arm. Together, they headed across the wide brick drive of the house.

Dena Ramsey McPhereson was pulling open her front door before Taurus could ring the bell. With everyone getting settled in and seeing to various responsibilities left unattended; during Pike and Sabella's wedding event in Las Vegas, she hadn't seen or heard much from her family in the last few weeks.

Dena pulled her brother and sister-in-law into a double hug. "I want to hear all about everything! The wedding, Vegas, everything!"

A Lover's Sin

"Honey where's 'Los?" Taurus asked, smoothing his hand across Dena's arm beneath the chiffon sleeve of her robe as they headed through the foyer.

Carlos was arriving in the living room just then. He set aside the stack of folders he'd been leafing through and met Taurus and Nile for handshakes and hugs.

"What are you guys drinking?" Dena asked as she broke into a slow sprint across the room to the bar nestled between the bookshelves that claimed the entire back wall.

"Hold off on that, babe." Taurus barely raised a hand toward his sister. "We can't stay long. It's gonna have to be an early night."

Dena blinked, exchanging a quick look with her husband while turning from the direction of the bar. "Taurus-"

"Have you talked to Moses?" Taurus directed the question to his brother-in-law.

Carlos raised a shoulder. "Not for a few days, why?"

"We got a call from Kraven in Paris- he and Darby went over to meet County and Fern on their honeymoon-" Taurus blinked, surprised by a sudden inability to continue the explanation. He kissed the back of Nile's hand when she gave his a supportive squeeze.

"Fernando's been shot." Taurus said.

Dena cried out. Both hands flew to her mouth as her eyes widened to dark moons.

"Is he-" Carlos massaged his eyes, unable to finish the question.

Taurus shook his head. "We don't know much. Kraven called right after the ambulance took Fern. I haven't talked to him since."

Carlos' olive colored gaze narrowed. "But he's alive?"

Taurus nodded. "Kraven says it looks like he's losing a lot of blood, though."

"How's County?" Dena asked in a small voice.

"Pretty much in shock, according to Kraven," Nile said and left Taurus' side to go comfort her sister-in-law. "He says she and Darby haven't let go of each other since..."

"Jet's being prepped," Taurus said then, massaging the bridge of his nose. "We'll be ready to leave by ten in the morning."

Dena nodded promptly. "I'll get us packed."

"No, you won't."

"Carlos..." Dena's voice was a stunned whisper in response to her husband's decisive reply. Her bewilderment faded to resignation as she tried to read his guarded expression.

Carlos walked past Taurus and clapped his shoulder. "Get you that drink, man?" He offered his brother-in-law and kissed Nile's forehead on his way to the bar.

"*That's* why I couldn't go to Pike and Belle's wedding." Dena snapped once the men had their drinks and were gone from the room.

"Cherí..." Nile murmured reassuringly and went to pull Dena back into a hug. "Things could be getting bad again- he just wants to keep you safe. After all that's happened, can you blame him?"

Enveloped in Nile's embrace, Dena kept her gaze on the doorway Carlos had taken when he left with Taurus. "No," she said, "no I can't."

Josephine Ramsey had been a portrait of happiness that evening. Earlier that day, she'd received the surprise of a lifetime. That evening, she shared that happiness with two of her three sons and their wives over a festive dinner where she announced her engagement to her long time love Crane Cannon. The meal consisted of spectacular food, laughter and hearty conversation.

By dessert however, the mood had changed. Johari and Melina were seated on either side of their mother-in-law. Josephine had nearly fainted when Yohan returned to the table to share the details of the call he'd just received from Quest.

"Why can't they tell us anything?!" Josephine cried out to her eldest son.

Moses had followed his younger brother back into the private dining room that the family had claimed for the celebration. Johari relinquished her spot next to Josephine so that her husband could settle next to his mother.

Josephine studied Moses' face with a mix of hope and fear brewing in her eyes. Desperately, she curved her fingers into the front of his shirt.

"Kraven says they're doing everything they can for him." Moses squeezed both Josephine's hands in one of his.

"I should be there." Josephine trembled.

"We're heading over first thing in the morning." Yohan said.

"I should be there."

Moses was already shaking his head in reference to his mother's plan. "That's not a good idea, Ma. Let me and Yo handle it."

"Moses..." Josephine swallowed around the emotion lodged in her throat. Her eyes were flooding with tears. "I have to see him. You- you can't expect me to just- just sit here!"

Crane patted Melina's shoulder and she gave up her seat for him. Moses placed his mother in the arms of her fiancé and then he went to his wife and pulled her close.

Crane pressed a tender kiss to Josephine's temple and rocked her for several minutes. Moses and Yohan mimicked the action with their wives.

"Sweetheart," Crane cupped Josephine's chin and tilted her head up. He watched until her eyes met his. "I want you to listen to Moses."

"But Fernando needs-"

"Shh...now you know it wouldn't do him good to know you're there worried over him. You know that, don't you?" Crane tapped the corner of Josephine's mouth and waited for the nod that came some five seconds later.

"I can't just stay here worrying alone." Josephine shuddered the words into his suit coat.

Crane squeezed her jaw, urging her gaze to meet his once again. "You're not alone- you'll never be alone again. You know that too, don't you?"

Crane nodded to Yohan and Moses when Josephine was once again sobbing into his suit. "You two take care of your brother. Your mother will be just fine."

Moses and Yohan came close to kiss Josephine's head. Johari and Melina joined in and the family took refuge in a group hug.

***

Any intentions on the part of the Paris authorities to obtain a statement from Lord Kraven DeBurgh were thwarted by the two women commanding his attention then.

Darby had not strayed far from her husband. In truth, she'd only been gone from his side long enough to use the hospital facilities on two or three occasions. On the third occasion, Kraven came to seek her out; deciding that she'd been gone from his sight a little too long for his liking.

Contessa was not easily removed from her husband's side either once the ambulance arrived at the hospital's emergency wing. Kraven relinquished his hold on Darby just long enough to collect an almost hysterical County as she raged against the emergency room workers. She threatened them with gruesome bodily harm if they did not save her husband.

Kraven managed to convince her to come and rest with him and Darby in a waiting room that; wasn't as yet, filled to capacity at that time of morning. The three were in the midst of a discontented slumber when they were found.

Caiphus Tesano nudged his brother as they passed the open doorway and he noticed Kraven on a long seat across the room. Slowly, he and Hilliam entered the quiet, sparsely furnished room.

As softly as the brothers treaded however, it wasn't quite enough to allow them to catch Kraven unaware. His expression was nowhere in the neighborhood of inviting when his shamrock green gaze merely slit open to observe the men making their way toward him.

Caiphus greeted with only a nod and closed expression. Hill's expression was noticeably more animated as he grinned devilishly while surveying the scene meeting his ebony stare.

"Very nice," he complimented Darby who sat half-in, half-out of Kraven's lap. Her rump claimed a cushion while her legs were thrown across Kraven's thigh and her head rested on his chest.

Contessa dozed with her back reclined against Kraven's side as she clutched the arm he'd curved about her. Her legs hung over one of the arms of the long seat.

"Very nice indeed," Hill added in clear approval of his friend's lovely burdens. "I'm guessing she's yours?" He queried when Kraven tugged Darby closer and she turned her face into his neck.

"How's Fernando doing, Kray?" Caiphus brought the serious back to the conversation with his question.

Kraven's frown made his already uninviting expression even more menacing. "How'd you find out?"

"Ramseys already know." Caiphus shrugged.

Kraven grimaced. "Aye...I got word to them right after..." the grimace turned to a scowl and he'd say no more.

"Someone tried to contact Sabra in Vegas," Caiphus went on with the explanation. "Smoak got the call instead, called us- he hasn't told Sabra yet."

"How's he doin'?" Hill asked that time.

Kraven closed his eyes and rested his head against the wall. "No one's told us a fucking thing. He lost a lot of blood before they took him," he cleared his throat suddenly when his voice wavered on the last few words.

"So-"

"Hill? Not now," Kraven said, his eyes still closed.

Hill didn't abide by the warning timbre in Kraven's instruction. "Was this some freak shit, Kray? Or it connected?"

"Oh it's connected alright," Kraven's response came without hesitation.

"You found a note?"

Kraven nodded in answer to Caiphus' question. Then another scowl tightened his magnificently set features. The rich, sing-song tone of his voice harbored a cold, guttural undercurrent then. "How the bleedin' fuck do you two know about that?"

Caiphus looked to Hill who made quick work of filling Kraven in on the death of Brogue Tesano, Austin Chappell and Gram Walters.

"Austin was on his way to see Smoak when he was run off the road. His chest was crushed under the wheels of the car that did it."

"Jesus…" Kraven hissed.

"Brogue had his throat slit in his suite at Sabra's resort." Hill continued. "We found out about Gram through Moses. Taken out same as Brogue."

"Christ…" Kraven breathed that time.

"Notes were found with all the bodies. 'For your attention, E'," Caiphus added.

Kraven's stare locked with Hill's and they communicated wordlessly for several seconds. Darby shifted in her sleep and Kraven blinked as if to jerk himself back to the present. Turning his head, he grazed his mouth across her brow.

"Kray-"

"We can't talk about this here, Cai."

"Now calm down," Hill urged with a barely raised hand. "We know this isn't the time, but we're damn well gonna have to *make* time. Where're you guys stayin'?"

Still brushing his mouth over Darby's forehead, Kraven deflected his gaze toward some obscure point across the room. "Right now our residence is this damn seat. We could find ourselves visiting a funeral home next if you must know." He rolled his eyes and muttered another obscenity below his breath.

"You've got my number. Call me when you know more." Hill said, his pitch stare moving over Contessa again. "You shouldn't be so pessimistic here Kray. Fern's strong and he damn well knows what's waitin' for him back here." His fierce features softened slightly then. "You can best believe he's not gonna leave it without fightin'."

Kraven watched the brothers take their leave. Darby stirred again, her move claiming the brunt of his attention. Impressively long lashes settling over his eyes again, Kraven savored the stirring of her perfume and her curves beneath his hand.

"Kraven..."

In spite of the rage slithering inside him, he smiled when her lips moved across his neck.

"Shh...it's alright. Back to sleep, love."

TWO

Quinta do Lago, Portugal~

"**T**his is bullshit!" Evangela Leer was a woman fit to be tied. Such grotesque surprises didn't befall her- not anymore.

She shoved a platter of crystal coolers and a matching pitcher from the table. Her long, exotic gaze shimmered as it followed the shatter across the brick patio.

The earlier statement was indeed a false one for she had most certainly been the victim of a grotesque surprise. Ironically, it was one she herself had conjured to carry out, not to have turned around on her.

"Who ordered this?" She snarled, stalking the expansive patio like a caged lioness and she was just as beautiful. A train of white chiffon covered the matching satin gown beneath it. The material trailed her bare feet as she walked the patio.

"Well?" Evangela tossed the question toward Saffron Manoa, who simply threw up her hands.

The gesture didn't pacify Saffron's boss.

Evangela's licorice dark face was unreadable. She stalked over and braced hands to the table laden with four HD monitors from which Saffron worked.

"I pay you too much to throw your goddamn hands up at me," she hissed, "now surely a woman who can rig a dead man's cellphone can tell me how another man was shot before I gave the fucking order to put a bullet in him!"

"Calm down, E."

"Screw that, Cas!"

Casper M'baye sighed and pretended to maintain her focus on the Portuguese entertainment magazine she held. "Wouldn't be good for Mae to see you this upset," she softly cautioned.

The warning was effective in getting Evangela's attention which wasn't surprising. Casper had a knack for saying just the right thing to calm her friends. Such a talent in the midst of such a group had often meant the difference between life and death.

"Where is she?" Evangela came down from some of the anger she harbored to ask of her sister.

"Sleeping," Casper kept her tilted stare on the magazine.

"Do you think the new medication is working?" Evangela strolled toward the chaise Casper occupied.

"You know it's too early to tell." Casper's Senegalese lilt was soothing even in its firmness.

Evangela nodded, turning while bumping her fist to her delicately rounded chin. She retraced her steps to the table where Saffron worked. Walking behind the chair,

Evangela gave a playful tug to one of the woman's thick reddish brown dreadlocks.

"I'm sorry," Evangela dropped a kiss to Saffron's forehead. "Anyone who can rig a dead man's phone from another continent *is* the shit."

Saffron; who had been responsible for the call the late Brogue Tesano made to his cousin *after* his death, merely shrugged.

"I know I'm the shit, but right now I *feel* like shit for not being able to tell you why this happened or who's responsible." Saffron hung her head in order to massage the bunched muscles at her nape.

"Well at least we know one thing," Evangela folded her arms across her chest and commenced to bumping her fist against her chin again. "We know the bullet that took that son of a bitch down, didn't come from any of us."

***

Grindelwald, Switzerland~

Sabella Tesano played out a shaky tune along the stairway bannister as her fingers tapped the shellacked wood grained surface. She waited on her husband to finish his phone call, but then second guessed interrupting him for *any* reason when he slammed down the mobile and chucked a book at the nearest wall with a viciousness that caused her to flinch.

Belle took her courage in both hands, between her teeth and anyplace else that she could find it. Clearing her throat, she gathered the gauzy folds of her lavender negligée and took the few steps from the short staircase that led down into the chalet's living room.

"Isak?"

The murderous expression Pike Tesano wore, vanished the moment he saw his wife.

"Are you alright?" His deep voice was soft with the concern that enhanced it. "Did I wake you?" He asked.

"I needed to get up anyway," she shrugged one bare shoulder. "Are *you* okay?"

"Yeah," he went to pick up the book and set it to a black suede Ottoman. "I'm good."

"Right," Belle eyed the weighty hardback she'd seen him pitch clear across the room. "Who was that on the phone?" She queried carefully and saw the shadow reclaim his bronzed face.

He began to smooth fist to palm. "How much did you hear?"

"I only know that you were talking to Smoak." The liquid brown of her stare was riveted on his face as he came close and brushed his mouth across her forehead.

"Just family stuff," he murmured into her skin.

"Family stuff," Belle curled her fingers into the neckline of the lightweight sweatshirt he wore to prevent him from looking away.

"Just business stuff."

"That's a lie."

"Bella…"

"What happened?" She began to search his face with increasing intensity.

Pike squeezed her elbows and gave her a tiny shake. "Come sit down."

"No," she freed herself from his hold and stood her ground. The almond tone of her gaze shimmered with unshed tears. "Is it Sabra?"

"Baby no…" he closed his eyes and put a weary, apologetic smile in place, "she's fine," he swore, tugging her into the fiercest of hugs.

Sabella allowed herself to be handled for only a few moments. Then she was pushing him back. "Then what is it?"

"Babe-"

"What's wrong?"

"Bella-"

"Dammit, Isak!"

"Alright," he winced, tugging her close again. "Alright, alright, shh…" he spoke next to her temple. "It's Fernando." He squeezed his eyes shut for a moment when she shuddered in his arms. "Come sit with me now."

Belle had no choice but to oblige the command. Her legs had become water. She clutched Pike's wrists once they were sharing the loveseat that matched the black Ottoman.

"Is he…?"

"Baby no…" Again, Pike soothed her with the words and added the slow shake of his head.

"What then?"

"He's been shot- in France. Contessa's with him. He's being cared for, babe. They're giving him the best care." He took both her hands into one of his. "Your family knows. They're heading out soon to be with him."

Pike used his free hand to brush his thumb across a lone tear that had escaped her eye. "He'll be alright, babe."

Belle sniffled. "When do we leave?"

Pike bowed his head and worked the muscle along his jaw. After a moment, he set her back and fixed her with a stern look.

"Now listen to me, Bella. We aren't doing that. I'm not taking you over there."

"But why? I- why can't we?" The questions left her lips as quickly as the pleading tears collected in her eyes.

"That's it Bella. No."

"You're forgetting that he's *my* cousin." She put anger quickly in place of her upset.

Isak remained unmoved. "This wasn't a freak accident," he told her.

"How do you know that?" She stiffened and pulled her hands from his.

"Honey, Brogue's dead."

The sound of Belle's sharp intake of breath filled the room.

"Sabi-"

"She knows. Aside from your family and mine, no one else knows that it happened at her resort."

"But why?" The confusion in her warm stare cleared suddenly. "Did Smoak...?"

The inquiry made Pike smile. "He didn't kill him. But there is something... we don't have all the answers yet." His smile tightened. "Since that's the case, the last thing I can allow is for you- for you both to go into that." He smoothed his wide palms across her belly that was progressively swelling with their unborn child. "I can't have you walking into what could be certain danger."

But for the faint sound of the wind that stirred the freshly falling snow outside, silence hung heavy between the couple for the span of a few minutes. Pike could make neither heads nor tails of his wife's expression.

"I understand if you want to hit me," he tilted his head, trying to coax eye contact. "Have at it, if it'll help."

Sabella gave into tears instead. She didn't resist when Pike pulled her close again. "Tell me he'll be alright," she spoke amidst shuddering breaths.

Pike settled back on the loveseat and kept her near. "He'll be alright," he buried his handsome face in her chestnut brown locks and inhaled the freshness of her hair. "He'll be alright."

***

Fernando Ramsey's surgeons accepted that they would be unable to speak with his wife without Kraven and Darby DeBurgh at her side. Contessa was little more than a limp mass of flesh anyway. She could barely stand for more than six minutes before she was dissolving into a fit of tears and wounded moans.

That being the case, Kraven kept hold of his lovely, albeit distraught companions. He played the role of the rock even though his friend's injury had rendered him into little more than a bundle of nerves.

Dr. Claude Moritz met with the threesome in the waiting room where Kraven, Darby and Contessa had spent virtually all of the past seventeen hours. The doctor was in the midst of greeting them but County had no patience for such niceties.

"Will I lose him?" She blurted.

The surgeon's smile brought to life the laugh lines at each corner of his small mouth. Leaning forward in the chair he'd claimed before the long seat, he took County's hands into his own. "Madame Ramsey, it would appear that your husband has been blessed with an uncommon strength. In truth, we have never seen anything quite like it."

"Doctor, what are you saying?" Kraven frowned.

"We anticipated a serious injury- given the blood loss. However, the real challenge was in fact stopping the bleeding." Dr. Moritz looked back to County. "Monsieur Ramsey's wound wasn't life threatening. The shooter was eh...what is the word....? Clumsy. The bullet was in and out," the doctor slid his hand back and forth for emphasis.

"Still, the Monsieur lost a considerable lot of blood. The bullet grazed a vessel during its departure but we are confident that we've stopped the bleeding. Another few hours will confirm our belief."

County still hiccupped on sobs but her expressive brown eyes glinted with traces of hope. "He'll be okay?"

Claude Moritz nodded once perfunctorily. "We believe that he will, Madame."

The tears released themselves when County let go of a happy gasp and squeezed the surgeon's hands. Dr. Moritz smiled while the small group uttered a collective sigh of relief.

"Can I see him?" County scooted to the edge of the seat.

"I think that would be just fine. I warn you Madame that the Monsieur is still under heavy sedation. It could still be quite some time before he's able to converse with you."

"I don't care," County shook her head like a small child. "I'll sit in a chair and just stare at him if you let me."

Dr. Moritz was delighted and threw his head back for quick laughter. "I'm sure we can find you something more suitable than a chair, Cherí. Perhaps, you could use some of the sleep your husband is getting, yes?"

"Yes." Kraven provided his agreement. "The Madame could certainly benefit from better rest than she's gotten on this chair."

"Exactly my thoughts," Dr. Moritz stood and offered a hand to Contessa.

County suddenly showed signs of hesitation. She bit her lip and looked from the doctor's extended hand to Kraven and Darby on either side of her. After seventeen hours of a most hellacious experience, the three had bonded beyond explanation.

Kraven nudged County's knee with his and then he brushed a kiss across her cheek. Cupping her chin, he gave it a reassuring squeeze. "We won't be far, okay?"

"We can have my nurses provide bedding for the both of you as well." Dr. Moritz smiled at the DeBurghs.

"See love?" Kraven dropped a second kiss to the top of Contessa's head. "Now go be with him."

County nodded, blinking remnants of tears from her spikey lashes. She drew Darby and Kraven into clutching embraces and then nodded toward the doctor and stood to follow him from the waiting room.

Darby expelled the breath she had subconsciously been holding and at once drew her husband's focus.

"We should turn in too, lass." He squeezed her nape while drawing her down the seat towards him.

Darby set her forehead to his bicep hidden by the long sleeved shirt he had worn beneath the sweater he'd shed several hours earlier. She indulged in only a few revitalizing breaths before pulling away.

"You go on. I'll find you." She smiled with effort.

"Have you lost your mind?" He sounded half stunned, half amused. "Surely you have if you think I'll let you out of my sight."

"I just don't think I can sleep." Darby rubbed her eyes and then braced a hand to Kraven's thigh and shoved to her feet.

"Is that a fact?" Kraven didn't know if humor or exhaustion produced the chuckle he exhorted. "Not sleepy, huh? I could've sworn you were the other unconscious woman I was holding earlier."

"It's not helping," Darby hugged herself and crossed to the other side of the room. Her skin was gooseflesh under the black knit Henley top she'd worn beneath the sweater that was now stained with Fernando Ramsey's blood. "Every time I close my eyes I..." she shook her head.

"You what?" Kraven had left the long seat and come to stand behind his wife.

Darby hung her head, sheltering her face behind the mass of her curls. "I see it… the blood… so much of it, I…"

"Lass…" Realization hit Kraven so suddenly, it almost staggered him. Regret weighed heavy on his eyelids and he shut them. How could he have forgotten what that must have done to her?

He was intrigued and partly envious of the fact that she was so unaccustomed to the sight of violence and blood spatter. That the presence of such a thing could instill shock and unease was alien to him. Yes, he envied her that reaction. He'd spent his entire adult life in a world where such a thing was commonplace.

"Love," he murmured the lone endearment into her hair, having pulled her back flush against him.

Darby turned as though she were compelled. She hugged him with a desperation that should have stopped his heart.

"Will you lay with me?" His low voice was still muffled by her honey blonde curls. "I can't rest without you."

Darby sniffled and could only nod eagerly while her face was hidden in his neck.

***

"Do we have anybody there who can give us a report on his wounds?" Rain Su inquired during the conversation that carried on while she and her colleagues indulged in drinks that evening from the sitting room of the villa that had served as their base of operations for the past ten years.

Saffron had managed to locate the hospital where Fernando had been taken as well as the ambulance he'd been transported in and the surgeon who had performed the operation.

Evangela was studying the wine goblet recently emptied of her third drink. She was sorely tempted to smash it against one of the brick walls in the room. She recalled Casper's valid warning earlier and eased a look toward Maeva. The woman appeared content, chugging down a bottle of ten year old Merlot.

Concern filling the haunting dark of her lovely stare, Evangela shifted a glance toward Casper. The woman shook her head as if reading Evangela's question and assuring her that there was no real cause for concern that the alcohol would adversely react to Maeva's new medication.

"Hell, can't we put somebody in there?" Santi Dumont blurted, eyeing Saffron's fingers as they worked feverishly over a keyboard.

"What about finding the son of a bitch who stuck his nose in our business?" Lula Velez was almost as fit to be tied as Evangela.

"And *why* he stuck his nose in it," Saffron murmured, never once veering from her intense typing spree or pulling her eyes from the monitor she viewed.

Rain frowned. "You think somebody's trying to set us up?"

"Nobody knows us or what we were planning." Saffron's tone was matter of fact.

"Are you serious?" Rain set aside her glass and leaned forward in the red cloth swivel chair she claimed. "Have you forgotten about all those little pieces of paper we've been leaving at the scenes of our most recent crimes?"

Everyone looked to Evangela seated in the furthermost corner of the room. It had been her idea to leave behind the messages.

"Sorry E," Rain studied the bridge she made with her fingers. "I know you had your reasons, but maybe we should have waited to reveal all that once the job was completely done."

"Evan knows what she's doing." Rough and disconcerting, Maeva Leer's voice rose from the corner she resided in with her bottle of red wine.

The rest of the group exchanged covert looks, but made no comment. They had all privately questioned the truth in *that* statement since Evangela's insistence that Maeva maintain a place in the group.

The woman's erratic and clearly psychotic behavior had cast little; if any, doubt in her sister's mind that Maeva was up to any and all tasks assigned to her. Given that many of the more brutal requirements of their organization were often delegated to Maeva, no one complained much. Over the last several years however, it had become apparent that Maeva was dissolving into an increasingly unstable state.

"Maybe we can make lemonade out of this piss," Evangela left her spot, twirling the stem of the empty wine glass between her slender fingers. "Somebody in that hospital might be able to tell us about his injuries. We might have the chance to get to him after all."

"Make him suffer…" Maeva chuckled and downed more from the bottle she gripped by the neck.

"Don't we have someone there already?" Casper asked, smoothing both hands across the red leggings she wore.

A Lover's Sin

"Think, think…" Evangela commanded herself as she walked the artfully designed room. Then she stopped and turned with one hand tapping the top of her head.

"It'd be easy to get somebody in there," she boasted, "but we need to know what we're dealing with first. Chances are, every member of the bastard's family is either already there or on the way." She perched on the corner of the long table where Saffron worked. The vibrantly colored satin skirt swung gracefully at her ankles.

"We need to know all this, before we make another move…" Silence held while Evangela thought over the next part of an impromptu plan. She snapped fingers in front of Saffron's face without turning to look at her.

"Get me a clean line," she said.

THREE

At Dr. Moritz's urgent request the attending nurses found the DeBurghs a room one floor down from where Fernando was in recovery. Though she'd joined her husband so that *he* could rest, it was Darby who fell off to sleep shortly after they were snuggled against each other in a small yet surprisingly comfortable bed.

The orderlies had brought in two of the standard sizes but Kraven opted for sharing one with his wife. Darby wasn't about to complain. The steady, strong beat of Kraven's heart willed her into a contented snooze.

Kraven sadly acknowledged that he wouldn't be visited by sleep anytime soon. He was satisfied enough however by Darby's breathing as she slept. Nevertheless, his mind raced with memories of the last several hours and what the immediate future was about to bring.

Revenge. It was revenge pure and simple. Though it was still unclear what deed was actually being avenged. There had been so many vengeance-worthy deeds that he and his cohorts had carried out 'under orders' and of their own accord.

Kraven closed his eyes and attempted to rub disturbing images from behind his eyes. As they were in his head, they weren't going anywhere. They'd been with him for too long. They had however blessedly dimmed the moment he met Darby Ellis. He smiled then, the action narrowing his deep set greens in a manner that was soothing rather than harsh. He inhaled the soft fragrance of coconut that held her curls.

He had pursued her with a ruthless intensity. Using every weapon he could conjure to woo her, she fell as deeply for him as he had for her.

He didn't doubt his wife's love in the least. But now; as those 'vengeance-worthy' deeds began to regain sharper focus, he had to wonder whether she might have second guessed becoming Lady to a Lord with a past as dark as his.

The annoying thought was punctuated by a dull grinding which radiated from one of the two phones on the night table near the bed they shared. Gently, so as not to awaken Darby, Kraven eased his free hand from beneath his head and grabbed the shuddering phone by its third vibration.

It was Darby's mobile and Kraven smiled at the sight of his mother-in-law's name on the face panel. "Well, well if it isn't the very lovely Miss E," his soft spoken greeting lacked nothing in the way of charm.

It worked wonders if Lisa Ellis's resulting purely girlish giggle was any proof. Kraven's smile transitioned into a more genuine grin when the sound emerged from the phone's speaker.

"Kraven this is a surprise. I thought I had dialed Dar's number." Laughter still colored the woman's words.

"Please don't hurt my feelings by telling me this is a bad surprise?" Kraven teased.

"Hearing *your* voice?" Lisa blurted. "Sweetheart, any woman who believes *that* should have her ears checked."

Kraven joined Lisa in a soft melding of laughter and then explained that he'd answered Darby's phone while she napped.

"Well that's good news." Lisa's tone was a sigh. "I was just telling that girl last week that she needed more rest from that business of hers. Kraven... is she just tired? She's not ill, is she?" Concern had overtaken the ease in Lisa's voice.

"She's just very tired, Miss E. Starting that business wasn't easy, but she's worked wonders in a short span of time," Kraven championed.

"*Working wonders* can take its toll, though."

"Agreed," Kraven looked down at Darby sleeping against him. He wound his index finger about a curl and watched it cling. "Don't worry yourself Miss E. I won't let your little girl out of my sight. I'll see she gets the rest she needs."

"You're a sweetheart Kraven but don't you spend so much time with my hard headed child that you neglect your own sleep, you hear?"

"I hear you Miss E."

"I mean it, hon. You sound pretty drained yourself."

Kraven grinned. "Miss E, is this a mom thing? Sensing this stuff?"

"It's a *parent* thing. I think you'll understand that better once you and my daughter give us our grandkids."

Kraven uttered another soft round of laughter. "How's the Colonel?" He referred to his father-in-law Sean Ellis.

"Doing well and just as eagerly awaiting those grandkids I mentioned."

The faintest furrow between Kraven's brows drew the heavy onyx lines closer. "I can promise you both that we're at work on it." He grimaced over the lie. The fact was that his wife wasn't quite on board with the whole grandkids thing yet.

From her home in Monterrey, California, Lisa Ellis appeared pensive. She didn't need to use her 'mom sense' to hear the tension in her son-in-law's deep, melodic voice.

"You just have Darby give me a call when she's feeling up to it." Lisa instructed, deciding against questioning whatever else may have been amiss.

"I promise. It'll do her good to hear your voice." Kraven cleared his throat in an effort to mask his weariness.

It didn't work and Lisa Ellis decided not to ignore her instincts that time. "Honey, what's wrong?"

Kraven hesitated only briefly before apologizing for upsetting Lisa. He proceeded to inform her of their whereabouts and then quietly filled her in on the awful events that had transpired.

"Does she need us there?"

Kraven listened to Darby's soft breathing for a few milliseconds before responding. "I think she'll get through it just fine but maybe once we're back in Scotland a visit would be a good idea."

"Take care of my baby, Kraven." Lisa's words travelled on a shuddery breath.

"It's the most important thing to me." Kraven pushed Darby's hair away from her face. "Say hello to the Colonel for me," he used his preferred handle for Darby's father who was retired Army.

Once the call with Lisa Ellis had ended, Kraven returned the phone to the nightstand and gingerly slid down into a more prone position on the narrow bed. Despite the care he took with his movements, Darby roused just slightly from her sleep. Lazily, she attempted to make room by moving nearer to the wall the bed was set against. Kraven wouldn't have it and kept her snuggled in tight next to him.

"I heard you talking..." Darby's sleep-drugged voice was a whisper.

"Ah damn, you caught me..." Eyes closed, Kraven smiled. "I was on the phone with an incredible looking older woman."

"Mmm..." Darby smiled drowsily. "I always suspected there was something between you and Ms. Elena." She referenced Elena Wallace who owned a lovely dress shop in Near Invernesshire, Scotland- the place the DeBurghs called home.

"I miss it." Darby's voice sounded more lucid. Her words quieted Kraven's full laughter over her earlier comment.

"I want to go home," she said.

"Soon petal..." Kraven murmured the endearment into the top of her head while planting a hard kiss there. "I just asked your Mom about her and your Da coming over when we get back. Miss Lisa's who I was talking to."

Darby pressed a hand into Kraven's broad chest. The unyielding surface felt like iron beneath her touch when she used it to push herself up slightly. "Why didn't you wake me?" her emerald eyes narrowed as she struggled to stifle an unexpected yawn.

Kraven closed his eyes again. "Miss Lisa made me promise not to and I always do what I'm told." He set a free hand behind his head and appeared completely relaxed.

Darby bit her lip and studied the fiercely beautiful features crafted upon the rich copper-toned pallet of his face. "So if I were to tell you to let me handle a little business?"

"I'd say you need to rest."

"I *have* rested."

"Not enough. Besides," he gave her waist a pat and then tugged her down more securely against him. "I'm missing home too."

"In what way?" She could feel her heart zoom right up into her throat and was riveted by the intensity of his stare.

Kraven focused gaze and attention on undoing the short row of buttons at the bodice of her top. "I miss our bed- miss you in it." His rich, sing-song tone held a ravenous heat. He tugged at the open top until it; along with a black lace cup bra, revealed one heavy breast.

"I haven't had you there in weeks," he muttered as if he were speaking to himself.

"You've had me other places," her words were a lengthy gasp and she felt her intimate walls contract when he fondled a nipple.

Kraven gave her a rough tug, drawing her up high over him. "I do what I must," he groaned just as his perfectly sculpted mouth covered the nipple he'd uncovered. He suckled madly, while keeping his wide hands in place at Darby's hips.

48

A Lover's Sin

Her lashes fluttered as she ground herself against the shocking length of his sex under the jeans he wore. "The doors don't lock," she cautioned.

"Be quiet then," he spoke amidst tonguing her glistening, rigid nipple. He made quick work of her jean fastening and unceremoniously tugged down the denims along with the panties and tights she wore.

Their movements were awkward in the narrow bed, yet there was a poetic beauty to their endeavors as they took off or merely shifting clothing en route to obtaining maximum closeness. Darby pressed against the thick slabs of muscle forming Kraven's awesome chest and she angled herself upward to remove her disarrayed shirt and unfastened bra. The hunger heating her took on a scorching quality wholly due to the man beneath her.

As usual, one look from her husband beckoned her mind and body. She was at once willing and desperately eager to surrender to whatever erotic intentions that came to his mind... or hers.

Little time was taken with foreplay however. Too many hours had passed; too many horrors had clouded over and crowded out previous pleasures. They needed each other far too much.

Kraven's lop-sided grin sent Darby's heart flipping when he settled intimately against her.

"Apologies, Lass..." he murmured, trapping her thighs in his grasp, "I should be taking more time with this body."

"Make it up to me later, then," she moaned. The words had scarcely cleared her lips when the generous length and thickness of his sex filled and stretched her.

"Over and over again," Kraven groaned the promise while lowering his magnificently crafted face into the fragrant crook of his wife's neck. "Over and over..."

The helpless softness of his tone sent triumph surging through Darby. The ability to render weakness over someone so powerful was beyond heady. She pushed her fingers through her hair, nuzzling her head deeper into the pillows and curving her hips into his deft thrusts.

"Hell," Kraven winced as the commanding need for release took charge of his hormones. He wanted more of her, but his body had other demands. "Stop moving," he groaned in Darby's ear.

"Get out of me if you want that."

He laughed weakly. "You're a mouthy wench."

"So I am... you've never had a problem with that before."

"Shut it," keeping his face sheltered in her neck, he gave her his index and middle fingers to suckle.

Darby hungrily obliged, moaning as she licked the digits and increased the wicked rotations of her hips. The moves of course did nothing to stifle Kraven's stormy need to come heavy and immediately inside her. Her tongue stroking and gliding over and between his fingers was sure to be his undoing.

He took his revenge however, pulling one of her thighs away from his hip and pinning it to the thin mattress. Darby fisted her hands against his incredible and unyielding chest. The chiseled wall of muscle was partly visible beneath the shirt she opened but had not pulled off his back. She bit her upper lip to silence the cry that his increased stroking depth instilled.

Darby felt stretched anew and in the most delicious way. Impossibly, Kraven seemed to widen and lengthen the deeper he buried himself inside her. Darby felt potent levels of moisture streaming from her core. The wetness pooled beneath her bottom to fuel the volume of the slurping sounds that colored the air with sex.

Kraven cradled her ample derriere, lifting Darby high into him. He groaned tortured when his fingertips grazed the wet spot she'd made in the bed.

"Nurses aren't going to like that," he chided.

"The orderlies might appreciate it," she nibbled his ear while uttering the tease.

Kraven's eyes crinkled to green slits when he chuckled. "Good to know my efforts are appreciated." Seconds later, his tongue was engaging hers in an explicit battle.

Darby raked her fingers through the lush, pitch locks that framed his darkly gorgeous face. She assaulted his tongue as sensually as he did hers.

Too soon, Kraven was breaking the X-rated kiss. He rested his head at her collarbone, chanting her name while she finished him in the sweetest way. Darby cried out when his hands flexed almost painfully on her body. Whatever discomfort the move may have roused though, was fleeting- ushered away by wave upon wave of delicious sensation.

Darby climaxed on the feel of his release filling her as potently as his devastatingly crafted endowment. Her rounded nails grazed the scars that provocatively marred his body. She left faint bloody half-moon impressions when orgasm forced her to dig the French tips into his taunt, bronzed flesh. Sweat-drenched and satiated, the lovers drifted into a weighty sleep. Their limbs entwined and their bodies remained intimately connected.

***

Las Vegas, Nevada~

"Is she very upset?" Smoak Tesano was asking his brother when they spoke by phone early that morning.

Pike's resulting chuckle held a half-hearted quality. "I think she can't decide whether she wants to beat me to death or strangle me."

"Not the honeymoon you expected, huh?" Smoak noted with a sympathetic smile softening his fierce dark face.

Pike's laughter was slightly more robust that time. "So long as she's with me, I don't give a damn."

"Understood," Smoak grinned, comforted by the genuine happiness in his older brother's voice.

"So how's Sabra doing?"

Smoak felt the muscle flexing along his jaw when he stroked it. "I haven't told her yet. She'll want to be on the first plane as soon as I do."

"That a good idea?"

"Hell no," Smoak nudged his fingers against a sheaf of papers along the edge of the massive walnut desk in the study he now shared with Sabra. "But I've learned how to pick my battles with her and this is one I don't have time for with everything else on my plate."

"How many guesses do I get to figure out what that means?"

"I'm not interested in waiting for Hill to tell us what he wouldn't before."

"So what do you want to do?"

"Everything that's happened is connected." Smoak had left the study and was then walking through the large dim apartment en route to the bedroom wing. "I think I've got enough of the pieces to find the rest and I need to put more of this shit in place before I talk to our brother again."

"This is a fuckin' tangled mess," Pike groaned over the phone line. "Dad wants us to clean up the family and now comes *this* crap out of nowhere. You think the murders are connected to what he told us in Vegas?"

"I think they are, but I don't have enough to go on to say for certain." While he walked and talked, Smoak absently massaged the silky hair that tapered at his neck. "I hope that's about to change…"

"What the hell are you planning?"

"Planning on tracking down that bitch who came knocking on Sabra's door a year ago, for one."

The line carried on silence for a time. On the other end, Pike was recalling his brother's description of the strange visitor whose arrival prefaced the death of Austin Chappell an old friend of Hill's.

"That won't be easy, man." Pike forewarned. "Hill won't tell you a damn thing and Sabra didn't know her- it was like she just popped up out of thin air."

"Not thin air," Smoak stopped by the long message table behind a sofa in the living room. There, he studied the photographs of the woman that had been generated from the security cameras in the corridor outside the suite at Sabra's resort where Brogue Tesano had met his death.

"Someone knows who she is," Smoak sounded confident even though his research into Rain Su's background had as yet proved unfruitful.

"I'll turn up something soon," he said while studying the woman's image.

"Can I do anything?" Pike asked.

Smoak dismissed the photos and continued his stroll toward the bedroom suite where Sabra still rested. "Just take care of my sister and my niece," he grinned.

Pike's laughter was at its most genuine then. "Predicting a girl, huh? Getting soft in your old age?"

"There's too much testosterone in our family." Smoak rubbed his fingers across the washboard slab of muscle that was his abdomen. "Tables been stacked against

Ma for too long," he added, heading into the room and over to the double king bed in the corner.

"Got a point there. I'll let you know when *we* know." Pike promised.

"Good deal." Smoak had settled to the edge of the bed and toyed with Sabra's hand where it peeked out from beneath the coverings. He brushed his thumb across his engagement ring on her finger. "I'll talk to you soon, alright?" he said to his brother.

"Watch your back," Pike cautioned before disconnecting.

Smoak bounced the slender mobile against his palm and then set it aside before he leaned close to rest his face against Sabra's shoulder. He allowed a few more seconds to pass before he kissed her cheek.

"Wake up, Sweet."

***

Dena inhaled sharply and then slowly moved into her husband's office. Carlos McPhereson could not be classified as a homebody by any means yet that was precisely the role he had been playing since shortly after reconciling with his lost love and re-claiming her for his own.

Dena paused on her trek into the study and observed him. She watched him ensconced in the work space he had fashioned from their home and wondered how long he'd be content there. After all, men like Carlos McPhereson *made* things happen. They corrected things, righted wrongs.

They protected their own- a silent voice reminded her. Dena accepted that as the reason she had been a virtual prisoner in her own home. Not that she had complained much over her present circumstance. It was certainly no hardship to be at Carlos McPhereson's beck and call.

Dena sauntered up behind him where he sat on a worn black and gray sofa. She raked her nails across a heavy bicep that was bare thanks to the wife-beater he wore outside faded sagging denims.

Carlos had already sensed his wife's presence the moment she'd arrived at his study door. "Wondered how long it'd take you to walk in here," he idly noted, the soft olive green of his gaze focused on the notebook he held.

"You looked busy," Dena's dark eyes followed the path she trailed on his skin.

Carlos tossed the notebook to the coffee table before the sofa and waited. Dena recognized the cue and walked around in front of the chair. Raising the flowing hem of her rose blush satin and chiffon lounge dress, she straddled herself across his lap. At once, Carlos was cupping her bottom to settle her more appreciatively against his groin.

The move stimulated the most exquisite sensations and Dena tilted back her head while savoring them. She rotated herself into him, her fingers traveling to the scoop bodice of her dress where she lowered the thin straps from her shoulders.

Carlos toyed with one of the straps where it dangled. "What do you want?" He followed the movement of her lowering the second strap.

Dena blinked, the barest hint of surprise taking hold of her dark, doll-like features. "I want *this*," she gasped at the feel of his fully extended sex; a result of her grinding efforts.

"And what else?" His other hand roamed the length of her thigh.

The query effectively ceased Dena's grinding. She fixed Carlos with a stale look. "I want to go. I want to see how he is."

55

AlTonya Washington

"No." Carlos' rich voice was flat and held not an ounce of sympathy.

She shook her head and looked incredulous. "But why-"

"Because I said so."

"He's *my* cousin."

"And you're my wife."

The counter reply stirred the heart flutter that never quite settled when Dena simply thought of the man who held her then. How long had she mourned the ending of their relationship all those years ago? Having him again was like a dream that she never wanted to awaken from.

"Now may I please have what's beneath this?" Carlos was asking, already gripping a mound of the delicate dress material in his fist.

Thoughts returned to pleasure, Dena resumed her grinding.

***

The previous evening had been blissfully uneventful. The nurses had informed the DeBurghs that the Ramseys were resting comfortably. The couple even received a room to room call from County who told them the doctors were very encouraged and satisfied that they'd stopped the bleeding.

Morning arrived and; with the dull shimmers of sunlight working its way through the blinds, Darby enticed her husband into more of what they'd shared hours earlier. Needless to say, the linoleum flooring beneath the bed would require an extensive buff job upon their exit. Kraven promised to leave a check for the damages.

He had gone to get them a more filling breakfast than what they'd scrounged up from the hospital cafeteria. During his absence, Darby made use of the shower, dressed in her same clothes and attempted to entertain herself and be productive at the same time.

The decision to begin her own PR firm had not just been some idle plan to fill her days until Kraven returned from the intense work required to ready the hunting lodge he was establishing inside the castle on his family's lands. She had been interested in the public relations field since before going to work exclusively for Nile. Handling PR for the acclaimed artist had been a full time job and then some.

How their lives had changed! Darby thought while settling to one of the simple armchairs that occupied a far corner of the room and flanked a low coffee table.

Nile was happily married and living in Seattle with her husband Taurus Ramsey. Meanwhile, a more than capable staff handled the daily operations of Nile's youth studio located just outside Compton, California.

Darby herself had ventured a tad farther but had never regretted marrying the devastating Scottish Lord who had swept her utterly and completely off her feet. Still, she had never been a pampered damsel and she didn't intend on transitioning into the role then.

PR by Ellis was still in the baby stages but already Darby could claim an impressive list of accounts. Clients; who had craved a bit of the magic she'd worked for Nile, were among the first to reach out when she announced the opening of the firm.

Settled with a bland, but passable cup of hospital coffee, Darby pulled out her phone and flipped through the hand-written notes that were always tucked in her tote bag. She was ready for a morning of catch-up. She had yet to hire an assistant and could imagine the backlog of emails and voice messages that had accumulated.

Darby had barely gotten through the third of seventeen messages when Kraven returned. She smiled his way, wriggling her fingers in greeting before jotting down the information left by the caller in the message. She was in the midst of returning the call, when the phone was taken from her grasp. Stunned, Darby watched her husband shut off the mobile, pocket it and then calmly set about unpacking the meal he had returned with.

FOUR

"**E**verything okay?" Darby asked once her surprise had dwindled enough for her to leave the chair and cross the room to where Kraven set out the breakfast.

"Time to eat," Was the only explanation he offered.

"May I have my phone?"

"I'll think about it."

"Are you serious?" She almost laughed.

His reaction was not one she could have predicted.

"You're damn straight I'm serious," he actually bit out the words. "You get your phone back when we get the hell out of here."

Mouth agape, Darby only shook her head until she could manage speech.

"Are you forgetting that I have a business to run?"

"Been trying like hell to forget it," he muttered.

"Kraven…" his words crushed her and the fact was echoed in her voice.

He bowed his head. "Eat your breakfast, Lass."

He looks like my husband, Darby tried to reassure herself though her thoughts were muddled by surprise and confusion. Kraven kept his brilliant gaze averted from hers, but Darby could see that he was gnawing the inside of his jaw with a determined intensity. She decided to put their impending argument in the 'unwinnable fights' category. Quietly, she took a place at the small food-laden table. Their breakfast passed in silence until Kraven's hand closed over hers when she reached for a silver decanter filled with orange juice.

"It's best if you don't phone anyone just now, petal."

Darby squeezed his hand. "Why?" She leaned forward to whisper. Her eyes narrowed in sudden realization and she tilted her head a fraction. She spared a quick glance at the closed door to their room. "Is this about what happened to Fernando?

"He wasn't just in the wrong place, was he?" She questioned when Kraven kept quiet. "Someone shot him on purpose." She shuddered when his expression confirmed her suspicion.

"But why?" She settled back in her folding chair to breathe the question. She didn't really expect an answer although she suspected he had quite a few.

Appetite waning, she picked a fork at the eggs and biscuits that had already gone cold. "What does Fernando being shot have to do with me not using my phone?"

It was Kraven's turn to slump back against the chair that seemed dwarfed by his size. He pushed aside the Styrofoam plate filled with sausages and oatmeal as though the contents disgusted him.

Darby watched him rubbing at his eyes while she summoned the boldness to ask. "Was Fernando the only one they intended to shoot?"

Finally, Kraven set his deep stare to her face. "No love. My guess is there's a bullet with my name on it as well."

***

"Quay and Ty?"

"Staying here," Quest promised his mother as he held her close. He and Michaela had paid a personal visit to his parents to tell them of the shooting.

"Quay's got stuff to handle for Ramsey," Quest spoke against Catrina Ramsey's temple as he rocked her slowly. "He doesn't want Ty traveling being pregnant."

"Well we sure as hell don't like the idea of you taking our girl halfway around the world," Damon Ramsey snapped. "Either of them," he added and squeezed Mick whom he held onto.

Michaela stood on her toes to brush a kiss across her father-in-law's square jaw. "I need to be there for County," she smiled up at him pitifully. "And we've gone off too much without Quincee to leave her again so soon."

"We understand honey, but that doesn't mean we have to like it." Catrina said.

Mick left Damon's side to gather her mother-in-law in a hug. Arm in arm, the two walked off together speaking softly.

"This was no accident." Quest shared when he and Damon were alone in Damon's home office.

Damon rolled his eyes. "Fuck," he muttered and walked a slow path toward the bay windows overlooking the rear portion of his and Catrina's Seattle home. "Just when we thought it was safe to claim the name Ramsey."

He smirked, sparking the dimples on either side of his mouth.

"I don't think this is specifically about the family, Dad." Quest went to sit on the edge of his father's desk and fidgeted with a football paperweight there on the corner.

Damon turned from the window. He fixed his son with a look that said further explanation was expected.

"I talked to Pike last night."

"And?" Damon lowered to the padded sill before the window and settled in to listen to Quest's re-telling of the events regarding the mysterious deaths, the notes left behind and how Fernando connected.

"I haven't talked to Roman in weeks," Damon stroked his jaw. "It's understandable that Gabriel will take his son's death badly," he referred to Brogue. "This will be very bad for that family," he smoothed both hands across his handsome molasses-dark face. "My friend will have to wait a little longer for that peace he's been wanting. So what's the next move?"

"We're pretty much stumblin' in the dark here, Dad." Quest lost interest in the paperweight and rubbed the bridge of his nose. "All this came out of nowhere."

"Maybe not..." Damon pushed to his feet. "Could be a diversion to keep you from other tasks."

Quest considered his father's words, knowing the man was referring to Roman Tesano's charge. The younger generation had been asked to take the reins and clean up the filth that his brother Humphrey had started and subsequently drawn Damon Ramsey's older brothers Marcus and Houston into.

Quest shrugged beneath the gray shirt he wore over a stark white tee. "Guess that's as good a reason as any of the others we have." He took note of his father's silence then and walked over to clap Damon's shoulder.

"Don't worry, Dad. We'll get there."

Damon smirked and then drew his son into a hug.

***

"Anything?" Evangela asked Saffron when she arrived in the kitchen that morning.

Saffron toyed with the fuzzy end of one of her thick dreads. "Will you make me eat my laptop if I say no?"

Evangela managed a smile before she went to fill a mug with fragrant black coffee.

Comforted by the reaction, Saffron left the settee in the kitchen alcove. "If it helps to know, I think we can scratch one of those numbers off our list."

Evangela turned with her steaming mug and saw the list Saffron held. The woman tapped her finger to a phone number.

"Moved from here well over a year ago."

"Shit. Has it really been that long since we've talked?"

"Time flies…"

"Don't we have a new address? Phone number?"

Saffron only shook her head and bumped the page of numbers to the leg of the camouflage Capri pants she sported.

"Shit Saf…" Evangela set down the coffee and tugged a hand through the straight hair that hit her shoulder blades. "No email? Fucking social network accounts? Anything?"

"None of that. But you know it won't take me long to find out the deal."

"I know… doesn't stop me from being mad as hell though." Evangela was slamming her fists to the cutting board countertop when Maeva arrived in the kitchen.

"What?" She inquired in an eerily flat, suspecting tone.

"Nothin' hon, just business," Evangela tossed up a dismissing wave.

Maeva's stare, which she'd changed from green to a vibrant shade of hazel, reflected increased skepticism. "What?" She repeated.

The tone was a clear warning that a more adequate reply was necessary. Evangela walked over and hooked her hand through the crook of Maeva's arm.

"Let me fix you some breakfast, sweetie. We're just trying to locate an old friend is all…"

***

"They're that certain?"

Kraven nodded at Caiphus Tesano's question before answering it through the phone line. "It all still depends on what the tests show but they're in awe of how fast he's healing."

"They don't have all the facts." Hill's voice rumbled through the line in a more morose tone. "Does it look like they'll hold him longer to try and figure out how he's healing so damned fast?"

"Doesn't look like it." Kraven spoke through a yawn. "I honestly don't think they'll try keeping him longer to solve this particular riddle. Besides, I don't think they want to feel any more wrath from the newest Mrs. Ramsey."

"Fern's got himself a beauty. Figures she's a bad ass too," Hill noted once laughter settled over Kraven's remark.

"Thanks for being there Kray," Hill continued. "I know how you hate bein' cooped up. You gotta be goin' stir crazy in that place."

Kraven drew a hand through the thick blackness of his hair and shifted his position on the bed. Darby was upstairs visiting with Contessa while he stayed behind to make the overdue call to the Tesanos.

"Being cooped up has its advantages," he sighed.

"Another beauty," Hill complimented Darby while his brother chuckled on the line. "You're a blessed man, Kray."

"Blessed, huh?" Kraven eased a hand beneath his shirt and smoothed it across his abdomen as he considered the words. "Sometimes I wonder if she was meant for me or whether I just recognized a blessing when I saw it and took her for my own."

Silence carried the line long enough for Caiphus to figure it best to end his part in the chat and let Hilliam and Kraven close out.

"Don't wimp out on me, Kray,"

"You're one to talk." Kraven chastised his old friend.

"You're loved by a beauty. There's nothin' better than that."

"I see. And why is it, you let *your* beauty walk away?"

Hill had no response and Kraven hadn't expected an answer anyway. "Wonder how long she'll be mine once she finds out?"

"Don't do that, man." Hill's rough voice took on a harsher quality. "We've done too much good to be defined by that stupid shit."

"That *stupid shit* isn't something that can be swept away- 'specially when the wronged is insane with a group of equally insane followers."

"Why don't you tell her about it?"

Hill's suggestion ignited a laughing fit on Kraven's part.

"I like being married very much."

Hilliam sighed a wicked curse. "She'd never leave you over that."

"And why is it that Persephone walked away from you?" Kraven bit out the words, unable to deny the darkness that was slowly overwhelming his mood. "Sorry man," he grated out eventually.

"Forget about it," Hill's voice held the same grated quality. "I got too much to make up for with her... looks like I'll have to wait a little longer to do that. We need to settle this, Kray. We need to find them and settle this- put this shit behind us to move on to what's important."

Kraven didn't bother inquiring of what ideas Hill could have to settle their current predicament. "There're no apologies that can make this go away, Hill. They want blood and they've already collected a shite-load of it."

"We better fuckin' think of something else then, my friend. Tell me about the lodgings on Near Invernesshire."

Kraven smiled. "I'll set it up." He looked over at the door as Darby entered. "I'll be in touch once I talk to Fern's doctors." His vivid gaze made a slow, appraising sweep of his wife's curvaceous honey brown frame. "You're sure you've got something to accommodate the bed and all the monitors?" he nodded in response to Hill's reply and promised to be in touch before shutting off the phone connection.

"Am I allowed to know what that was about?" Darby folded her arms over her chest.

Kraven averted his gaze and smiled over her phrasing of the question. "I'm getting air transport for Fernando back to Scotland to complete his recovery."

Darby uncrossed her arms. "Will the doctors allow that?"

"We'll find out soon enough."

"Are you having problems making the arrangements for the flight?" She asked.

Kraven peppered his soft smile with a shrug. "Well among the aircrafts I own, I don't have anything that'll handle Fernando's bed and all the equipment to monitor his condition. How's Contessa?" He asked after a few beats of quiet.

"Still a wreck," Darby swung her arms and moved further into the room. "She's not as beaten as she was though... so how long are you going to hold my phone hostage?"

"We've had this conversation, Lass." Kraven exhibited a lithe grace for someone his size when he left the bed. "You'll get it back when I feel the time is right."

"You're my husband, Kraven not my dictator."

He leveled his stare her way just shy of a full minute. "I'm not dictating."

"Easy for you to say when you've got all the power."

The leveled stare filtered with unmasked hurt. "You think I'm overpowering you?"

She understood what he meant and examined his toned frame pensively. "Not physically," she lifted her chin, "you'll probably wait 'til we're back in Scotland to try that."

"I don't believe this," he took a step toward her, "you're angry with me for trying to keep you safe?"

"Keeping me safe from what?" Darby stepped in closer as well. "Don't forget, you never told me why you believe you're in line for a bullet."

"Darby," he was regretting that he'd even said *that* much.

"Don't bother. I already know," she threw up her hands, "I'm *safer* not knowing, right?" She meant to walk past him and her temper spiked a few degrees when he blocked her way.

"So we're gonna start the physical overpowering early, huh?"

The hurt returned to his eyes and could be heard through the heavy breath he expelled. He went to claim one of the chairs in the corner of the room.

Regret took residence in Darby's shamrock gaze and she went to the chair.

"Kraven?" She knelt before him.

He wouldn't- or couldn't look at her. "I'd never touch you that way." He shook his head stubbornly. "I'd never... hurt you like that."

"Kraven-baby I, I'm sorry, I know that." She put a kiss to his denim clad thigh. "I know you're not that kind of man."

"Do you, love?"

"Yes," she hissed the word, her lovely features tingeing with certainty. "But I won't break, Kraven. I'm not made that way. I've never looked for or *asked* a man to fight my battles. I take great pride in that and great...enjoyment in taking care of myself when the situation calls for it."

The softness in his stare then rivaled the touch he placed upon her face when he cupped her cheek and used the pad of his thumb to outline her mouth.

"Talk to me about this," she pleaded.

At once, his resolved returned to harden his features into a stony mask.

Darby's temper reheated when she saw his reaction. "Give me my phone," she demanded.

Kraven pulled his hand from her face and let it dangle across the arm of the chair. "They're things about me that I'd rather die over than have you know. The man you see before you now is not the man I've always been. I should have told you more about him a long time ago but when I saw you..." he placed the back of his hand to her cheek.

"All I could think of was what I wanted and what I planned to keep forever," his hand drifted downward across her neck.

Darby squeezed his hand. "I don't care about who you *were*."

Kraven's smile was both sad and slightly humored. "Don't be so sure, love."

"Kraven-"

"That's it, Lass." He kissed her mouth hard, vaguely punishing. "Please believe that I'm sorry." He spoke against her lips before pulling away and leaving her alone in the room.

FIVE

"Hey you."

Contessa straightened in front of the window where she'd been taking an absent appraisal of the city streets below. Whirling then, her eyes widened in tandem with the shuddery breath she expelled at the sight of her husband's striking translucent stare. At that moment, it was fixed on her and for a moment she forgot to breathe.

"Ramsey…" County broke into a run toward the bed but stopped just short of throwing herself against him.

"Get here," Fernando ordered with a slow shake of his head against a pillow.

"But-"

He caught her wrist and tugged her down flat against him. There, he treated her to a hard, through kiss that County melted into without a second thought.

"Am I hurting you?" She managed to ask when he freed her mouth.

"Never," he put a lingering kiss to her cheek.

She couldn't help it. She cried. The tears served as a purging of fears, frustrations and a welling of elation.

Fernando drew his wife closer, keeping her face sheltered in the crook of his neck. "I know babe... I know and I'm sorry."

"You shouldn't be apologizing," County gave an awkward shake of her head. "And *I* shouldn't be on you."

"Are you serious?" His handsome caramel kissed face was a picture of amazement. "*On* me is the only place I want you."

"You were shot." She cried as though he had forgotten.

"I recall." Fernando followed the stroke of his thumb across her jaw. "And it hurt like a bitch," he growled.

County blinked. "But not now?" She watched him curiously.

He shifted his head slightly to the left, signifying no.

Her curiosity turned to shock. "How is that possible?"

Humor conquered his bright gaze. "Would you believe that I've got super powers?"

County's sudden laughter carried on a happy sob. "I don't care. I don't care why it doesn't hurt," she splayed both hands across the solid wall of his chest beneath the gray hospital gown he wore. "I only care that you're here with me. Don't do that to me again, Ramsey."

Fernando jerked her close, putting a hard kiss to her forehead and squeezing her. The look he aimed above County's head shimmered with anger.

* * *

The afternoon saw the arrival of family. The fact that Fernando was awake and alert after such an ordeal wasn't half as shocking as the fact that he was sitting in a chair with his wife on his lap when his brothers walked into the room.

Moses and Yohan Ramsey weren't accustomed to being surprised by much. They were undoubtedly surprised speechless just then. It took several moments before Fernando even noticed his brothers. He only turned his head toward the doorway at Yohan's rough clearing of his throat. Until then, Fernando had been more than satisfied in reacquainting himself with the soft flesh behind County's ear.

She gasped upon noticing the men in the room. "Ramsey," she murmured, trying gingerly to slip off his lap.

Fernando had no intensions of making that an easy feat. He simply flexed a hand over her jean covered thigh and stilled her.

"Let go," she encouraged politely but through a strained smile. She took advantage of her freedom the second he loosened his grip. Approaching her brothers-in-law, County graced them with a playful demure smile, hugged and kissed them dutifully and then left the men to talk.

"What the hell are you doin' out of bed?" Moses questioned his little brother.

Fernando left the chair and grinned. "Waiting on my hug." He spread his hands.

Annoyance melted along with Yohan's and Moses' fears for their brother. Gratitude for his well-being rained down in a wave. Soon, a three-way hug was taking place in the middle of the room.

"Bonjour, Cherì."

Darby barely raised her head from the pillow. She'd taken to bed shortly after the exhausting conversation with Kraven earlier that morning.

Now I'm hearing things, she reasoned knowing her muddled and confusing thoughts had all of her senses in disarray. But oh how she could have used her best friend's presence just then.

"Darby?"

She cocked her head a bit more distinctly. "Nile?" She whispered once a few seconds had ticked by. Fingers threaded through her hair then and she squeezed her eyes closed.

"I'm here, Cherì."

Darby shivered, relieved. "I thought I was going crazy."

"*Going* crazy?" Nile teased, waiting for her friend's reaction and joining in when she heard the woman's laughter.

Darby turned on the bed. Tears sparkled in her jade stare the second she set eyes on Nile.

"It's alright, Cherì," Nile soothed, drawing Darby's suddenly trembling frame closer. Kicking off the beige platform pumps she wore with coordinating trousers and a wrap shirt, she joined Darby on the bed and began to rock her slow.

"It was awful," Darby sobbed the words.

"I know, love. I know…"

Smirking sadly, Darby acknowledged the truth in her best friend's words. Nile Becquois had watched as her father was gunned down by her mother and then seen her mother killed right before her eyes. Yes- Nile knew.

"I hear that Fernando is making great progress with his recovery, Cheri."

"It's a miracle," Darby confirmed, sniffling while she shook her head in wonder before she shuddered again. "County...she was so scared..."

Nile squeezed Darby tighter, listening as her friend recounted the awful event.

"I thought the blood was Kraven's- he thought it was mine..."

"Mon Dieu..." Nile pressed her face into the top of Darby's head. "It's over now."

"No," Darby shook her head on Nile's chest. "Something's wrong with him."

"It's been a very difficult time for him, for you all," Nile excused, very disturbed by the hollow tone in Darby's voice.

"It's more than that," Darby eased back from Nile's hold. "He said there was a bullet meant for him. Why would he say that?"

Nile blinked her expression blank as the news gave her pause. She could only shake her head.

"He won't tell me anything. Can you believe he took my phone? Won't give it back until we leave here, can you believe that?"

"Maybe he wants you to rest."

"That's not it. Not all of it."

"Cheri," Nile soothed, pushing curls from Darby's face. "Maybe you should wait and talk to him when things calm down."

Leaning into Nile's touch, Darby offered up another morose shake of her head. "Something tells me things won't be calm for a long time."

Michaela Ramsey hadn't become an acclaimed investigative journalist and author by not learning how to read between the lines. As she sat in the waiting room, she knew there was much more going on than what had been shared up until that point.

What Kraven had told them about the shooting was pretty much what they'd been told by the inspector they had met upon arriving at the hospital. The man had just taken statements from Kraven and Darby. He was to return the following afternoon to speak with Fernando and Contessa. Mick was pretty sure that Quest and Taurus realized they had been given the cover story, but she knew they weren't going to call Kraven on it. Not then, anyway.

That told her one very important thing. The feminine element was to be kept out of the loop. It was clear that the guys were going to close ranks around whatever the real story was behind what had happened there. All she and her...*girls* could count on was being protected-*over* protected and kept in the dark.

Michaela smirked then faintly and took in her husband's alluring profile as he sat hunched over in one of the seats with his elbows braced on his knees. She was pretty certain she could *tease* the scoop out of him, but it'd be damn tough especially once they were back in Washington.

Quincee, seated in her mother's lap, raised her arms to wave her prized rag doll in Mick's face.

Smiling then, Mick's pensiveness dwindled and she laughed. She caught one of Quinn's tiny fists and planted a kiss to the back of it before nuzzling her face into her little girl's hair. The child giggled hysterically.

"Michaela?"

Mick looked toward Kraven who had called to her.

"Will she come to me?" His vivid gaze was soft as velvet when it settled to the baby.

Mick shrugged her brows and smiled. "Only one way to find out," she turned Quincee around and sat her up straight on her lap.

Slowly, Kraven left his seat across the room and crossed the brief distance to Mick and Quinn. He knelt before the chair they occupied and then tilted his head a bit.

"Hello little, Lassie," he greeted Quincee in a voice that melted the heart of every woman in the room. He looked to the tiny rag doll the baby clutched and brushed a thumb across the toy's dingy face. He then leaned in to place the softest kiss upon it.

Quincee beamed, clearly impressed by the gesture toward her beloved possession. Gracing Kraven with a four-toothed grin, she offered him the doll. He accepted and then spread his hands to silently request Quincee join her toy. She accepted.

As Mick had done moments before, Kraven settled his face in the softly scented curls that crowned the child's head. Unfairly long lashes, shielded his eyes as a serene smile defined the curve of his mouth.

County arrived in the waiting room shortly after Kraven returned to his seat with the baby.

"Moses and Yohan are with Fernando," she announced when everyone looked her way. The smile she attempted to hold wavered when she saw Michaela.

Mick wasted no time leaving her seat to meet her friend. They embraced tightly until they were joined by Melina, Johari, Taurus and Quest.

"You look a hot mess," Mick teased once she'd pulled her friend close again.

County laughed through her tears. "Always the truth from you."

Mick shrugged. "Of course," she laughed and put a hard kiss to County's cheek. "So how's the coffee in this place?"

County scrunched her nose. "I expected better- it being France and all."

"Well maybe we can scrounge up some tea instead."

The women were preparing to head off to the cafeteria when Mick turned back to Kraven. He was still holding a very content Quincee.

"Kraven would you please help Quest watch her?" Mick asked, her amber eyes alight with playful warning. "She can be quite a hand full."

"*Three* hands full," Quest added, directing a loving smile and hazy gray gaze toward his daughter.

Kraven grinned and gave Quincee a little bounce that caused her to giggle. "Nothing I'd like better Mick, thank you."

The women made their way out and the easy expressions worn by Kraven, Quest and Taurus transitioned into grim masks.

"What happened?" Quest's voice was like gravel.

"We know what happened." Taurus countered in a voice as rough as his cousin's. "*Why* did it happen?"

"Do you know who this 'E' is?"

Kraven's chest expanded as he sighed and absorbed the questions directed his way. He shook Quincee's doll before her round, dark face and smiled when she cooed merrily.

"It's someone from our pasts- mine, Fernando's, Hill's…"

"And Brogue?" Quest asked.

Kraven nodded slow. "He was a part of it."

"What is *it*?" Taurus asked as though he were speaking to a child.

"I can't say, T."

"Fuck that, our cousin's shot in there," Taurus snapped, his crystalline stare was sharp as daggers.

Kraven merely grimaced. "I can't say 'til I talk to Fern."

"And how is it that you're not laid up in there with him if all this is about a past you share?" Taurus challenged.

"Been wondering that myself, considering what happened. Fernando was a bystander... of sorts."

"Guilt by association," Taurus reclined in his chair, folding his arms over the front of his hay-colored crew shirt.

"Guilt by association," Kraven spoke the words in slow agreement. He blinked when Quincee began to gnaw on her doll. "I suggested to Moses and Yohan that Fernando and County stay with Darby and I in Scotland until he's a hundred percent." He toyed with Quincee's thick onyx curls. "It'd be better for Fern- for them both being there instead of this bleedin' hospital or on a long flight back to Seattle." He leaned down to inhale the baby scent on Quinn's hair. "I'd like it if you'd *all* come."

"We need to know what this is. *All* of it." Quest said. "You know we'll be on your ass 'til we get the story."

"And on Fern's too when he's- as you say- a hundred percent." Taurus promised.

"You'll have your answers. I swear it. You'll all be safe there. The place is like a fortress- more so now with all the modifications I've made to prepare for the lodge."

Quest and Taurus traded looks and then Quest fixed Kraven with a knowing expression.

"You think whoever did this will try again, don't you?" He asked.

Kraven commenced to bouncing Quincee on his knee again. "I'm pretty sure of it."

***

"Maybe it was a mistake to take Gram first." Lula Velez wondered while browsing tracks on her IPOD.

"I wanted them to know I was coming for them." Evangela drained her glass of Courvoisier. "Wouldn't have mattered who we took first."

"But you wanted the Ramsey to be last, why? E?" Rain queried from her place behind the bar.

Evangela approached the massive walnut furnishing to refill her drink. "The bastard was the event planner. Wouldn't have been fair to cut him out of the party, now would it?"

"Wonder who else wanted him dead…" Casper murmured.

"Hell Cas, someone else with a score to settle," Santi rolled her eyes and paused from brushing her waist length blonde locks. "I'm pretty sure the man hasn't been a saint all these years."

"Timing was piss poor." Santi noted.

Evangela abandoned her drink and turned to brace her elbows back against the bar. "Maybe it wasn't."

"Come again," Rain encouraged.

"Maybe the timing wasn't piss poor but perfectly executed."

"Why?" Lula asked.

"To screw us up," Maeva spoke from her leaning position against the den doorway.

Santi looked back to Evangela. "Who'd want to do that?"

"That's not the right question, Santi. Who'd even know there was anything *to* screw up?" Evangela pointed a finger across the room to Saffron then.

"No more bullshit. You find someone in that fucking hospital to tell me what injuries that son of a bitch sustained." She sneered and gave a firm toss of her hair. "I'll bet you cunts anything that they weren't life threatening."

SIX

"**Y**ou said it, girl." Darby murmured when Quincee uttered an indecipherable slew of phrases that Darby took to be ones of surprise and certain confusion.

The two of them stood before a gargantuan-sized aircraft that would carry the lot of them to Scotland- to Near Invernesshire- home.

"Sure is big, huh?" Darby gave Quincee a bounce as she eyed the silver vessel in as much awe as the baby.

Quincee appeared to have taken as intense a liking to Darby as she had to Kraven. Those who knew her better said little Quincee Mahalia Ramsey had simply found more suckers to charm and wrap around her tiny fingers.

Moses and Yohan agreed with County that Fernando would do well in the fresh, open spaces of Kraven's homeland. The doctors were of one mind that Fernando's recovery was indeed remarkable. Still, they cautioned that he was in need of abundant rest and relaxation. It wasn't hard for them to permit the trip as they each believed a few weeks among the Scottish Highlands would serve their patient well.

The aircraft Kraven had secured with the help of Hilliam and Caiphus Tesano was well suited to say the least. There was more than enough space to accommodate everyone comfortably. The vessel was more than adequate for handling all the hospital equipment Fernando would require during his recuperation.

Darby gave a little shiver and realized in that moment how happy she was at the promise of returning home. It had been almost two months including her trip to Edinburg for business which was followed by an additional three weeks spent there with Kraven while they waited to join Fernando and Contessa in Paris.

The shiver returned that time due to the memories of the most recent weeks spent with her husband. Love and desire had seemed like almost tangible things between them, but that was nothing new. Darby was as happy with Kraven as she had ever been. She loved him with every part of her, but this situation involving Fernando was eating away at him terribly. Of course the shooting had been an awful occurrence but Kraven's... attitude was about more than that. He had made it more than clear that he had no intentions of cluing her in.

Darby laughed then as she responded in kind to Quincee's gibberish-speak but her eyes remained focused on her husband. She'd caught sight of Kraven talking with members of the hospital residency staff who had come to assist the medics in readying the plane for their patient.

Perhaps going home would be a period of recovery for them as well, Darby imagined. With any luck, Kraven

might relax enough to share with her what had him…
rattled.

She didn't realize he was standing right before her until he was touching her face. He moved a curl behind her ear once he'd wrestled it from the wind's grasp.

Blinking to dismiss the anxiety from her eyes, Darby gave an easy smile. "That's some plane. Is the staff having second thoughts?"

"Not one," Kraven glanced across his shoulder before turning back to his wife. "They're very pleased with it and their sister facility in Meulan will be sending staff to make sure Fern's getting the proper care." He explained, citing the town some forty-five minutes northwest of Paris.

Darby smiled at Quincee when Kraven leaned close to rub noses with the little girl making her giggle.

"This is a good thing you're doing for Fernando." She commended him, studying the way the breeze tousled his thick dark hair over his head and against the collar of the dark taupe hoody he wore.

Kraven kissed Quincee's cheek and rose to his full height. "We've been like brothers since we were kids. He's like family," he grinned thoughtfully. "He *is* family. I don't apologize for doing what it takes to keep my family safe."

"And would you agree that keeping family safe means keeping them informed?"

"Lass…" Kraven's features tightened over the challenging question. He massaged his neck while casting an agitated stare toward the ground.

"I won't stop asking."

"Even though you know it'll upset me?" His gaze was still downcast.

Darby rocked Quincee slowly and smiled. "That sounds interesting."

Kraven looked up then. "People don't care much for upsetting me."

Her smile remained. "That's even more interesting. People don't care much for upsetting me either and since you've never seen me upset, it might be *interesting* for you to witness it."

Kraven cupped her chin. "Don't count on it." He kissed her mouth and then returned his focus to Quincee.

"Come little one; let's go find your Ma." He said.

Gently, Darby uncurled Quincee's fingers from the tassels lacing up the V-neck of her chocolate ribbed sweater. She relinquished her hold on the baby to Kraven and watched his departing figure with a guarded glare.

***

Near Invernesshire, Scotland~

Kraven had arranged rooms for Hill and Caiphus at the Angus Inn. The four story rain washed establishment was located at the edge of the borough's main road and was within walking distance of the Baird Pub and Wallace Café. Although the rustic beautiful stone inn boasted a popular eatery, Hill and Caiphus decided to venture out.

The brothers stretched their legs for the brief trek to the Baird Pub. Of course word had already spread of the visit. Kraven DeBurgh's guests were treated as VIPs and they generated all the conversation and speculation such a label stimulated.

Such a thing would've happened anyway however. The men were walking enticement if such a thing could claim physical form. The women had who captured a glimpse of them through shop and salon windows, made no attempt at concealing their appreciation. The men of the borough spoke softly among themselves as they tried to solve the mystery of why such a dangerous looking pair had paid a visit to their quaint, quiet town.

Thankfully, the unrest and suspicion didn't last long. Caiphus and Hilliam Tesano weren't only walking enticement, they were charm personified. They effortlessly utilized every attribute afforded them to gain favor among the wary crowd.

Caiphus dropped $500 into Reese Baird's till and told the man that should cover the tab him and his brother expected to run up during their stay. He told the proprietor that they'd settle up any additional charges on their way out of town. The Tesanos tipped generously and let themselves be bested at a few hands of poker with the locals. They even talked weather with Reese Baird's wife Margaret. The woman hoped they'd packed warmly as it seemed winter might visit them early that year given the extreme cool of the past several months.

"Early winter," Hill remarked once he and his younger brother were tucked away in the candlelit pub at a booth with mugs and two pitchers of ale between them. "That's fitting," he proceeded to chug down half a mug of the flavorful ale.

"Why haven't you told Smoak and Pike about what you suspect?" Caiphus had had his fill of talking weather.

"Because what I suspect could be wrong."

"But you know it's not." Caiphus rolled the sleeves of his woven brownstone shirt above powerfully chorded forearms and kept his brother's ebony gaze locked with his sapphire one. "Even *I* recognized that description of Maeva Leer and I never met her before in my life."

Hill grimaced, breaking eye contact with Caiphus then. He realized that was due to the fact that he'd clued his brother in on virtually every aspect of his past.

"I'm beginning to regret choosing you as my confidant," he downed more ale and then used the back of his hand to remove remnants of the liquid from his mouth.

"Well there's no goin' back on the choice." Caiphus lifted his head in a quick up and down move as a gesture of challenge. "What gives?"

"One thing has nothing to do with the other. Maeva and Evangela Leer have nothing to do with what Dad and the others expect us to do about taking down the family."

"You're sure about that?" Caiphus hissed an obscenity when it appeared Hill would say no more. "So when was the last time you checked on Persephone?"

"What the fuck, man?" Hill's fierce features sharpened with a more savage intensity. "Where'd *that* come from?" he slammed down the empty mug.

Caiphus wasn't put off. "Tell me all this hasn't made you want to find her again."

"Find her and what, Cai? Keep her?" a cunning smile emerged, adding a dark humor to Hill's expression. "I get it… as usual, seeing your scrumptious little Bee has you thinking with your heart…and your dick."

Caiphus' expression tightened over the mention of Sybilla Ramsey. Hill was right of course.

Regardless of that, Hill appeared to regret his words. He kicked Caiphus' booted foot under the table and shrugged. "I've gotta clean up this mess before I can even look at her again- now more than ever."

"Why are we here, man? You've got to know none of this is gonna remain secret not with half Fernando's family here."

Hill filled his mug with more ale. "I'll go along with whatever Kray and Fern say. If they want to bring the whole gang in on it, so be it."

***

The group was almost ready for takeoff en route to Scotland. Most everyone had selected their seats and were securing their things in overheard storage units. Others were already catching up on the much needed sleep that the events of the last several hours had robbed them of.

Once they had taken off, Darby decided to take advantage of the few minutes of solitude before Kraven joined her in their flight compartment. Her husband had yet to return her phone but she'd made good use of her e-tablet and had sent emails to her clients in hopes of rescheduling various meetings.

Darby made a quick check outside the compartment before logging into her email. She frowned when no return messages greeted her in response to the rescheduling. She checked her sent file and bit her thumbnail as it appeared the messages had certainly gone through to the intended recipients.

Silently, she told herself there was nothing to worry over. After all, she had just sent the messages the previous day. Still, she worried. Surely at least one of her clients should have replied. Darby tapped her nails to her thigh, visible thanks to the sleep shorts she'd changed into in hopes of indulging in a nap during the short flight. She contemplated resending the messages, but reconsidered when she heard Kraven's voice rumbling throughout the cabin as he entered the compartment corridor.

Sparring a few last moments of silent debate, Darby shut down the tablet, slipped it into her tote and dimmed the lighting. She eased down between the coverings of the pull out bed that filled the space.

Kraven had to duck his head before entering the compartment. He doffed his socks and boots and then fell flat to the bed on his back. He inhaled deeply for a few seconds and then sat up to remove his shirt. He tossed it to

the floor along with his boots and then unfastened the
button fly of his loose fitting jeans but didn't remove them.

Darby kept to her side of the bed- her back to
Kraven. She didn't want to react when he tugged her
against his chest and into a spooning embrace. Not reacting
wasn't an option especially when he pushed her hair from
her neck and roamed the column with his lips. Slowly, he
added the tip of his tongue to the caress.

Darby regretted having slipped into such flimsy
sleepwear. Not that she didn't want his touch- thoughts of
his touch had the power to render her helpless to do much
else. Of course, she knew the way men's minds tended to
work. Giving into sex might give him the impression that
she was seeing his side of their latest argument and she
didn't want there to be any misunderstandings there.

If only... she could resist reacting to what he was
doing to her. He was suckling her ear just then. An arm had
slipped beneath her and he'd insinuated a hand inside the
T-shirt that molded to her generous cleavage. Darby bit her
lip, yet moaned when she turned her face into a pillow.

Her thighs weakened, parting when she was
overcome by the sensation stoked from his thumb grazing a
nipple. When he ceased the caress and flattened his palm
over the breast, she rubbed her nipple into the center in an
almost desperate fashion. Her muffled moans gained
volume when his hand journeyed to her aching sex. She
bumped herself against it, rolling to her back when his
middle finger lunged high.

Kraven pounced then, lowering his dark head to her
chest once he'd tugged her breasts free of the T-shirt's
scooped neck.

"Wait..." the command was barely audible and
again Darby bit her lip. Her hips writhed on the covers

while she rode his long fingers. Soon she was ordering him to fill her with another part of his anatomy.

Low, rough sounding groans roamed from Kraven's throat as his mouth worked over one puckered nipple. He then manipulated the other between thumb and index finger. Darby flexed her fingers but they were restless for the feel of his thick hair between them. She gave in, all the while cursing her weakness.

She arched more of herself into his mouth, working herself feverishly on his fingers inside her when he sucked her nipples harder. Three of his fingers were at work inside her and they just managed to compete with the delicious power of his well-built cock.

"Please…" the faint command wisped from her lips. She needed his sex to replace his fingers despite the fact they they'd managed to coax a puddle of moisture from her core. She didn't want to climax, but knew it was eminent.

"Kraven…" blindly, she worked her hand down his ribcage, across the carved perfection of his abdomen and past his waist. Her nails grazed the silky ebony curls there and lower until she tried to close her hand around his shaft.

The feel of him sent her convulsing on the sensation of orgasm. Her weak curses mingled with breathless cries of satisfaction. She wanted much more though and worked her hand up and down his length to encourage him to do more.

Kraven let himself be pleasured and he shuddered over a glistening honey brown nipple when he came hard in her hand. He was finished, but far from sated.

"Please Kraven," Darby continued to beg, still stroking his semi-hardness but she was denied.

Kraven circled his tongue inside her ear. "Sleep," he urged.

"Kraven-"

"Shh… I'll have you good and proper when we're home."

Contented by the promise, Darby drifted into sleep.

SEVEN

Home. In her mind, Darby was already curling up on the burgundy window seat that overlooked her favorite portion of the property from the master bedroom chamber of the manor house. She imagined an oversized mug of her favorite Chai tea in hand. It would be the perfect accompaniment- the perfect welcome.

The group was touching down in Scotland just after lunch. A caravan of Rovers took them on into Near Invernesshire from the private airstrip. Taurus and Nile would reside in the manor house that Taurus had kept there for years. Moses, Johari, Yohan and Melina would join them there. Fernando and Contessa would stay with Kraven and Darby along with Quest, Mick and Quincee.

The estate was quickly transformed into an area alive with the sounds of vehicles, conversation and laughter. Fernando's recovery was still an unbelievable miracle. The man was moving about with so much ease, no one could have guessed he'd recently been shot unless they were told. It would take the group's combined efforts to ensure Fernando got the rest the doctors had insisted upon. The newlyweds would command an entire wing along with the small staff of hospital personnel that met the group on arrival.

Kraven handled his duties as host and checked in to make sure everyone was getting along properly. All was well, until he happened upon a squabble between the happy couple. Kraven couldn't say it was a totally bad thing to witness. The fact that one of his best friends had pretty much walked away from certain death, was still unreal to him.

County stood with her hands on her hips in the middle of a huge, elegantly furnished room. She glowered at her husband who had just finished a long conversation with his mother and was then exchanging hiking boots for sneakers.

"You're crazy if you think you're going anywhere except to bed."

Fernando didn't veer from the task of tying a pristine pair of black New Balances. "You knew I was crazy when you married me," his tone was sickeningly delightful. "I didn't misrepresent myself."

County stomped her bare foot. "I'd like to see you fight those two orderlies when I make them strap your ass in there."

"Now see…that hurts," Fernando rested an elbow to his knee and winced. "I don't believe you'd sic the orderlies on me after all I've been through."

"Ramsey…" County whined, pivoting on her heel when she heard the knock on the door. "Thank God," she said finding Kraven there.

"I heard," he was saying before she could launch an explanation.

"Will you talk some sense into him, then?"

Kraven took her hands in his. "I've been told that it's usually best to let a difficult child *think* he's getting his way."

Contessa blinked while Fernando reclined in the huge armchair and grinned.

"What do you mean?" She asked.

"I'll keep him company while he has his walk."

"Well…" County slid a quick, sullen look in her husband's direction.

"County I almost went crazy in that place myself but at least I had the freedom to leave- unlike this guy."

"Thanks man," Fernando breathed but silenced quickly and lowered his eyes when County sent him another look.

She began to nod after a few long seconds. "I guess…"

"Come 'ere," Kraven tugged her in for a squeeze and forehead kiss.

"Promise that you'll come back if it looks like he's getting tired."

"I promise, love." Kraven bumped her chin with his fist and smiled.

County went to her husband. "You're a jackass," she mumbled while easing into a pair of flip flops near the chair he claimed.

"I love you too," Fernando tilted back his head for the kiss he expected.

County made the peck brief, but sweet. "Goin' to
find Mick," she grumbled on her way out of the room.

"She ask you any questions yet?" Kraven inquired
when they were alone.

"Thank God, no." Fernando rubbed a hand through
his light brown curls. "I think it's the horror of seeing me
shot that I've got to thank." He tugged up the sleeves of a
black sweatshirt. "She's still in too much shock to start
asking the questions she'd be asking otherwise." He shoved
to his feet then. "Guess you're not havin' the same luck
with Darby, huh?"

"Oh she's in a state of shock, but it's manifesting in
a different way." Kraven paced a slow circle around the
room. "She's got a ton of questions. So far, taking her to
bed has been the only way I can get her to shut up."

Fernando grinned. "I'm havin' a hard time feeling
sorry for you."

Raucous male laughter filled the room for a time.

"Thank heavens for that option," Kraven sighed.

The laughter that had flourished, waned to be
replaced by a surge of seriousness as reality came barging
in. The friends met in the middle of the room for a tight
hug.

Kraven clapped Fernando's shoulder when they
broke apart. "Let's get the hell out of here," he said.

"Would it be too much to ask for you to keep it to
home for a while, Miss?" Kraven's houseman Seamus Hale
was giving Darby another hug as he put forth the request.
"I'm an old man who can't take the scares you've given
me."

Darby smiled lovingly at the man who looked like
he made his living wrestling alligators as opposed to seeing

to household matters for aristocrats. She moved in to kiss his grizzled, sun-bleached cheek.

"I promise and I'll have you know I've been thinking so much about this place 'specially since all this happened."

Seamus' mouth thinned into his version of a smile. "I'll hold you to that." He squeezed her elbow and backed toward the door. "I'm off to see about dinner."

Alone then, Darby turned to her window seat and the tray of tea and biscuits that Seamus didn't trust to be delivered by the newly hired cook staff.

A knock vibrated through the door as it opened. Darby laughed when she saw Nile's face.

"I've got another tea cup!" She announced.

"Just what I wanted to hear," Nile hid her hands in the front pocket of her navy blue smock top as she crossed the grand room that was as warm as it was stunning.

The friends were soon curled up on the long window seat. They shared a fleece blanket tossed over their legs and feet. Each cradled a mug of vibrantly flavored tea.

"So, how is it?" Nile asked once they had absorbed the view of the unending waves of green beyond the window.

"Fine," Darby kept her eyes fixed on the mesmerizing view. "If only my husband weren't treating me like I'm some fragile Scottish rose or daffodil or whatever the hell they have here."

"Has he seen your temper yet?" Nile spoke the question in a hushed tone while blowing across the surface of her tea.

Darby grinned, still looking out over the view. "No reason for him to. He's been... perfect in *every* way Nile."

"I've seen the man. You don't have to sell me."

AlTonya Washington

"That's not what I mean. Well- not totally. He's... he's sweet, Nile. Genuinely, I mean. We don't agree over everything but there's a give and take, you know?" Darby finally exchanged her view beyond the window for one inside the depths of her tea cup.

"We have an appreciation for each other's ideas and opinions. Since *this* happened... it's like all that's gone out the window in favor of Kraven's word being law."

"Have you told him that?" Nile tilted her head when Darby sipped her tea and didn't answer. "So you've decided to let it go?"

Darby set her mug to the sill. "I don't want to explode and have there be so much tension between us that I can't... encourage him to be straight with me."

"Encourage?" Nile's confusion lasted barely a second. "You mean, 'seduce'?"

"The opposite, actually."

"What?"

Darby looked at Nile pointedly over the bridge she made with her fingers.

Nile's dark lovely face was a picture of wonder. "You'd try... withholding?"

"If he can use sex then I sure as hell can."

"Ha!"

Darby rolled her eyes. "Thanks."

"Honey... I'm sorry." Nile paused to laugh shortly. "You know that plan rarely works."

"Shit Nile, of course I know that but he'll keep treating me like a China doll if I don't do something. I'm tired of not being able to keep my legs closed when he comes near me." Darby cursed again and bolted from the window seat. "Weak," she muttered.

"You're wrong." Nile turned on the seat to watch her friend pacing the room's alcove. "It's almost impossible denying a man you love. Especially when he's sexy as sin."

"Remember what I told you?" Darby smoothed the mosaic print lounger beneath her butt and perched on the edge of a cream settee. "Kraven said whoever shot Fernando had the same in store for him. Now how could he expect me not to question that?"

"Maybe he doesn't have all the answers, Cherì."

"Bullshit- he's got enough."

"It might be better for you to focus on other things. How's the business doing?"

Darby tried speaking amidst the laughter she suddenly burst into. "He doesn't even want me working. He's already taken my cell, remember?"

"Right," Concern began to shadow Nile's face.

Darby noticed. "So do you still think I should take a back seat to finding out what the hell is going on?"

"Are your brothers asking how you recovered so fast?" Kraven inquired while he and Fernando walked the east side of the estate. They were heading in the direction of DeBurgh Castle which sat off far in the distance. The family seal and banners decorated the massive windows of the anciently beautiful dwelling.

Fernando swatted a slender tree branch he held against the tall grasses they walked through. "They'd never think there was anything weird about it- just that the bullet wound wasn't serious, is all."

"Maybe some good *did* come from our time there, eh?" Kraven walked with his head bowed against the wind that stirred his hair.

Fernando broke the branch in half. "I'd rather be dead."

"Liar," Kraven wasn't surprised by his friend's proclamation. "You don't really feel that way. Not now. Not with Contessa by your side."

"Fucking bad ass timing," Fernando rolled his eyes.

"Makes sense though. Now we've all got things we care about."

"You really want to tell them?" Fernando stopped to lean against the chest-high wooden fence.

"It's the last thing I want," Kraven followed suit resting against the fence he'd scaled as a boy. "But we've got very smart wives. They'll hound us 'til we crack."

"Or until some of our old friends inform them of our checkered pasts."

"I took Darby's phone," Kraven risked a sideways glance at his friend. "It was stupid, I know. This shit has me acting like a goddamn idiot."

"You know if blackmail was the case, they wouldn't be out to kill us." Fernando reasoned.

Kraven pushed a hand through his hair and smiled at the truth of the statement. "I can't buy that the set back of this botched attempt is the end of it." He leaned his head back as if to draw strength from the crisp air fragrant with trees, flowers and the mist creeping down from the Highlands.

"Maybe they'll try again, successfully take us out and that'll be the end of it. We'd never have to worry about Contessa or Darby or either of our families ever knowing what we'd been- what we've done."

"Well it's like you said, mate, we aren't much interested in dying anymore, are we?"

Fernando's annoyance was mirrored in the striking clear depths of his eyes. "I'm not fond of opening this can of worms, Kray."

"Looks like it's already been opened for us."

"I want to talk to the guys first."

Kraven nodded. "Hill and Caiphus are here."

"Since when?"

"I'll arrange for us all to get together in a day or two." Kraven said once he'd shared the details about the Tesanos visit.

The discussion was interrupted by the sound of Kraven's name being roared somewhere in the distance. After a couple of minutes, a body came into view. Kraven and Fernando saw a Jeep heading from the direction of the castle. It looked to be filled to capacity with the man who called out to Kraven standing in the passenger side and waving.

"Wood!" Kraven sent the greeting when the man jumped out of the vehicle when it slowed.

"Wood Cairn, Fernando Ramsey." Kraven made the introductions once he and Wood had clasped hands. "Wood's the foreman overseeing the castle renovation." He explained. "Any pains in the ass I should know about?"

Wood grinned, rubbing at the bushy auburn sideburns that filled out his face. "All's well but if you've got the time I'd like to show you what progress we've made during the weeks you've been away."

Kraven nodded his understanding but turned back to Fernando. "Shall we take you back first, mate?"

"What for?" Fernando eased both hands into the pockets of his sagging dark cotton sweats.

"I've got another Jeep waiting that can carry you both over." Wood shared. "There're also a few additions to the staff you should meet." He waved towards the men in the Jeep he'd rode out with. "They've been overseeing the special carvings and engravings you requested for the castle doors and fixtures- wait'll you see."

Kraven's laughter carried on the crisp air and he clapped the older man's back. "Wood if I didn't know better I'd swear you were giddy with excitement!"

"Bah!" Wood waved a hand. "Nothin' wrong with bein' proud of your work, lad! I tell ya, your guests may be too mesmerized by the beauty of this place to feel up to venturing out to make a killin'."

Fernando and Kraven both broke into roaring laughter then.

"If it's alright with your boss here Wood, I think we'll walk."

Kraven rested a hand on Fernando's shoulder. "You're sure?"

"Hell yeah," Fernando slanted his friend a wink.

"You heard the man," Kraven waved Wood on ahead and then continued his trek with Fernando to the castle.

***

"*...was on holiday when the gunman struck. Authorities have no leads at this time...*"

Persephone James exchanged her tea cup for the television remote to rewind the news broadcast she'd only been halfway listening to. Slowly, she stepped out into the living area of her hotel suite and replayed the report.

She listened aptly when the anchor stated that Fernando Ramsey had been carried to an undisclosed location for further observation and that speculation was that he'd been placed on an aircraft headed for Scotland.

Persephone clicked off the TV and sat in silence on the arm of the sofa. After several moments, she tossed aside the remote and sprinted from the living room.

***

A Lover's Sin

Kraven arrived in the bedroom to find his wife at her vanity pinning up her hair. The short, lacy peach robe she wore left little, if anything, to the imagination.

Darby felt her stomach do one of its crazy flips when she heard the door close and the lock being set into place. She finished with her hair and stood, but Kraven was there behind her before she could move away from the vanity.

He took full advantage of her bare nape, grazing his mouth across her heated skin. Cupping one breast through the robe's lacy fabric, he eased his other hand beneath the robe's hem to insinuate his fingers between her thighs.

Darby melted into him for barely a minute before she caught herself. "'Scuse me," she cleared her throat and wiggled out of his loose hold.

Kraven watched her head into the bath and followed her there to observe her starting the shower.

"Is there room for me?" He leaned against the long, lilac tinted marble counter space and delighted in the tone of her curvy brown body standing half in, half out the glassed in shower space.

"Don't know…you seem to prefer my cell over me…"

Kraven blinked and bowed his head over the sudden need to laugh. He didn't dare give into the urge though and couldn't believe his actions had made her so angry, regardless of how stupidly he'd behaved. Then, he stroked his jaw as a bit of logic filtered in. He supposed he'd be pretty pissed if someone had nerve enough to lay claim to his property too. Besides, there were better ways to do what he felt was necessary.

Without another word, he left the counter and went out to the bedroom. Darby was pulling off her robe, when he returned with the phone, waved it in the air and placed it on the countertop. His jade eyes were helplessly fixated on her body when she let the robe fall and puddle around her feet. Sadly, he was not to be rewarded for his return of her property.

Wearing a sweet smile that hinted of naughty intentions, Darby walked up to him, rested her palm in the middle of his chest and pushed him out of the bathroom. She slammed the door shut in his face and went to enjoy her shower. She had lathered and rinsed twice before her privacy was invaded.

Kraven had stripped and was turning her to face him once he'd joined her in the spacious shower room.

"A slammed door isn't an invitation," she balked, her fists at his shoulders.

His expression was pure arrogance. "I don't need one," he finished the statement milliseconds before his tongue plunged deep into her mouth. The kiss didn't last long. Soon, he was trailing his alluringly curved lips down the front of her body. When he hit the spot he obsessed over, he spent several minutes plying her with an intimate treat.

Darby kept her fists clenched until weakness had rendered them incapable of maintaining their shape. Shamelessly, she rode his tongue unable to resist the need he roused with the expert thrusts and rotations inside her. When he rose to his full six and a half feet to kiss her again she, of course participated.

"I didn't want company," she still managed to argue amidst the hungry tangling of their tongues.

He took her thighs, parting them further while lifting her in an effortless display of strength. "I'm not company," he informed seconds before he took her. Water beaded and sluiced across his muscular back that rippled with a captivating savagery beneath his exertions.

Darby let her head fall back, her lips forming an O as her mouth filled with water. The strong jets from the shower head pummeled her skin almost as deliciously as Kraven plundered her body. His wide erection ventured deep and forced wavery moans from her throat as the rigid organ journeyed high.

Heated and needy, Darby pushed back locks of his black, water-slicked hair. She trained her green eyes on his as they took one another to the cliffs of desire, where they lingered on peaks of pleasure, after diving into lakes of sensation and returning to do it all over again.

EIGHT

The next morning was more brisk and overcast than the one before. The couples pretty much kept to themselves the previous evening. They all opted for dining in their rooms and making an early night of it. That morning it seemed that everyone had opted for a late start to the day.

Given all the travel, unpacking and settling in *sleeping* in seemed to be a fine idea. Darby however, wasn't interested in extra sleep time that morning. She and Kraven had carried their explicit love scene from the shower to the bed where they enjoyed each other until well after midnight.

A late night though, hadn't prevented Kraven from rising at dawn and heading out to the castle to check in on the day's tasks. Once he'd headed out, Darby got up, showered and dressed comfortably in jeans, a button down khaki shirt and low-cut leather boots. She then made a discreet exit from the property using one of the Jeeps stored in the garage.

She headed into town, deciding to personally look in on one of her clients. Following tea and biscuits with Nile the day before, she had checked for return messages regarding the meeting reschedulings. There were none. A suspicion was growing in her mind, but she wouldn't give into to it...until there was reason to.

Elena Wallace had run her quaint dress shop for decades and had achieved modest yet comfortable success in the trade she loved. When Darby suggested she reach out to the myriad of tourists searching for authentic Scottish creations to mark their travels, Elena was uncertain. Yet she was intrigued by the possibilities that a public relations campaign might afford her. Elena Wallace became one of Darby's first clients.

Essentially, Darby was just getting her feet wet and hadn't really expected her efforts with the countryside dress shop to bring forth abundant results. She was wrong. Within a few months of Elena's website going live, her business nearly doubled. Traffic to the site had quadrupled within six months so much so that one of the shopkeeper's high school aged nieces took over the job of updating the site as Darby had yet to hire additional personnel to oversee that particular responsibility. As most of her other clients employed their own IT departments to handle such needs, Darby provided input on improvements for better site presentation and placement to increase visitation.

Things were going quite smoothly for the elderly entrepreneur. Darby's meetings with Elena were usually informal and in person. Still, as the rescheduling messages were sent to every client, Darby decided to pick the woman's brain about whether or not she had received it.

It would have to be done delicately of course. Darby
visited the shop under the guise of dropping in for a quick
hello after being gone so long. She was pleased to find the
dainty, pastel-toned shop filled with patrons she didn't
recognize from the borough. She did recognize another of
Elena's young nieces working the front counter and Darby
waved from afar. The girl pointed and Darby followed the
direction to where Elena Wallace stood talking with a
customer. Darby milled about, pretending to browse a rack
of sweaters until the woman was free.

The sharp, seventy-nine year old had already
spotted her PR person and rushed over the moment the
customer had gone to browse another area of the split level
shop. Darby received a tight squeeze and a kiss to the cheek
but there the hospitality ended.

"What in the world are you doing here, Dear?"
Elena's blue eyes glistened with concern. "Is Kraven
prowling about somewhere taking a break from all that
commotion at the castle?" She asked.

"Well you know him, in the thick of the commotion
as usual," Darby tried to laugh.

"I see... does he know you're here?"

Darby narrowed her emerald stare over the strange
question. "I'm a big girl, Miss Elena." She managed to
pepper the phrase with a halfhearted laugh that time.

"Does he know you've left the estate?"

"He's not my father." Darby didn't bother with
laughter that time.

"He was quite clear about you not coming to town."

"Quite clear... when?"

Elena blinked as if she realized she may have said
too much since Darby didn't appear aware of the decision.
She shrugged her fragile shoulders then as if accepting that
it was too late to do anything more than to move forward.

AlTonya Washington

"We all heard the news about what happened in France, Dear." Elena braced a hand over Darby's forearm. "I called first thing to see if all was well. Kraven answered your phone, I think you were resting and he was sweet enough to take my message."

"Sweet," Darby grimaced.

Elena acknowledged the flat tone of Darby's voice but cleared her throat and continued. "Kraven said you needed to rest and he's right, you know?" Elena pursed her lips when Darby merely continued to stare down at her stonily.

"Anyway, he said you would be cutting short your workload until this was all behind you. Rowan told me about the computer message you sent about rescheduling meetings." Elena glanced toward the counter at the niece she referred to and then looked back to Darby. "I called Kraven again but he said that nothing had changed and that his people would be in touch when you were ready to get back to work," she chirped, rambling a bit in light of Darby's continued glaring. "He said all your accounts would be monitored and you'd be contacted if there were any emergencies."

Darby realized all the strength in her body had been routed to her hands. She stood clenching the sweater she held in an ever tightening grasp as Elena spoke.

"Dear one," Elena pressed the back of her hand to Darby's cheek. "Do you feel faint?"

"I feel something," Darby forced herself to breathe. "Is there a quiet place I could sit?"

"Why yes, love, you can have the office." Elena took Darby's elbow to lead her from the sales floor. "Perhaps you'd like a nice cup of hot tea?"

"Yes, several cups. I'll be here a while. There're some calls I need to make."

***

Kraven hadn't gone back to his and Darby's bedroom since he left earlier that morning. When he returned to the manor house, it was to grab a quick bite to eat and check in on his guests including the patient in residence. His plan was to return to the castle afterwards.

It seemed that everyone had decided to converge for breakfast together in the dining hall that morning. The kitchen staff had the chance to show off their talents by putting on a *Full Scottish* for the group.

"I'm issuing a challenge!" Kraven called out over his chattering guests. "For the so-called men especially," he grinned when laughter rumbled. "Taking bets on who'll be able to do anything but head back to bed after eating!"

"Well I'm already out of the running." Yohan decided, his canyon-deep voice was as thick as sweet maple syrup. "Eating like this, I'll be big as a house."

Taurus walked past and clapped his cousin's sinewy shoulder. "I'm afraid you've already achieved the 'big as a house' stage, brotha."

The room roared with laughter at Yohan's expense.

"All muscle!" Yohan accurately boasted. "Help me out, girl," he looked to his wife.

Melina took her place on Yohan's lap and linked her arms about his neck. "That's right, baby." She plied him with a kiss that roused applause and more laughter.

Quest and Michaela were last to arrive in the dining room along with Quincee. Quest took the baby while Mick went to the hutch for coffee.

"Are you sure about this high chair, man?" Quest asked when he approached with Quinn. Kraven had insisted she use the chair for the duration of their stay. Quest wasn't so much concerned about the safety of the chair as he was for its expense. It looked like a priceless antique if he'd ever saw one.

"This thing dates back at least a century and I'd rather see it used than collecting dust mites in some museum." Kraven waited for Quest to set Quincee to the cushioned seat and then he secured a polished cherry wood table in place before her.

The little girl studied the empty table and then looked up at her father with question sparkling in the hazy gray eyes she'd inherited from him.

"It's comin' Cocoa Puff," Quest read her inquiry with ease, tweaking her chin when he bent to kiss her tiny mouth.

Kraven watched the delicate exchange and his heart seized with an emotion he could not shake.

Nile arrived in the dining room then. "Breakfast is in the serving room! Everyone can help themselves!"

"Is there a hungry woman in this corner?" Nile queried when she approached Kraven, Quest and Quincee. She held a bowl that carried what looked like oatmeal.

Quincee obviously recognized the bowl emblazoned with the replica of her rag doll, for she began to clap and display her four-toothed grin.

"Thanks, Auntie," Quest kissed Nile's cheek and then set off to grab his own breakfast.

"Need help?" Kraven asked, watching Nile settle before Quincee and prepare to feed her.

"Nooo…" Nile cooed the word to her niece. "Nobody can accuse this lady of eating like a bird. Isn't that right, Mademoiselle?"

Kraven tucked one hand beneath the arm of the lightweight cobalt blue hoody he wore and rested his chin in his other hand while taking in the scene. Nile 'yaayed' each time Quincee took a spoonful of the creamy cinnamon and sugar laced oatmeal. Quincee chewed enthusiastically and clapped joyfully.

"Sure you don't need any help?" Kraven spoke as if mesmerized.

Nile finally paid attention to his rapt interest. She winked at Quincee while passing her another spoonful of the oatmeal. "I think *this* guy would like to have a little doll of his own."

Kraven eased his hands into the side pockets of his carpenter's jeans and bowed his head slightly. Nile looked up and smiled at the embarrassment flushing his darkly gorgeous face.

"Does my friend know this?"

"She knows it very well," his voice was soft, solemn, "She knew it before we were married."

"And she married you anyway? Sorry." Nile shook her head, sending tendrils flying from her messy ponytail. "Here we go, Cherí," she fed Quinn more oatmeal. "Darby loves kids, Kraven but she's terrified of having one of her own since..."

"I know she doesn't have the best relationship with her dad's family."

"Hmph. She's got *no* relationship with them. Too afraid they'll spit in her face because she's black." Nile twisted her mouth in anger. "They basically disowned her dad when he married her mother."

Kraven muttered something foul and finally took a seat in a wide maple chair at the head of the long, rectangular dining table. "I hoped one day she'd be convinced that I don't care about that."

"Oh she knows that, Kraven." Nile leaned in to wipe a bit of oatmeal from Quincee's plump cheek. "Guess it'll take her a while longer to trust *herself* and drop the guard she's spent a lifetime building, you know?" She 'yaayed' when Quincee swallowed a larger spoonful of the oatmeal that time.

"I don't think it'll take her much longer," Nile slanted Kraven a wink. "She's completely in love with you. That kind of love guarantees babies, babies, babies," she looked over again and laughed at the sight of him blushing.

Kraven was still a bit solemn. "I'm pretty sure all she's in love with right now is the idea of kicking my ass for repeatedly sticking my nose in her business since all this happened."

"Well... taking her phone may've been a touch much." Nile shrugged beneath her empire-waist tee. "I'm surprised she didn't hit you for that. My girl can have a pretty bad temper."

"I've seen glimpses of it."

"Well, I advise you not to bring any more of it to light."

"This is serious, Nile."

"And you think she doesn't realize that? It's painfully obvious how serious this is. More so, because we thought all the drama was behind us. Talk to your wife- don't let it go too long."

Kraven nodded sending tufts of onyx hair tumbling into his copper toned face as he considered Nile's warning.

"Is she in the kitchen?" He asked.

"Haven't seen her yet this morning." Nile fed Quincee the last of the oatmeal.

"She must still be asleep." Kraven frowned.

"I doubt it. She wasn't in your room. I went up to check in on her when we came over."

Frustration churned its way through Kraven then. Any thoughts for a calm honest talk with his wife were the farthest things from his mind then. The admirable measures of control he now wielded over his temper; and had fought to keep in place since the shooting, were beginning to unravel. He gave a start when Nile patted his knee and he saw that she was standing with the baby.

"Talk to your wife," she ordered and bent to press a kiss into the top of his head. Quincee waved as the two of them left the dining room.

Kraven braced his elbows to his knees and studied his scarred hands while silently promising that a talk with his wife was just what he had in mind.

***

"I say we let them handle it," Casper was telling Evangela that afternoon as they cleaned the fish they'd have for supper.

"Fuck that," Evangela used the back of her hand to swipe away a trickle of sweat from her temple. "I'm sick of hiding out here while this thing gets away from us."

"The worst thing we can do now is to let our emotions turn this whole thing to shit, E."

"Second that," Rain grumbled.

"And just where do you bitches think it's at right now?" Evangela snapped again, scaling the fish she held with a greater intensity. "They're scramblin' as much as we are right now. I want to take advantage of that."

Casper rinsed her hands at the deep sink they worked from. "You're not doing yourself any favors by veering from the plan here. Let our people in place take it from here. You can't afford to get pinched before seeing this thing to its end."

Saffron walked into the tool shed at the rear of the property where the women worked with the fish. She watched them silently until they noticed her in the open doorway.

AlTonya Washington

"You're a scary bitch," Saffron told Evangela once everyone had stopped what they were doing to look her way.

"According to our source at the hospital," Saffron continued, "Fernando Ramsey suffered a bullet wound from what the doctors referred to as a 'lucky shot'. It seems the bullet went through and through."

"What the fuck did I tell you?" Evangela threw her boning knife into the sink and stalked off.

"It looks like his condition was touch and go there for a while though. The bullet nicked a blood vessel or artery or something, they had a time getting the bleeding to stop."

"But I'm sure it didn't take long for things inside that incredible body of his to… right themselves." Evangela sneered, rinsing her hands from a water hose in the corner of the concrete structure.

Saffron looked glum. "The doctors are in awe of how fast he's bounced back. They're crediting his excellent physical condition with his recovery."

"Bullshit," Evangela kicked at the bucket that caught the fish guts and scales she'd rinsed from her hands.

"I'm with E on that," Lula said as she too joined the group in the shed. "The bastards are scramblin' to perpetrate a story. I've just heard a broadcast that says he's still at death's door. We should strike while they're panicked and confused."

"We've had it if they get organized." Evangela murmured, while drying her hands on the seat of her denim cutoffs.

Casper was regarding her friend with a mix of suspicion and doubt. "How'd you know his wounds weren't serious?"

Evangela's agitated expression, slowly transformed into one of devilish delight.

***

Darby wasn't feeling nearly as confident and bad assed when she returned home as she'd been when she left that morning. She hadn't planned on being gone the entire day, but she was sure that someone in town had called to report her whereabouts to Kraven.

She knew he had to be climbing the walls and; while she hated to upset him with everything going on, she wasn't used to being managed. Her father was the only man who had ever done that. No man since had ever come close or even dared to.

Darby knew her husband had his reasons. But as he had yet to share those reasons with her... to hell with him, she thought.

Confidence somewhat re-set, Darby strolled into her beautiful home that was alight with electric golden candles that filled every window and corridor and glowed with a brilliance against the dusk of the evening. Soft music- a genre she couldn't quite identify- was piping in through the speakers that were posted in almost every room.

The inviting smells of dinner and the soothing timbre of mixed conversation stirred in the air. Darby set down her things and followed the voices to the den beyond the dining room.

The gang was all there. Everyone, including Quincee and a recuperating Fernando were in attendance. Laughter entwined throughout the discussions. The group appeared relaxed and in high spirits. That changed when Kraven saw his wife in the den's tall, curved doorway.

Nile was first to notice the change in his expression. She followed his stony look toward her friend and smiled.

"Hello, Cherí. Dinner smells wonderful. We were about to start without you."

"Sorry everybody. I was in town taking care of business all day." She slapped her hands to her thighs and shrugged. "Time got away from me, I guess." All too aware that she was playing around with gasoline and lit matches, she directed the explanation toward Kraven and threw him a deviously beckoning smile when his expression merely darkened. After a few seconds, she rolled her eyes and smiled happily at her guests.

"You guys get started and I'll be down before the main course." To add more kindling to the fire pit she was building for herself, she locked green gazes with Kraven again and then winked and blew him a kiss.

He was out the den and storming the back stairway shortly after Darby made her exit from the front of the room.

NINE

Whatever calm Darby had managed to hold onto for the scene downstairs, vanished just after she slammed the bedroom door. It opened and slammed again minutes later to announce Kraven's arrival.

"Where the devil have you been all day?" The melodic lilt of his voice held an eerie quality.

Darby feigned surprise, careless of his tone. "You mean you don't know? Please! Do you really expect me to believe that?"

"What the hell is wrong with you? Do you have the slightest fucking clue about what's going on?"

"No!" It was the opening she'd been waiting for. "I have *no* fucking clue! And if that's the way you want it, so be it!" She spat with a rigid wave of her hand before slicing the air with an index finger. "But if you think I'll let you run roughshod over my business, you can fuckin' well think again!"

Kraven observed her for barely a second before tossing up a tired shrug. "I won't do this with you now."

Darby trailed one hand through her hair and gave the curls a yank as she paced the room restlessly. Needing more of an outlet, she stormed over and kicked one of the oak doors leading to Kraven's wardrobe room.

"And what if *I* want to do it now, dammit?!" She blinked then, ordering herself not to budge when he suddenly bolted toward her. Effectively, he eclipsed her view of the room behind his broad frame.

"You can either come down and dine with our guests or I can lock you up here."

Darby's mouth fell open.

His gaze was livid when he bowed his head to rake her body. "I'll be back after dinner and you won't much care for my actions when I get here."

Anger roiled in her eyes and Darby was ready to blast him.

"The first words past that luscious mouth had better be 'yes Kraven'."

Darby knew *no* words would be forthcoming. She was too enraged to do anything more than scream. She stepped to one side, intending to move around him. Kraven moved as well, continuing to block her path.

"Yes, Kraven," she tightened her fists and quietly obliged his order. Brushing past him, she decided to forego a shower and change of clothes.

Kraven rolled his eyes when she threw open the door and stalked out. He muttered a hushed prayer for control and then took his leave from the room.

Silent tension accompanied an otherwise outstanding meal. Following Kraven's and Darby's heated departures from the den, Michaela put Quincee down for the night leaving the adults without the little girl's antics to bring much needed comic relief to the evening.

The couples filed into the elegant dining room and took their places at the beautifully set table beneath the tray ceiling that showcased a massive crystal chandelier above. The long rectangular table was complete with blazing candelabras set amidst large bowls teaming with an array of items for the evening's menu. A fire roared in the huge stone hearth across the room, casting wicked shadows across the tapestried walls.

Judging from the looks worn by the Lord and Lady of the manor, there was no mistaking that there had been no kissing and making up upstairs. The diners prepared their plates quickly and quietly. Kraven didn't care much for being a quiet diner, unfortunately. He made a show of slamming the silver dipping spoons to his deep ceramic plate as he filled it with loads of potatoes, greens and meats.

Darby sat rigidly at her end of the table. Stubborn and seething, she refused to eat.

"Kraven um…tell me about all the artwork I've seen around here." Melina tried to dispel the tension. She took advantage of her seat closest to him to inquire of the exquisite pieces she'd viewed since arriving.

In spite of his agitation toward his wife, Kraven allowed none of that to filter in when he addressed Melina. "Isn't it great?" He asked Mel. His voice was soft and colored with enthusiasm for the topic.

"My mother and grandmother were the collectors," he said, fork poised over his plate while he remembered his late mother and grandmother.

"Well they both had a great eye," Nile, seated across from Melina, joined in on the conversation.

"Thank you both," Kraven's brilliant stare sparkled when he smiled. "The castle has even more fantastic pieces. I can't wait to show them off when the lodge opens."

"It must have taken them forever to collect all this." Mel sipped from her wine goblet and waited on Kraven's reply.

"This isn't even the half of it." Kraven split a smug look between the women. "But I'm afraid you'd have to venture out to various museums in and around Scotland to see the rest."

Darby let loose a blast of laughter that sent all eyes toward her. "Good luck with that, y'all. The great *Lord* here has decreed no leaving the grounds." The sudden gasp she uttered carried an air of sarcasm. "Oh I'm sorry- does that decree just pertain to me?"

"Well since you brought it up," Kraven leaned back and began to wipe his hands on the embroidered hunter green napkin near his plate. "We've decided it'd be best for you all to stay close to the grounds."

Darby laughed again. The gesture was wrapped up in wickedness. "Let me make sure I understand. *We've*- as in the men and *you all* as in us women folk."

Kraven regarded his wife with a bland smile. "You're very smart Lady DeBurgh."

"So you're making good on your threat to lock me up after all?" She sneered.

He tossed aside the napkin. "Like I said, love- you're very smart."

Kraven concentrated on devouring more of his meal while Darby watched him scathingly. The silent seconds that passed seemed like hours. Then she was slamming her fists to the heavy table and forcing herself to dismiss the shards of pain firing through her wrists as a result.

"Locked up here without so much as an explanation about why-"

"Someone did just try to kill Fernando."

"You know that's not what I mean."

"I won't talk about this now Darby."

"So that's it?"

"That's it!"

Kraven's roar sent everyone shifting in their seats then. Nile risked a look at her girlfriend and recognized the vicious glower that usually prefaced Darby coming to blows or raining down some other angry display on a poor soul. She was about to speak out calming words when Darby shoved her chair away from the table and stood. She placed her hands flat against the damask tablecloth. The look she aimed at her husband only hit the top of his dark head which was bent over the plate he was scraping clean.

"Well I sho is sorry, suh. If it be pleasin' you, I be retirin' to my quarters now, massuh."

There was a dual gasp from Melina and Johari. Michaela and County pressed their lips together and studied the intricate patterns that were woven into the tablecloth. Nile cradled her brow in her palm and shook her head. The guys all figured it best not to make any movement.

Darby shoved her chair back again harder and stomped from the dining room with her head high.

For the second time that evening, Kraven went storming after his wife.

Darby refused to cower following her outburst. Instead, she waited in the kitchen. Luckily, the cooks had already gone home for the night after preparing the evening's meal. Hands folded on her hips, she waited for the approaching confrontation. Kraven halted his steps just after crossing into the kitchen. He recalled what Nile had said about his wife's temper and he could have commended the fact that the woman he loved possessed such a fiery spirit. Sadly, she'd had the poor judgment to direct it his way.

Darby measured Kraven's scowl and realized she'd never seen him truly furious. Good, she thought, tilting her head up a smidge higher, it was past time that he was as angry as she was.

"Was I unclear earlier?" He didn't yell, but his rich voice carried on an octave that was just as powerful.

"I asked that we not discuss this yet."

"*This*," Darby let one hand slip from her hip. "The 'this' *you're* referring to being why Fernando was shot, who did it, and why you figure there's a bullet meant for you. Well *this* isn't about that. Who the hell gave you the right to re-route handling my client's needs to *your* control?" He blinked and she could see that he at last, understood her fury.

"Miss Elena was very helpful." She told him and boldly closed a bit of the distance that separated them. "She was so concerned about not going against your wishes involving *my* business!"

"So sue me, Lass," he shrugged, but the easy gesture did nothing to remove the tension from his darkly fashioned features. "Do you even realize how little rest you've gotten since all this happened? Are you so dense that you don't expect that I'd do everything I can to see that you're not bothered?"

"So my business is a bother?"

"Christ, would you stop behaving like an idiot?! It doesn't become you."

Darby knew she was seeing red but she chose to let it rule her instead of backing down from it. "Is this about the fact that the bulk of my client list right now are *your* people- *your*... subjects? You think you can just command them to shut me out until you give permission? Jesus Kraven, how am I supposed to run a business like that?!"

He turned away from her then, dragging all ten fingers through his hair in an effort to summon calm. It didn't work, so he knocked a stack of glistening Dutch ovens to the brick flooring and kicked the lot of them for good measure. That did nothing to summon calm either.

"I don't give a good goddamn about that bleedin' business of yours! If it were up to me, the only business you'd be workin' at is fillin' this house with my kids!"

It was Darby's turn to blink in surprise. An emotion other than anger pooled the emerald orbs of her eyes then. She watched Kraven turn and kick more of the pots out of his way as he left the kitchen.

"I should go in there." Nile put her napkin on the table and pushed back her chair.

"Let 'em be, babe," Taurus took the sleeve of her paisley print shirt dress and drew Nile back to her seat.

"I've seen her physically attack men more than twice her size." Nile shook her head ominously. "She'll try to kill him."

Fernando reached for County's wine glass only to have his hand slapped by his wife. The grim faces at the table brought on the need to toss back more than a few swigs.

"Oh well..." he sighed, grimacing at the water County had set before him. "If things get ugly, at least we've got a hospital staff on the premises."

Quiet settled for only a few seconds until someone sniggered. Soon, the dining room was filled with sounds of loud and necessary laughter.

Darby had seen Kraven heading in the direction of the castle following his departure from the kitchen. She took the same route and found him in the castle great room when she arrived. She watched him there for a long while. He was seated on the edge of a wide teakwood table. In one hand he gripped a broadsword that Darby was certain she couldn't lift using both hands and every ounce of her strength. He held a cloth in his free hand and used it to polish the already glistening steel blade.

Darby smoothed her damp palms across the seat of her jeans and stepped reluctantly into the gymnasium-sized room.

"That for me?" She teased uncertainly and relief flooded her body when she saw him smile.

"Never," he set aside the sword and tossed the cloth across it. He massaged the base of his neck and then extended a hand in her direction.

Darby was already posting up on the soles of her boots in anticipation of running to him. She closed the distance quickly, throwing all of her weight into the force of the hug. They held onto one another fiercely.

Kraven buried his face in Darby's curls and inhaled their coconut fragrance as if the scent were an empowering drug. "You know I could never hurt you."

His voice was muffled but Darby heard him clear. She pulled back as far as he would allow. "I know that," her gaze thinned to emphasize her sincerity. "I know it," she took his face in her hands and shook him a bit.

"I'm sorry. I really am sorry for being so difficult," she sniffled as a sob crowded her throat.

"Don't, Lass," he brushed away the tear that left her eye. "You've had every right to be difficult. This is a fucking bloody situation. I'm very proud of how you ran with the business- making it a success in such a short period of time." He shook his head, his eyes never leaving her face. "I'm sorry for being such an ass about it."

"Kraven..." she sniffed. "What I said at the table-"

"It's okay."

"No, no it was crass." She followed the path of her hand over his cheek. "It was out of line and you had every right to be upset about the firm given this *bloody situation* and all," she smiled pitifully.

"What I said about kids...Darby that came out of nowhere."

"But it didn't," she tugged on the open collar of his shirt. "I know how much you want them." Her smile brightened. "If I had any doubts, seeing the way you dote on Quincee is proof enough."

He kissed her palm. "We have time." He dismissed the voice that said he *hoped* they had time.

"But my mood can stand some improving." She said when he hugged her again. "If you can understand me being on the fence about kids, the least I can do is to try and get off it."

"You've got good reason for being afraid. Rushing you over it is the last thing I should be doing." He squeezed her hips, drawing her more snuggly between his thighs. "I love you and you're enough for me. You'll always be."

"I love you too," she bit her lip when he sent her a wink. "Enough to stop nagging you about what's going on."

"I should have told you everything long ago. As in 'before I married you' long ago."

"Kraven-"

"I was afraid to."

The admission stunned Darby and it showed. So much, that Kraven grinned at her reaction.

"It's true, I swear it." He shrugged his thick brows. "Shocked the hell out of me when I realized it. Losing you is the only thing that truly scares me."

Darby pressed her forehead against his. "More than your fear of spiders?"

He laughed. "Maybe not the *only* thing."

"I can wait 'til you're ready to talk about it." She said after they'd shared a sweet kiss.

"This isn't just about *me*, darlin'." He patted her hip methodically and appeared thoughtful. "If you could give me time to talk to the others involved," he brought his eyes up to meet hers, "I swear I'm done being a coward here, I only need a little more time."

"Shh…" she urged with another sweet brush of her mouth across his. "I trust that you know what's best. I just want you to know that I'm here and I'll *be* here."

The woman had no idea how much strength she gave him, Kraven thought. He searched her eyes with his and tugged her into a crushing kiss.

TEN

Despite the fireworks of the evening, the group enjoyed the rest of the night. Fernando even made a point of offering Darby the use of his hospital staff should she feel the need to give her husband another *talking to*.

Spirits remained high throughout dessert and after dinner drinks. Everyone turned in, prepared for a fantastic night of relaxation after the hearty meal and spectacular... entertainment from the host and hostess.

By morning, Darby felt wonderfully rested. She had no more to go on about what else had Kraven so unnerved but she was content that they had made valuable headway and perhaps understood each other a little better.

That was certainly true on Darby's part and she decided to act on her promise to try 'getting off the fence' about growing a family with her husband. Of course, that meant facing the family demons that had ruled her for far too long.

That morning, she waited for Kraven to set off for the day and then she placed a call to her parents. The sound of Sean and Lisa Ellis' voices brought such contentment, that Darby was happy to still be nestled among the quilted bed coverings. She snuggled deeper while chatting with her parents about all that had been going on.

Unfortunately, the conversation wasn't all cream and sugar. Sean Ellis was appropriately peeved by the danger his daughter had found herself in ten days prior. He expected more of an explanation than what he'd been given so far.

"Hmph," Sean grunted when Darby made an effort to provide more details. "I should be calling more instead of spending so much time at the base."

"You're entitled to give an occasional lecture, Daddy."

"Well you can be sure I plan to speak with my son-in-law before any more time passes."

"Daddy please, Kraven's had a lot to deal with handling all this."

"Don't worry, don't worry I'll be sweet." Sean's promise stirred laughter from his wife and daughter.

"So Daddy... I um...I wanted to ask about contacting the family uh- your family in Ireland." Darby rambled the words when she felt spirits were raised as much as they were going to be.

The line held a ghostly quiet, but not for long.

"What in the fuckin' hell do you want to talk to those sons of bitches for?!"

"Daddy!"

"Sean!"

Darby and Lisa spoke in unison. The decorated colonel rarely cursed in the presence of women. That he had done so was evidence of how heated his temper had become.

"Answer me, Darby."

"Well…" Darby worked to keep her voice soft and 'Daddy's little girl' sweet. "It's just that Kraven and I have been talking about giving you grandchildren, is all."

"Dar!" Lisa gasped.

"Baby," Sean's gruff tone softened over the line. He cleared his throat before it became too syrupy however. "I don't want any grandchild of mine around my family. Ever."

"And it's because of that, that I can hardly talk to Kraven about it." Darby sat up in the bed. "Daddy can't you understand where I'm coming from? I've been afraid all my life that they'd jump down my throat if I so much as knocked on any of their doors… all I can think of is my child going through something like that."

"Honey… you never have to worry about that." Lisa soothed.

"But Mommy the fact is that I've never dealt with it- faced it. I don't know how they'd react one way or another and it's kept me on edge all my life- kept me from moving past it. If they spit in my face then so be it."

"I'll be damned if-"

"Sean." Lisa stifled her husband's reply.

"Daddy if that ever happened at least I'd have the experience of it- good or bad and I'd know how to handle it should my child ever have to deal with such a thing." She flopped back into the covers. "I can't go into motherhood with that kind of fear and tension in the back of my head, Daddy. I've lived with it for a long time and I'm sick of it."

Idly, she studied the captivating etchings in the eggshell crown molding along the lofty ceiling.

Sean's sigh held a rough undertone. "You talk to her," he said to his wife and left the line for the women to chat.

"He'll come around, Honey." Lisa promised once she and Darby enjoyed brief laughter at the man's expense. "That kind of ugliness is something we tried to shelter you from- we *still* want to protect you, the same way you'll protect *your* child."

"I know Mommy…"

On the other end of the line, Lisa Ellis smiled. She knew her daughter's words meant that she appreciated her parents' point of view but that they would in no way sway her plans to seek out her father's estranged family.

"I'll talk to him, alright?"

"Thanks Mommy."

"I love you too much."

"It's never too much. I love you too. Kiss Daddy." Darby snuggled back into the bed covers when the connection silenced.

***

Melina and Nile had asked Darby to give a tour of the property that morning for those who had not had the pleasure of viewing the exquisite estate. As Nile had seen the beauty of Kraven's lands, she eagerly awaited another turn about the grounds. Mick and County would join as well and the excursion would take place as soon as their hostess arrived downstairs.

They waited in Darby's home office and Melina and Nile made use of the time to handle a little business. Mel's staff was in the process of planning the lay out of the gallery pieces for the upcoming show that would feature paintings from Nile's students. Proceeds from the show would benefit kids in the Pacific Southwest and would serve as the Ramsey's annual cause endeavor for the year.

Mel and Nile set up shop at the large handcrafted Maplewood desk. Kraven had the piece custom made for his wife when he'd commissioned work on the spacious office that occupied its own corner of the house and captured light from the northern and eastern portions of the property. Melina and Nile viewed work via Mel's laptop while web conferencing with Charm Galleries' staff as they provided direction on the best spots for the pieces.

"The kids are so excited about attending the showing," Nile worried the thin gold chain at her neck and bumped Melina's shoulder with her own. "I think the girls are *more* excited by the chance to get all fancy and mingle with the grownups."

Mel laughed while moving her finger across the mouse pad. "Bet the fellas aren't too keen on that part."

The art connoisseurs were still laughing when Contessa and Mick arrived with Quincee.

"Now if we can get my slow-ass cousin and our fiery hostess down here we can get this thing started." Mel said.

"Johari's getting her camera and lenses together for some pictures she wants to take of Quinn." Mick explained.

Melina's exotic slanting stare softened when she looked toward the busy little girl. "I can't believe how much she's growing, Mick."

"Yeah," the proud mom smiled over at her daughter who was smoothing down the matted brown hair on her doll's head. "It's so weird she's gonna be two soon."

Quincee responded with an indecipherable sentence that made the women laugh.

Melina's laughter ended abruptly though when she noticed something behind mother and child. She frowned, leaving her spot next to Nile behind the desk.

"Mel?" Michaela's amber stare reflected concern when it appeared that the woman was going to walk right into the sofa where she and Quincee were seated.

Mel however was headed for the wall behind a singular armchair and antique looking reading lamp.

"Mel?" Concerned then as well, Nile exchanged a look with County.

"This Darby's?" Melina posed the question to no one in particular when she stood before the canvas on the wall.

"Well um- yeah, it's from all those anonymous pieces." Nile explained, leaving the desk to join the group across the room. "We're showing them along with the kid's works."

"Right…" Mel's gaze was riveted on the painting.

Mick had turned on the sofa, but her eyes were riveted on Melina instead. "What do you see?"

"Work by an artist I recognize."

Frowning, Mick glanced back at Nile and Contessa.

Mel finally looked away from the canvas and graced her family with an indulgent smile. "I recognize the style of the work. The artist we're featuring in the gallery show is the same one who painted this, right?"

Nile hooked a thumb through an empty belt loop on her jeans and nodded. "This piece came from the donated work you fell in love with."

"Now I understand why." Mel crossed her arms over the lavender off shoulder top she sported. "He was definitely talented…"

County tilted her head and sat on the arm of the sofa. "He?"

Mel nodded. "This is the same guy who did Sabra's scandalous nude portraits. This was done by her friend Austin Chappell."

Michaela's smile was thin as she regarded the landscape portrait through narrowed eyes. "You mean, her murdered friend."

***

Vilanculos, Mozambique~

Oscar Navarro sat trying to hide his smile as his boss read and then *re*-read the card he'd pulled from the envelope that had just been hand delivered by his fiancée. Oscar held a similar card and he took great delight in watching the reserved, intelligent man he respected look as stunned as an expectant father.

Carmen Ramsey's lovely, honey-toned face took on an animated expression. Gold bangles chimed at her wrists when she clapped her hands and turned to her fiancé's top man.

"So Oscar, may I have *your* RSVP since this one's tongue appears to be tied?"

"I happily accept." Oscar grinned.

Carmen Ramsey had taken it upon herself to arrange the nuptials for her and Jasper. The ceremony would take place in two weeks' time. According to Carmen, the entire village had been invited in addition to Jasper Stone's expansive staff.

Carmen looked back to Jasper who hadn't moved an inch on the chair he held at the head of the dining table on the terrace that overlooked the waters of the San Sebastian Peninsula.

"Why Jasper Stone if I didn't know better, I'd swear you were trying to give me the brush off."

Jasper took her waist a split second after she'd uttered the last word. One easy move had her snug in his lap.

"Oscar leave." He told the man without looking his way.

Chuckling softly, Oscar took no offence to the order and discretely made his exit.

"You're starting to hurt my feelings." Carmen pretended to pout.

"Stop," Jasper patted a hand to the back fastening of the high waist color block skirt that accentuated the shapeliness of Carmen's hips and thighs. "You know how much I want this."

"Are you upset because I took over the preparations?"

"That's not it," the hand pats to the beige and black skirt became more stroking. "Remember I mentioned a man called Gram Walters?"

"The man who died."

"A bit more than that. He was killed."

"Jasper," she laid a hand on his shirt over the designer logo near his heart.

"He was a good man. Went on to do very good things. This makes no sense and I want to get to the bottom of it."

Carmen let the toe of her leopard print heels hit a table leg and she absorbed Jasper's words. "And this is more important now than me becoming your wife?"

"No. Christ no."

"Then what?"

"It's complex, Sugar."

Her hand fisted on his shirt. "Try."

"It's best if I don't yet."

"Then give me what I want."

Jasper cupped her jaw and squeezed a tad. "I do that every night."

Carmen smiled, lowering her sparkling gaze in a demure fashion. Her cheeks were still burning when she reached for the invite on the table. "Then give me this."

"I love you," he said.

Carmen reciprocated the claim seconds before they kissed.

* * *

Westport, California~

"You say you have the means to find her?" Rae Su squeezed her husband's hand and regarded the tall, striking couple seated on the other side of the table.

"That's right Mrs. Su." Smoak spoke softly to the woman who had mourned the loss of her daughter for over twenty years. "I have considerable means to do just that or to at least find answers so that your family can finally put her memory to rest."

The parents appeared on the verge of ease, yet flecks of apprehension continued to stir in their dark eyes.

"Why are you helping us, Sir?" Li Su's voice was as soft as his wife's. "Why are you-" he nodded respectfully toward Sabra. "Why are you looking for her?"

"A member of my family has been the victim of a crime and we believe Rain may have inadvertently seen something when she was in the area." Smoak's delivery of the lie was smooth. He'd come prepared with the falsity knowing the Sus would question strangers appearing out of nowhere offering promises of hope and closure.

"Is she in danger?" Rae's small hands folded over the edge of the dining table as she inched closer to it.

"We don't think she was noticed." Smoak kept his tone as soft as his expression. "Photos from the security camera where my family member was staying show that she may have passed by the room. She could have heard something that could give us a clue."

Rae's eyes glimmered then with tears... and tentative happiness. "You have a picture?" her fingers flexed on the table with unrestrained anxiousness.

Smoak took the shots from the portfolio he'd set across the table. He slid them over to the Asian couple.

Rae's hands shook over one of the glossy 8x10 black and whites. The cry she uttered was one of recognition and joy.

Li Su blinked and leaned in slowly as if he were hesitant to do so. He submitted however and studied the photo of the woman who was a definite match to his daughter. He then looked up at Smoak, eyes glimmering in similar fashion to his wife's.

"How can we help?" The grieving father shuddered the words.

"It's as I said over the phone Mr. Su, any information on your daughter might give us a bead on where to begin looking."

"It's been over twenty years," Li spread his hands palms up on the table in a gesture of exasperation. "One day she- she was here and the next she was just-just gone..."

"Mr. Su, I know this is difficult," Sabra leaned closer to the table. "I believe there's a reason for everything- something- no matter how insignificant or unrelated could be the spark of the most outrageous situations. My own life is proof of that." She curved her hands around Smoak's arm braced on the edge of the table.

"Did anything seem strange about Rain before she left you so long ago? Maybe there was something with a friend or boyfriend?" Sabra posed her questions gently; far

removed from her usual boisterous manner. She knew very
well that a more insistent manner might have the distraught
parents wondering what their daughter's disappearance
some twenty-odd years prior had to do with her being a
possible eye-witness to a present day crime.

"She had no boyfriend…" Rae looked beneath her
lashes spiked with tears. "We were lucky- we thought…"
she clutched a handkerchief of the same rose blush color as
her button down dress.

"She wasn't yet sixteen- not yet bothered with the
drama of boys…"

"And her friends?" Sabra smiled encouragingly at
the woman.

Rae was shaking her head. "No friends. Not that she
wasn't liked. She knew many girls, but always spoke of
them like they were beneath her. 'Stupid little girls with
stupid little problems like what boy would ask them to a
dance or if their parents would give them a raise in
allowance for a new outfit'… this is how she talked of
them."

"And she hasn't tried to contact you once in all
those years?" Smoak asked.

"Shortly after she left…" Rae looked to her
husband.

Smoak and Sabra watched Li Su present a small
accordion folder that he'd brought to the seafood restaurant
where they'd met.

"She sent us a letter," Li explained, unwrapping the
folder. "She said she was fine and we shouldn't worry.
Even sent a picture."

Sabra leaned closer to Smoak as they studied a
fifteen or sixteen year old Rain Su on a pier with three
other girls. Smoak flipped over the worn photo and scanned
the scribbling on the back.

"The letter she sent… finally told us that she'd found somewhere to belong." Li told them.

"We took the letter to the post office." Rae eyed the paper sadly. "The postmarked stamps proved it came from Europe. Europe! How in the Heavens did she get there?" The woman broke into a soft crying spell. She kept her handkerchief pressed tight to her mouth and turned her face into her husband's shoulder.

"We gave our daughter a good life." Li Su told Smoak and Sabra while rubbing his wife's arm. "At least we thought we had. When she disappeared… we didn't have money to hire anyone to look for her." His expression hardened.

"The police were no help especially when they saw the letter. A missing Chinese girl is of little worth." He added.

Determinedly, Rae pushed the folder and photo closer to Smoak. She claimed the 8x10 security glossies for her own and pressed them to her chest.

"Excuse me," her words were hushed as she left the table.

Li came to his feet along with Smoak and Sabra. "My wife has been through much," he watched the woman make her way through the semi-crowded restaurant. "We have two grown sons, hardworking men. They've given us beautiful grandchildren and daughters-in-law, but the loss of Rain is an unhealed wound."

"I understand, Sir." Smoak said.

"I hold no hope that we'll ever see her again, but knowing- *seeing* proof that she lives…" he reached for Smoak's hand to shake. "Thank you." He graced Sabra with a nod and smile, and then went to catch up to his wife.

Smoak's broad shoulders hunched a little beneath his shirt once the Sus had cleared the dining room. "Damn," he massaged the bridge of his nose.

"Shh..." Sabra kissed his jaw.

"I hate this."

She lingered close, tightening her grip on his arm again. "You've given those people more than they've had in decades. Rae Su will treasure that picture as all she'll ever have of her daughter."

"Her daughter could wind up dead once all this is over."

"So what now?" Sabra asked once they'd stood in silence for a time.

"Scotland."

"When do we leave?"

"You're not going, Sweet."

"Smoak don't-"

"Understand me on this," he turned and tugged the cuff of the understated yet flattering black blouse dress she wore. "It's a dangerous situation that I don't want you around."

"They're my family too, so stop wasting your time arguing with me." She kissed his cheek and let her lips linger there. "Please Smoak?"

"Hell," he grumbled and drew Sabra into a smothering hug.

***

Darby had arrived downstairs to claim her tour party and the group set out to walk the property. Some twenty-five minutes after the women left, Kraven had the men gather in his study.

"So is this it?" Taurus asked once they had enjoyed two rounds of drinks in virtual silence.

"It's time we had a little talk." Kraven watched the expressions change around the room.

Quest looked from Kraven to Fernando and back again. "This about what I think?"

"Long overdue wouldn't you say?" Kraven's grin held little humor.

"This may not go over too well if we get the scoop before Darby." Taurus sighed.

Amusement flooded Kraven's grin then. "I don't fancy playing with fire, but there's more going on here than you know. It needs to be discussed."

Moses smoothed a hand across his shaved head. "We're a little short on all the interested parties, aren't we?"

"We'll have Quay and Pike on speaker." Kraven was saying as the front door bell chimed. "I haven't been able to get a hold of Smoak yet."

"What about Hill and Caiphus?" Yohan's question prefaced the study door opening.

Seamus Hale stepped inside the room. "Mr. Tesano and Mr. Tesano," he announced.

"Gentlemen," Kraven nodded, "let's get started."

ELEVEN

"**A**re you sure it's the same artist?" Darby asked once she'd claimed a seat on the hillside. She and her guests had stopped to take a breather from the walk along the grounds.

"He had a very distinctive style," Mel explained as she slathered on a touch of sunscreen. "Use of colors, shadows and such are like an artist's signature. Very hard to mistake especially when you get paid to notice 'em."

Michaela reclined at her spot on the hill, inhaling the fragrance that carried on the air and among the vivid green that rolled around them in a never ending wave. A mixture of concentration and contentment commanded her expression as she listened to Melina and Darby debate. She smiled, watching as Quincee toddled around trying to pull at the large, colorful flowers dotting the hillside.

"What are you thinking?" County noticed her best friend's unreadable look.

"Don't know…" Mick shrugged and leaned back to rest on her elbows. "Something I can't…can't put my finger on…"

"Mmm hmm…" Contessa turned her face toward the sun. She knew that Mick didn't suffer long from not being able to 'put her finger on' anything.

"I can't figure why Darby's mysterious donor would give her a painting done by a man who *coincidentally* worked on paintings for Sabra *and* was then murdered. There had to be a connection between her and Austin Chappell." Mick went on.

"Which means there could be a connection to why Fernando was shot?"

Everyone looked to County when she spoke the words.

Johari stopped fiddling with the camera she'd been using to snap shots of Quincee. "It's one hell of a coincidence." She said.

"Too *many* coincidences for it not to all figure in." Darby muttered while removing her sneakers. "You guys realize that our husbands know a lot more than they're telling."

"Or *will* tell."

Darby didn't respond, but she knew Mick's foresight was valid. While Kraven had promised to share with her soon, she knew him well enough to know he'd never tell her all of it. She answered Mick's prediction then. "Guess we'll have to decide if we can live with that."

"This could be to our advantage," Taurus said, once Hill Tesano had explained their use of fictitious news broadcasts regarding Fernando's injuries.

Kraven swiveled in his desk chair and tossed a small soccer ball back and forth. "I find it hard to believe

you thought up such an advantageous idea on your own,"
he grinned when soft laughter followed the jibe at Hill.

The clearing of a throat came from the vicinity of
the speaker phone situated on the corner of the massive red
oak desk.

"What point does putting out false stories serve?"
Quay's voice followed the sound of the gesture.

"Might be good for the other side to think they were
successful- *somewhat* successful." Quest answered his
twin.

"But won't that discourage them from trying
again?" Pike's clear timbre was next to come from the
speaker. "That might make it hard to draw them out."

"I think the point is to encourage them to move on
to who they missed." Kraven watched as all eyes turned
toward him.

"Fuck," Fernando spoke the expletive that had been
on the tip of everyone's tongue.

"Why am I now regretting this little couple's
getaway with our wives?" Moses went to freshen his drink.

"The place is secure, Mo." Kraven defended his
homestead. "They're only a few more improvements I need
to complete for the lodge and they were well underway
months ago." He fixed a steady look toward Quest.
"Everyone will be safe here. I wouldn't have insisted on
having the women here if I thought otherwise."

"And why did you...insist?" Quay asked.

"The folks we're dealing with are too unpredictable
and with everyone wanting to be there for Fern, my home is
the perfect place to keep them properly guarded."

"So now, the question is how will all this affect us
going after Gabe and Vale?" Pike questioned.

"From what I understand, this *does* connect to our
uncles." Caiphus re-crossed his ankles on the navy suede

ottoman set before the matching chair he occupied. "This part though is on a more personal level. It's safe to say that the ones behind what happened to Fernando were affected in some way at least by what Uncle Gabe and Uncle Vale were involved in- specifically these clean up projects."

There was a collective curse from the group spurned either by first hand memories or by what some had been told.

"So this is some kind of revenge thing." Quay's voice was akin to a growl.

"That's probably a safe bet," Pike's voice followed.

"It's a bet you'd win," Caiphus said.

"Talk to us, guys." Yohan urged, his bottomless ebony gaze was fixed on his brother.

Hill's and Kraven's faces carried the same haunted look as Fernando's. Each man was remembering in mounting detail what had happened when they were boys and where the promise of adventure had really led them.

"Some, like me, arrived by boat," Kraven set the soccer ball in his lap and braced his chin on the bridge he made with his fingers. "Others got there by plane, train, some by car-"

"Or wagon for those who lived closer." Fernando recalled.

"Took us forever to get there," Kraven continued. "It seemed longer than that for us to discover we were somewhere in Africa- Madagascar to be specific."

"It was like nothin' we'd ever seen." Hill rested his head back along the sofa he shared with Quest. "Nothin' but kids everywhere. It was like that Neverland in Pinocchio. All the games and food and fun you could stand."

"But there was a price." Kraven's words returned the solemn air to the conversation. "We were there to work and the business was sinful."

"At the end of that first week, we took these tests and then they divided us into groups." Fernando leaned over in his chair to set his elbows to his knees. "They told us what our price was. Wasn't a monetary price and that was fine with us. So long as we got to keep on havin' fun, we didn't mind the cost."

"And what was that?" Moses asked from where he leaned against the bar crafted in the same red oak as Kraven's desk.

"Death," Hill said.

"The death of others," Fernando clarified.

"The place was like a boot camp," Kraven began, shifting in his chair again. "We were trained to be soldiers," he laughed. "It was absurd. Most of us had never even been in a real fight and just like that we were being trained to use weaponry like somethin' out of a movie."

"'School' consisted of learning how to strategize and read schematics." Hill grunted. "They would've loved having the Kid there." He referred to Smoak who designed weapons for a living.

Yohan tensed visibly. "Are you saying this place taught you how to be mercenaries?"

Fernando merely nodded at his younger brother.

"Did you have the chance to put your training to use?" Moses asked.

"Oh yeah…" Kraven replied.

"I'm guessin' there was more to it than training exercises." Pike said.

"Much more than training exercises little brother," Hill confirmed.

"After our... first time, a lot of kids couldn't handle it. They were screwed in the head for life." Kraven mopped his face with both hands.

"They were weeded out." Fernando looked ill. "We don't know what happened to the ones who didn't make the cut."

"How long were you there?" Quest asked his cousin.

"A month was too long for some- but I put in almost two years 'til Marc found me." Fernando smirked, "but then I guess it was my own involvement with the powers that be that led to my early release."

Moses and Yohan traded closed looks before focusing on their brother.

"Ma made such a fuss to get me up out of there. Daddy was content to let me rot." Confirming to his brothers what he had only pretty much hinted at, left a sour taste in the back of Fernando's throat but he continued. "Marc sent me there, y'all."

"Colossal pile of shit," the glass Moses had just refilled with bourbon splintered into hundreds of glistening shards as he cursed his deceased father.

"Give the man a break, Mo." Fernando's sarcasm was evident. "Wasn't like I wanted to be under his roof. I *did* run away many times- was more trouble than I was worth. Besides, the jackass always had issues with me. My running away- getting into trouble that last time just gave him the excuse he needed..."

"But Aunt Josephine made a fuss," Taurus quietly noted.

Fernando grinned. "Guess she threatened to draw too much attention to what they were up to."

"Boy soldiers... Jesus..." Quay's voice that time came through as a whisper through the phone line.

"Why is it no one's taken this shit down?" Moses' pitch stare was hard and fixed on Caiphus. "Hill knew what the fuck was goin' on and he's obviously confided in you."

There was a hush as loaded looks passed between Kraven, Hill, Fernando and Caiphus.

"Ah-hem," Pike's voice drifted in from the speaker as he faked clearing his throat.

"There was a lot more going on there than turning teens into mercenaries." Fernando said.

Taurus' fair extraordinary features tightened into a harsh mask. "Ovaries," he said.

"Which brings us back to Mr. Roman's charge for us to shut it all down," Quest added.

"As kids, our part in this was about bringing down the bad guys or so we were told." Hill directed his explanation to Quest.

"It seems we were *working* for the bad guys." Kraven resumed his tossing of the soccer ball.

Hill raked a hand through the shoulder length onyx waves crowning his head. "We didn't find out about the ovary mess 'til much later." He looked to Taurus. "Issues within the Ramsey family were instrumental in uncovering *that* part of the mystery. That's when we knew it wasn't over and was up to us to shut down."

"And the so-called authorities?" Quest's left dimpled smile appeared in reference to the word. "Where were they in all this?"

"You're right, it's laughable." Caiphus massaged his eyes. "I've got a damn good team behind me, but even *I* know that the reason we can write our own ticket is because my last name is Tesano. Our family's at the helm of this decrepit shit and they've got a slew of partners and … customers- many who make their livings at all levels of governmental circles.

"So far I've only brought down those with no Tesano affiliation which is why I'm still in business… and alive."

"Naïve…" Hill referred to the lot of them. "We actually thought we were doing good back then."

"'Ridding the world of evil elements', was how they put it." Kraven's chuckle was hollow and then he was flexing his hands around the ball, squeezing until it popped. The air seeped out in a slow hiss. "Finding out about the ovaries told us what the girls were *really* there for."

Quest shook his head. "What did you think they were there for?"

"They used them as rewards," Kraven tossed the massacred ball to his desk. "Higher your body count, the more tactical your strategy, the more girls you were rewarded with."

"Which brings us back to what happened to Fern," Hill grumbled.

"So this *is* payback." Quay said. "What? Did you guys botch some mission, take out the wrong person's favorite uncle, what?"

"It wasn't about a mission." Hill said.

"But Quay's right," Kraven made eye contact with everyone in the room. "It *is* payback."

At once, a collective male groan filled the room.

***

Smoak made sure that Sabra was sleeping soundly before he resumed work on the unfolding puzzle he had taken upon himself to solve. At the very least he hoped to collect all the pieces. The meeting with Li and Rae Su had given him more headway than he expected it would. Now, with the envelope containing the letter and photo of Rain Su, Smoak had a key piece to the puzzle. But how to unlock the rest was the question then.

Smoak paced the living area of the suite that he and Sabra shared in a hotel just outside Westport, California where the Sus lived. He strolled the room, one hand fisted at his thigh while the other clutched the photo of Rain and her friends. There was nothing in the background to give any hints about the location. Likewise, the letter Rain sent to her parents, held no clues as to her whereabouts.

A muscle danced at his jaw, beneath the taut blackberry skin. He felt feverish as his anger crested. He was more frustrated then than he'd been during all the time it had taken him to piece together what little he had about the origins of his cousin's murderer. Now, he was stumped again and such a thing was rare for him.

Smoak considered going to bed, waking Sabra and having her... distract him as only she could. It didn't take much for him to approve of that course of action.

The matter settled in his mind, he headed back toward the bedroom. He dropped the photo to the message desk near the windows that offered a calming ocean view. Reflexively, he flipped over the worn photograph and stopped. His dark stare scanned the scribbling on the back- a list of names. He stopped on one in particular.

"Evangela Leer. E..." he muttered an obscenity. "Can't be that simple," Still he took a seat behind the desk and logged into his netbook. Once the razor-slim device was booted and ready, he began his search.

***

"Good Jeez! If I'd known I'd have to come *this* far to check on that fool, I'd have thought twice!"

The women were returning from their touring expedition when Sybilla Ramsey arrived in time to meet her family in the dirt drive outside the manor house. Once she'd been introduced to Darby and all hugs and kisses

148

AlTonya Washington

were exchanged, Bill pulled County aside for a second lengthier embrace.

"How is he? How is he really?"

"Recovered just like that," County snapped her fingers. "Walking around like nothing ever happened."

"That's what Mommy said when I talked to her." Bill's dazzling gray eyes reflected disbelief. "That's incredible. Can I see him?"

"Sure, he's probably off somewhere climbin' a tree." County waved tiredly.

"Where're you stayin', Bill?" Darby asked, moving to and fro as she held Quincee. "We've got plenty of room here and you could be close to your family."

"That's sweet Darby thanks, but if I could have a rain check and use it when this bunch leaves, I'd love to come here for a...quiet vacation."

"Deal!" Darby laughed along with everyone else.

Quincee clapped amidst all the laughter. Soon, Darby was handing her over to Bill who raved over the little girl's red and black overall set.

"Y'all are spoilin' that girl too damn much," Mick complained, watching Sybilla dancing in place with the baby. "It'll take Quest and me a month to get the little princess tiara off her head when we get her back home."

"Hush Mommy, someone *this* adorable is made to be spoiled."

"Just remember you said that Bill when I bring her spoiled butt over for *you* to take care of."

"Anytime," Bill spoke in a baby tone directed to Quincee who giggled wildly.

Sybilla was still making animated faces at the little girl when the front door opened and Caiphus walked out of the house. He spent time greeting the women attentively though his turquoise stare shifted towards Bill more than once.

"This is a surprise, Caiphus," Mel noted when she moved in to hug the man.

"I was in the area," he said when they drew apart. "I heard about Fern and called Moses and then Kraven about driving out to see him."

"So what are you really doing here?" Sybilla asked when he finally made his way over to her.

"There's a possibility that what happened to Fernando links to my case." He rubbed noses with Quincee and tweaked her cheek.

"How much of a possibility?"

"Tsk, tsk," Caiphus' deep set eyes narrowed playfully over Bill's obvious interest. "For a full explanation you'll have to be part of my crew."

"Hmph," Bill rolled her eyes toward Johari across the driveway. "If Jo's here, Moses isn't far behind." She lifted a shoulder that was bare except for the thin straps of her black tank top. "I can find out what I need from him."

"True, but however will you put what you learn to the most effective use without my backing?" He fingered one of her short, light brown curls. "You know you won't get the results you're after until you join me."

Bill set her forehead against Quincee's and refused to acknowledge the truth in Caiphus' statement.

"How long will you be here?"

"Just here to check on Fern," she sighed. "I have a room in town."

Bowing his head, Caiphus shielded his smile. Since there was only one inn in the borough, he didn't dare tell her that they were probably neighbors. Instead, he gave Quincee's earlobe the gentlest of tugs and laughed when the little girl giggled in response.

"Motherhood would be a good look for you," he said to Bill even as his eyes remained on the baby.

Sybilla blinked, stopped by the unexpected comment.

"I expect to be involved should you ever decide to go that route, Bee." He moved on across the driveway toward the truck he and Hill had driven out to the estate.

The earlier meeting had adjourned. Quay and Pike had already signed off. A few attendees lingered while others made their way down one of the long corridors leading to the foyer. Hill, Moses and Quest stood talking to Kraven who reiterated what he'd said about the place being able to withstand any attack. Dogs already roamed the estate in addition to several other breeds that Kraven planned to add to his stock once the lodge opened.

"The trainers are here along with their dogs while I look them over and decide which I prefer." Kraven leaned on the doorjamb of his study while explaining to the men. "Hill can attest to the weapons I keep."

"Damn right," Hilliam complied without hesitation.

Kraven spread his hands. "There's no better place we can defend ourselves."

"This woman believes she has the right to kill you all." Quest massaged his T-shirt sleeve and the fraternity brand that pained his bicep when he was agitated. "This is a twisted situation, Kray. I'm sure you know she won't listen to reason- no matter how good the reason is."

"Time for talk has passed," Kraven pushed from the jamb. "Evangela Leer is most certainly deserving of taking her revenge and God knows we all played our parts. But if she comes here seeking blood instead of the truth about that night, I'll damn well see that the only blood she gets for her trouble is her own."

A Lover's Sin

TWELVE

The set of Ironwood doors flew open in Darby's wake as she raced from the front of the manor house that morning. The ankle-length hem of her eggshell chiffon housecoat; worn over a matching shift, beat against the brisk dawn air. She charted a course across the green dew-drenched hillside toward the castle.

Seamus had awakened her that morning with word that Kraven needed her at the lodge ASAP. She spared no time to change from her sleepwear and left the house with morose thoughts nudging her still sleep-clouded brain. At the massive entry way of the castle, she hesitated but a moment before crashing into the great hall.

"Kraven? Kraven!"

The place was so massive. Darby had no clue where to start looking for him. Finally, she settled on taking the wide staircase beyond the hall. She heard his voice before her slipper shod foot hit the first step.

"What the devil are you wearing?"

Darby turned, expecting to find him on his last legs given the urgency of Seamus' instruction. Instead, she found her husband looking decidedly pissed.

"Why aren't you dressed?" Kraven may have *sounded* pissed, but he didn't *appear* as though he minded his wife's morning garb. Frequently, his rich, emerald stare returned to her chest which almost heaved past the confining bodice of her shift.

"Seamus," Darby swallowed, "Seamus made it sound urgent," she took time to gulp in several refreshing intakes of air.

At that point, Kraven's eyes were helplessly fixated on his wife's distracting bust line.

Darby set a hand to her throat once her breathing began to slow. It was then that she noticed the very long hickory table across the room. The gleaming rectangular space was laden with an array of weaponry. Speechless, she crossed to the table until she was but a few feet from the selection of broadswords, dirks, bows and arrows, machetes, guns and more.

"What is this?" Horrified fascination claimed her lovely honey brown face when she looked to Kraven.

"I need to be sure that you know how to use all this." Kraven approached the table. "Makes no sense to have access to such weaponry and no idea how to properly handle it."

Darby scratched the top of her head and looked back at the grizzly selection of lethal equipment. "A pitch fork?" She queried.

"Anything can be a weapon, love."

She shook her head in wonder, "I didn't think I'd be expected to know..."

The alluring curve of his mouth thinned. "You're expected," his tone was flat.

"Kraven I-"

"Get the broadsword," he eased his hands into the deep pockets of the black cotton sweats he wore.

She laughed shortly. "Is this really necessary? I-"

"Now, Lass."

Tamping down her rising irritation, Darby decided to appease his wishes. She went to grasp one of the basket hilted Claymores that lined the section of the table closest to her. Of course, she was able to do little more than lift the sterling silver hilt. The sword had to weigh a ton. The steel blade hit the chilly stone flooring with a heavy clank once she'd pulled it from the table.

"Dammit Kraven, what the hell is this all about?"

His smile was soft with love and certain desire. He hadn't counted on experiencing such delight at the sight of her handling one of the gargantuan swords and looking so delicious as she did so.

"This is about teaching you to be at ease around vicious items that could save your life." He relieved her of the sword and effortlessly replaced it on the table.

Darby closed her eyes while she inhaled and exhaled once deeply. "Why is that suddenly so important?" She opened her eyes in time to witness the hurt claim his expression.

"It's always important, Darby."

"But why now?" She challenged, already knowing the answer. When he averted his eyes she hit her thighs with her fists. "How many times will you make me beg for an explanation?"

When he looked her way again, the intent in his gaze was easy to decipher. Darby backed away then, ready to barter for the clarification she sought. Kraven advanced;

his mind was of a singular intent as he moved. Darby retreated, until her hip bumped the high table.

"I deserve an answer," she breathed when he cuffed her neck in his palm.

"I know petal, and you'll have it but *this* first, hmm?" Keeping her neck in his loose grasp, he used his free hand to push aside the robe and untie the tassels of her shift.

"I missed you," he issued the confession while nibbling her ear.

"It hasn't been so long..."

"An hour is too long," he continued to work the tassels until he'd freed one breast.

When next Darby opened her mouth, it was promptly occupied by Kraven's thrusting tongue. Her chest heaved again, but for a wholly different reason. He molested a firm nipple between thumb and index finger. A cunning smirk curved his seductively shaped mouth when she gasped repeatedly in response to his handling.

Darby funneled her fingers through his thick hair when he lowered his head to take her other nipple captive between his perfect teeth. Gently, he proceeded to gnaw the rigid bud before bathing it beneath his tongue.

Darby's fingers weakened in his hair and her head fell back when he subjected the nub to a more devastating assault. Suddenly, he left the nipple glistening wet and puckered for more. His plan was to take Darby out of the flowing robe. She protested, tightening her fingers in the sheer material as she silently acknowledged where they were. Kraven didn't appear to mind. Again, he lowered his head, that time he used his teeth to tug the garment from her shoulders.

"Kraven no-" she gasped when he lifted her and took her to a thick mound of fur rugs set in a square clearing between four massive black butter suede sofas.

He settled her to one, straddling her across his lap as he resumed feasting on her breasts. He alternated suckling one and then the other, outlining the fullness with the tip of her nose before dragging his tongue up between the deep valley nestled between the honey brown orbs.

"Wait," she moaned when he began the process all over again. The moaned word carried on virtually no volume however. Instead of pulling away, Darby pressed more of her body into his mouth.

Kraven obliged his wife's unspoken request and gathered the folds of the robe until he was able to ease his hands beneath the material. He cradled her bare ass and broke off the suckling then.

"What the hell?" He tapped her flesh in silent inquiry of her missing underthings.

Darby felt her cheeks burn and she let her gaze fall to the emblem adorning his T-shirt. "I couldn't find them after... last night."

Kraven's chuckle was humor and devilment entwined.

"Wait," Darby summoned more force into her voice when his hand flexed on her bottom and she felt the other burrowing between them while he freed himself.

"Let's go back to-" Her suggestion was thoroughly stymied when he tugged her down, sheltering his sex inside hers.

Darby's low groans merged into cries and soon she was chanting his name without a care for whoever may have overheard. Her forehead rested on his shoulder as she rode him slow.

"That's it, that's it…" Kraven encouraged until his words melded into a mix of phrases that sounded ancient yet beautifully erotic. He groaned, provocatively long lashes sheltering his vivid gaze when he rested his head back on the sofa.

Darby felt cool air upon her skin and she realized the robe had drifted from her shoulders. She began to claw then at the worn Manchester United T-shirt he wore. She hungered for the touch of his bare taut flesh.

Kraven wouldn't allow it.

"Why not?" she could barely form the word amidst her cries.

"Are you serious? Anybody could walk in and see me, you know?"

His tease made her want to laugh but sensation had her too overwrought to do little else but moan. Kraven raised his head and began to treat the column of her throat to a delicious tongue kiss. He fisted a hand in her hair to clear a path for his mouth.

Darby was moments from coming. So was Kraven and he did the unthinkable: he pulled her off. Before she could argue, she found herself dumped on the fur coverings between the sofas. She bit her lip seeing the hunger dwelling in Kraven's shamrock stare and knowing it was mirrored in her own. She inched back on the furs when he doffed the T-shirt.

Greedily, her jade stare cascaded along the length of him. The scars he wore added an animalistic beauty to the chiseled expanse of his torso. Her eyelids felt heavy as the desire churned to a more potent level once her greedy survey drifted past his waist to the stunning endowment he possessed. Kraven finished removing his sweats along with the leather sandals he wore and was on his knees beside Darby in the next instant.

He covered her, treating her to another throaty kiss that Darby eagerly returned only to find herself disappointed again when he ended it. Like before, she didn't have the chance to argue. Kraven had flipped her to her stomach. Again, his hand fisted in her curls and he barred her neck for his mouth. Ravenously, he tongued and kissed the satiny softly scented skin there.

Darby nudged her bottom against him the entire time. Kraven responded by insinuating a hand between her and the luxurious tanned furs. He drove three fingers high and she buried her face in the coverings to stifle her cries.

Kraven continued his famished gnawing at her neck until he could no longer hold out. Darby's breathless cries for more than his fingers had finally weakened his determination to pleasure her out of her mind.

Satisfied that he'd done that, he was then focused on taking what he needed from her. Darby trembled uncontrollably at the feel of his hands covering her thighs, spreading them to more adequately accommodate him as he tugged her back to receive him.

He took her from behind in one lengthy, hard thrust and she could feel the moisture streaming her thighs mere seconds after he began to move in and out of her moist, puckered heat.

Darby clutched the furs between her fingers as she happily accepted the delicious slams he subjected her to. She tried to ease up a bit, but Kraven wanted total control. He spread her thighs further, thus increasing his penetration and subsequently their enjoyment.

"Am I hurting you?" he dipped his head to ask when she cried out again.

"I'll murder you if you stop."

Her breathy response sent him grinning and he leaned down further to drag his tongue between her shoulder blades. "As you wish, Lady DeBurgh."

Back in the manor house, the newlyweds lay cuddled after a morning of lovemaking and after-sex dozing.

"We shouldn't have done that," County sighed even as she tingled from her husband's affections. "You're recovering from a gunshot wound, dammit."

"Would you rather go for a healthy walk?" Fernando kept his eyes closed while he drawled the question.

"Don't be stupid..." County appeared equally relaxed but after a few moments of quiet, her eyes fluttered open. "Ramsey, you could have been killed."

"It was a scratch," he tapped her bare bottom beneath the covers.

"All the blood you lost," she turned amidst the tangled linens and looked down on him. "And then you recovered, just like that-"

Fernando covered her hand, preventing the snap of her fingers. He kissed them, taking time to study her wedding band before pushing up in the bed and taking her with him.

"You know this was no accident. I wasn't just in the wrong place at the wrong time."

"We don't have to talk about it." She stiffened against his steel frame.

"We have to," he cupped her chin and squeezed. "Chances are strong my attacker will try again."

Contessa bristled anew, her eyes watering.

"Hey," his entrancing gaze narrowed as he sought to console her.

County resisted the offer. "Tell me what this is about then."

Fernando sat up straighter against the mahogany headboard. "There's a reason why we're able to have marathon sex less than two weeks after I've been shot." He raked a hand through the close crop of curls covering his head.

"I'm the Ramsey's black sheep-always been trouble. Of course, my mother thought I was her angel. I could do no wrong." His smile mingled with a frown. "There were times I thought the way she felt had nothing to do with me. That she doted on me for some reason she'd never clue me in on…and as much as *she* doted on me, my father rode my ass every chance he got."

County scooted up to rub his shoulder.

"I couldn't do a damn thing right in Marc's eyes and just like it was with my mother, I believe his…dislike had nothing to do with me."

"Fernando what-"

He lifted a hand. "All the trouble I got into…maybe part of it was me tryin' to get *Daddy's attention* which was stupid because any *attention* I got was of the unpleasant variety. I guess I wanted him to pull me close, ask me what was wrong, act like he gave a damn." He rubbed a hand along the array of muscles defining his abdomen.

"He never did that though and so…when I had the chance to get the hell out of Dodge, I took it. Moses had this friend who said he'd heard about this place just for boys- food, fun, excitement…none of us bothered to ask what they wanted in return."

County studied the chords of muscle snaking up along the powerful line of his arm. "What did they want?"

"We worked out all day, even had school," he made a face, "but the nights were outrageous like one long party.

They didn't even call for lights out but our asses had better be present for roll call at six a.m." he pulled County over to lie across his chest.

"We trained like dogs, learned how to box, the use of martial arts, weapons."

"Why?" She whispered.

"They were growing an army."

"Training an army?"

His smile triggered the crinkles at the corners of his captivating eyes. "Only so much training before you have to go to work, babe."

Contessa shook her head. Something told her she didn't want to hear that part. "What's this got to do with your recovery?" She asked.

"Growing the army was only part of the reason we were there. Besides the instructors and teachers, there were a shitload of scientists and we...we were the lab rats."

She looked at him; haunting suspicion lurked in her warm brown eyes. "What are you saying?"

"We never trained or had a class or hell...played a video game without first havin' a shot in the arm or a pill down the throat. We never questioned why, not even when the side effects hit us."

He could feel the gooseflesh rising up beneath the flawless honey tone of her skin and he eased a sheet up over her back. "Josephine made Marc find out where I was and when he did, I realized that he knew where I was all along and he knew exactly what was happening to me. But I didn't waste time being pissed off. By then I'd seen and...done enough. I wanted out. Strange as it sounds, Marcus Ramsey was the lesser of two evils."

"But you found out? What they were doing- what they were giving you."

162

AlTonya Washington

"I kept in touch with the ones I was closest to back then. Some of us couldn't forget, didn't want to even after we said 'to hell with it' and got the fuck out of there." His hand fisted against Contessa's back. "The shit they shoveled into us it...worked at a cellular level. It was like a steroid making us smarter, stronger, bigger, faster...aggressive, driven...insane and we healed quick-like something out a comic book."

"A super hero," she recalled what he'd said the morning he woke in the hospital.

He smirked. "It was supposed to act as a vaccine, I guess- something to protect us from infection, post-traumatic stress...but everyone wasn't targeted by the same side effects except for the healing- that went right down the line. There was the tendency for scarring among some of us but little to no lasting pain."

"How were any of you allowed to just walk away from that?"

"They didn't see us as threats. Remember there was just as much they could hold over our heads as well."

"Fernando..." County sat up a bit. "You said Marcus knew," she frowned. "Is this related to the ovaries and all that happened with Nile and Dena?"

Fernando set his head back hard against the mahogany frame and dug the heels of his hands into his eyes.

"Yeah babe, yes I'm afraid it is."

"Mmm...where is everybody?" Darby slurred her words while curving deeper in Kraven's body. They lay nestled beneath the furs after their pleasure was spent.

"Shouldn't this place be jumpin' with construction folks, by now?" She asked.

"Gave them time off. We can stay here all day if we like."

Darby giggled. "And whatever will we do here all day?"

"Talk."

She blinked and a furrow marred her brow.

"You've been asking for so long. It's time I oblige your request."

Darby braced against him to push herself up. She realized what he meant, but said nothing and only watched and waited for him to begin.

"We believe Fernando was shot because of something that happened back when we were all kids." He trailed his fingers across her wrist and studied the area as he spoke. "Remember my telling you that I ran away as a teenager- the fun and adventure I hoped to find on that boat where I stowed away?"

"The oasis," Darby nodded and her heart lurched at the darkness that crept onto his face.

"Oasis," he practically snarled the word. "If *oasis* translates into a place of mayhem, deception and depravity."

She could have shivered from the ice flaking off his deep, usually inviting voice. "You make it sound like hell."

Kraven's smile was as chilled as his voice. "It's strange how easily hell can masquerade as heaven." He rubbed his eyes as he spoke. "I ran away a lot as a child, looking for excitement, something to prove my worth. I was named for an ancestor who everyone thought would amount to very little. He was born fragile, sickly...his father called him Craven which means coward." He smiled reverently. "The man grew to be anything but- he was a great man and as a boy, I dreamed of being as fearless as he was but I didn't have much chance to prove it in my safe little world here. I had to go looking for it."

"Tell me please," she leaned closer to cup his face. "What happened there? What did they do to you? What does it have to do with what happened to Fernando?"

He pulled away her hands and squeezed them. "Our fun wasn't free. There was a price to be paid and it wasn't cheap. But the dividends..." his smile went colder, stiffer. "They trained us to be soldiers- elite order takers." *Killing machines*, he said to himself. "For a teenage boy, there's only one thing better than blowin' somethin' up."

Darby waited for him to continue, but she didn't need him to not when his brilliant gaze trekked toward her chest and lingered there. Suddenly self-conscious, Darby folded her arms over her bare breasts as her lips conformed into a thin line.

Kraven tugged her arms down and then he retrieved the robe and pressed it to her chest. "They threw girls at us like they were scraps of meat- our reward for jobs well done. The girls didn't seem to mind, probably because they were zoned out on the same shite they pumped into us on a daily sometimes hourly basis." He stopped fingering the delicate material of Darby's robe and clenched a fist as though he were breaking a rule by touching her.

"They were training us to be super soldiers- at least that's what it seemed like on the surface. We never got the true story on what it was really all about."

"Were the girls being trained too?"

"Some, but we figured they were mostly there for sex until...Nile and Dena. Finding out about the ovaries put a whole new twist on it."

"Baby..." Darby didn't try to hide her confusion. "What does this have to do with-"

"There was a girl that we...we shared one night."

Darby swallowed. "We?"

"There were six of us."

Her heart sank. "Oh."

"It wasn't anything we hadn't done before." He raised a knee and set his arm across it. "That night, there was a new element to it. My friend Austin, he gave her something… he brought *party favors* for us as well. It was intense stuff- had to be. We were with her for two days. When it was all over, we didn't remember a bleedin' thing."

"Then how-"

"My friend Gram recorded some of it. Then Austin told us what he gave us-gave her. Hers was some kind of enhancer," he said when Darby eyed him inquisitively.

"The labs were…they were always experimenting with something. Austin's study track placed him there. He and Brogue used to try out the crap on their girls but this stuff was somethin' different." He scrubbed his face with his hands and kept his eyes closed for a second or three.

"We could see it on the recording, towards the end when the effects started to wear off. She…performed but didn't want to… it was like she was at war with herself."

"God…" Darby breathed, cradling her forehead as if it pained her to think.

Kraven watched as she pressed the back of her hand to her mouth as though she were going to be sick.

"We left it up to Fernando to choose the girl. He always found the best ones for our parties. That night when he got there he was high on somethin', passed out before he had his turn." He rested his head in his palm and fixed his gaze on a spot along the towering ceiling of the great room.

"We were all pretty dead on our feet anyway. This…event came on the heels of a mission- we called them clean-up projects. It was a success and we were entitled to the choicest piece of ass to celebrate a job well done." He clenched his fist and looked as though he were considering smashing it into his own jaw.

"Hill and I planned the job so the girl was ours to have first. We let Austin and Gram go first though. Austin administered the drug and um…he had her while Gram recorded and then they switched places…Brogue went next, then Hill." He shuddered. "The drugs worked excellently. She was more than willing but she was very small."

Darby needed no additional clarification on that score. She knew exactly what Kraven meant regarding…size.

"Men in my family received their *blessings* at an early age," his grim tone matched his expression.

Darby glanced south of his waist and recalled in vivid, heated detail the first time she'd tested her husband's family blessing. She however had thoroughly enjoyed it and been expertly prepared to receive it. Of course, she had been dealing with an experienced man and not a high and impatient teenaged boy.

"So this was about revenge? How can that be if no one remembers anything? She didn't see the recording, did she?"

"Not that I know of," He raked back a fall of onyx from his brow. "But revenge is the only explanation that makes sense. Besides, our squad was the most elite and the island was an intimate community. When we threw a party, everyone knew it."

Darby studied the range of beautiful battle scars marking the man's physique. "She won't stop, will she?"

Kraven reached up to tug one of her curls. "Could you?" He asked.

THIRTEEN

Darby could no longer allow the real world to remain at bay. She closed off in her office early the next morning in hopes of getting work done. She knew that meant making phone contact with her newly estranged clients. She knew that many of her clients still pledged allegiance to her husband and his wishes er-orders that they give her a break.

While waiting on her laptop to boot, her thoughts returned to the day before. The day before she knew more about Kraven's past than-what? Than she wanted to know? Bullshit. She'd badgered him enough to be straight with her, hadn't she? Now what? She had answers that would most likely give her nightmares.

Kraven was no fool. He'd seen how what he'd said had affected her and how could it not? But God, she still loved him. That emotion wasn't going anywhere no matter what he told her, was it?

The computer booted and she logged in and prepared to draft a blanket email to her clients letting them know that she was back on the job. Grudgingly, she added a line instructing them to contact Kraven if they needed confirmation.

***

Later that day saw the arrival of more visitors headed for the DeBurgh estate. Smoak and Sabra were checking into the Angus Inn when Sabra felt someone pinch her side. She whirled, her eyes alight with fire until they landed on Sybilla and Sabra screamed her happiness.

"How's Fernando?" Were Sabra's first words when they pulled out of a hug.

"Fine now and on the mend faster than anyone expected."

The cousins linked arms and strolled across the rustic, golden lit lobby. Smoak finished checking in him and Sabra and then joined the women.

"So who else is here?" Sabra asked while Bill and Smoak hugged.

"Just about everyone," Bill slipped her hands into the back pockets of her 'skinny' jeans. "Your brothers, except for Pike. Here in this very hotel."

That was welcome news for Smoak who kissed Bill and Sabra before returning to the front desk to get info on Hill's and Caiphus' whereabouts. Alone again, the ladies took time to chat about everything going on.

"I like this happiness I see." Bill knocked a finger along one of Sabra's bouncy curls and laughed when she hugged herself in contentment.

"You better snag your man before somebody else does." Sabra challenged as a naughty element filtered her almond shaped eyes. "He's as delicious as ever. You should take advantage of being in the same hotel."

"I should've known it'd happen this way," Bill studied the bellhops and guests zipping through the spacious lobby. She recalled her surprise at finding the Tesanos at the front desk when she returned from visiting with Fernando.

"Girl, at least stop lying to yourself. Even if you feel the need to lie to everybody else."

Sybilla folded her arms across her chest, unable to deny that was exactly what she'd been doing. "I'm thinking about taking him up on the offer to join his team. I've got to be part of this case."

Sabra fidgeted with the tassels dangling from her snug money green top. "You think it's connected to Brogue and Fern?"

"And Marcus *and* Houston," Bill added the names of their uncles. "It's all part of that same ugly mess the two of them stepped into all those years ago."

"Smoak found something..." Sabra's face harbored a far off expression. "We have an ID on the woman we think killed Brogue. But he's found something else." She shrugged. "He's not telling me."

"Probably waiting to share it with his brothers and our cousins first."

"You should be in on that meeting."

"Oh I'll find out one way or another," Bill sighed. "If not through Moses, then by way of my... new boss."

Sabra smiled deviously. "And just how long do you think you'll stay out of a bed with him if you start working together?"

Sybilla's smile was equally devious. "Unlike two women I know, *I* have no problem keeping my legs closed in the presence of a Tesano."

"Bullshit," Sabra rolled her eyes and sang the word. "I should be offended by your lack of faith."

"Oh I've got faith, Bill. Faith in the fact that you've never stopped loving your soon-to-be sexy-ass-boss," she bent to kiss her cousin's forehead. "I'm going upstairs to open my legs for a Tesano."

"Slut," Bill called.

"Don't hate," Sabra spoke over her shoulder.

Caiphus opened the door to Hill's roomy suite and was prepared to greet Smoak with a hug. The hard look his brother wore though, warned him against the gesture.

"Kid!" Hill's dark bronzed face lit up with a broad grin when he walked out into the small living area and saw who had rung the bell.

"When are you gonna cut the bull and tell us how Persephone fits into all this?"

Caiphus frowned and looked to Hill who kept a hard look fixed on Smoak.

"I found old news footage about a brutal slaying of one Cleon Raymond- stabbed over forty times with a butcher knife." Smoak revealed as he walked in and shut the door behind him.

"There was so much damage to his throat that it nearly severed his head." From the knapsack slung over his shoulder, he produced the old group photo of Rain Su and her new friends. He slapped it down to the coffee table before the chair Hill had taken. "This is the bitch that came to Sabra's door that day," he pointed to a tall gangly girl standing off a bit from the group. "Took me a minute before I recognized her. I don't think it hit Sabra when she saw it."

Caiphus edged in to check out the picture.

"According to the back of the photo, her name's Maeva." Smoak informed his brothers. "Cleon Raymond had a daughter named Maeva. They found her at the scene of his death, covered in his blood but they never tried her for the killing. One-because it was clear she was disturbed and two- because they found the deceased's stash of child porn in his closet. They figured he was molesting her and she finally fought back and won."

"Christ," Hill breathed, running a hand across his whiskered jaw.

"It gets better," Smoak folded his arms across the black crew shirt he wore. "Guardianship of the young Miss Raymond was given over to the mother of her best and apparently only friend Evangela Leer. Maeva was later adopted by Evangela's mother Tammy and her first husband Willard Leer."

Caiphus and Hill sat immobile in their seats, riveted on the story.

"The marriage ended abruptly. Mrs. Leer-maiden name Burnett was already... involved with her second husband to whom she's still married. His name is Brandon James and they have one daughter. Persephone." Smoak took a seat on the edge of the broad maple wood coffee table then. "How does she fit into all this, Hill?"

Hill swallowed, looking like he'd been blindsided. Not a common occurrence for a man such as himself. He was still for a long time, flinching when his brother called his name.

Smoak blinked as it all became clear. "You didn't know these wenches were her sisters."

It wasn't a question, yet Hill shook his head anyway. His obsidian gaze was set and stunned.

"I knew she was unreasonably close to... Evangela. I couldn't figure why, other than being best friends in that

172

AlTonya Washington

wild place. It makes sense now…" he left the chair and began to walk the room.

"Why do they want Fernando dead?" Smoak queried.

Hill fixed his younger brother with a crooked smile that held no amusement. "They want him dead for the same reason they want *me* dead. Although I now suppose their reasoning for my desired demise comes with a bit of a twist."

***

Seattle, Washington~

Josephine Ramsey's celebratory luncheon with Tykira, Dena and Catrina held the tone of anything but glee and celebration. The ladies met at Dena's where Josephine announced her engagement to Crane Cannon. The women were undoubtedly thrilled by the news. In light of recent events however it was difficult to let happiness truly take hold.

That became especially obvious when Josephine broke down into soft weeping after she made the announcement. Catrina moved over to hug her sister-in-law where they shared the sofa on Dena's sun porch. There, they had enjoyed tea and cakes following a lunch none of them really touched. When Josephine apologized they all ordered her to do no such thing.

"Honey, Fernando's going to be fine," Catrina kissed the smattering of fine hair at Josephine's temple. "He's walking around and everything. He told you so himself."

"I know," Josephine sniffed. "I'm so thankful. It's just the-the thought of it happening makes me want to shut down." She clutched the hem of Catrina's short-waist blouse. "You know," she said.

Catrina nodded. "The thought of my guys being caught in traffic can be cause for me to panic."

The admission brought about much needed lightness to the moment. Suddenly, Dena slapped her knees.

"We've got so much to celebrate." Her dark, doll-like face glowed as she regarded her family. "Fernando's going to be alright, Quay and Ty are bringing more Ramseys into the foal. Aunty's about to marry the love of her life. We've come too far to let this defeat us. I know *I'm* not gonna let it." She stood. "It's time for a party, or two, or three!" She laughed. "I insist on giving the official engagement party *and* the reception. We're gonna do it up big- news, tv, magazines, radio- the works. We've gotta keep the happy vibes going. I know I'm damn well in need of more of them." She shrugged.

"What do you say Aunt Josie? May I?"

Josephine raised her tea glass. "Hell yeah!" She cheered, laughing when the rest of the women followed her example.

***

By late afternoon, Darby was curled up on the bed with her attention stretched between a manila folder and legal pad. She was scribbling away when the door opened and Kraven walked in. The uncertainty in his eyes when he looked her way broke Darby's heart. She pushed work aside and offered him her hand.

It took less than a minute for him to press her back into the bed and cover her with his weight. The moment turned steamy in a second.

"Put your mouth on me." Darby was already unbuttoning the gauzy gray sleep shirt she wore.

Kraven brought a reluctant end to the kiss however. "You need to get back to work," he said.

"Later," she worked her bare nipples into his sleek chest. "Please," she arched up to suckle his earlobe.

Kraven thought he could have fainted from the pleasure but he resisted. "Back to work," he tried to sound firm but hunger gleamed in his eyes when they drifted toward her exposed cleavage. "Work," he shook his head once and pulled her shirt closed.

"I want to throw a party for my clients," Darby blurted.

"Lass," Kraven rolled to his back and worked the heels of his hands into his eyes. "You're killing me."

"I promised to be hands on and accessible and I haven't stuck to that in weeks. Half of them won't even talk to me unless you tell them you're okay with it." She lay across him then. "Can I have the party?" The blouse opened and she was rubbing into him again.

"I'll have to approve the guest list before anything's set," he said after only a few moments of her sultry pleading. "All the plus-ones will have to be approved and you'll have to have it right here."

"Not a problem," Darby's high ponytail bounced wildly as she nodded.

"If I can't approve the list, the party's off." He fought to keep his tone stony. "I mean it. No matter how much you beg or whatever you do to try changing my mind."

She leaned down to nibble his earlobe. "And what do you think I'll try?" She added her tongue to the caress.

"Doesn't matter- won't be good enough."

"Mmm… you're sure about that?" She intensified her suckling while easing a hand inside the waistband of his nylon sweats and boxer shorts to stroke his firming sex.

Kraven couldn't fight the demands of his hormones and turned Darby to her back. He feasted on her breasts but

gradually lowered to focus his attention elsewhere. Darby
lost herself in his touch. She forgot everything except
making love and Kraven didn't disappoint. His feasting
journeyed lower until he'd freed her of her underthings and
was tonguing her moistened sex.

He was thorough in his task, keeping his massive
hands sealed on her bottom and perfectly positioned for his
mouth. Darby didn't complain especially when his
ravenous repetitive thrusts had her quivering through a
climax in a few sweet moments.

When Darby was spent, Kraven did the unthinkable
and withdrew before treating her to the rest of what his
body had to offer.

"Kraven-"

"Shh...go back to work," he cupped her jaw and
gave her his kiss.

Darby moaned and hungrily suckled her taste from
his tongue.

Kraven quit the bed soon after and left the room
without a look back.

***

"I don't like it." Evangela dropped a fist to the
button silencing the speaker phone.

"Let them handle it, E." Casper massaged her
temples. "It's what we put them in place for. We've got
bigger fish to fry, remember?"

"Cas is right," Rain said, flexing her bare feet from
her spot on a chaise lounge. "You know the guys will make
them suffer."

"The fuckers won't die peacefully, E." Lula added
her opinion.

Evangela held gazes with Maeva for a long while.

"If they screw up-"

"E, they won't-"

"If they screw up," Evangela pointed toward Rain. "We do it my way- every step of the way. No questions." She whipped a towel from her bikini-clad frame and prepared to dive into the figure-8 pool. "I'm getting sick of these bastards cheating fate. It's about time for fate to win a round."

FOURTEEN

"**H**ow'd she take all that?" Taurus pulled a stalk of the high grass as he walked the rear wall of the DeBurgh lands with Kraven that morning.

"She looked like..." Kraven mussed his hair and winced, "like she was going to be sick."

"But?" Taurus heard the man's voice catch.

"She didn't turn away from me I...I was sure she would but we-we um- she let me..." he sent Taurus an awkward look and then grinned. "We made love again. Several agains."

"Your wife loves you." With an athlete's agility, Taurus hoisted himself up on the stone wall. "But you don't need to be reminded of that, do you?"

"I know it." Kraven hung his arms over the side of the wall and studied the vast scope of green waves beyond. "Monsters often have many lovable qualities. It's what makes us effective at carrying out the vileness we're capable of."

"Man please don't do this. You've spent a long time at this pity party of yours-you don't deserve it."

"Things I've done-"

"A long time ago."

"Yeah," Kraven threw back his head in a gesture of mock ease. "And how long before that reasoning just sounds like a baseless excuse?" He looked up at Taurus seated along the wall. "What happens the day she realizes that? I didn't tell her about the missions, the clean-up projects, and my life following all that, T."

Taurus frowned and slipped off the fence.

"I mentioned it while telling her about the island but I...I didn't explain what it was really all about."

"But she knows you were a soldier?"

"Hmph- soldier- and soldiers have never been known to cross the line, have they? And we definitely crossed the line, didn't we?"

"You need to tell her all of it."

Kraven set his strong jaw at a stubborn angle. "I rather she leave me than have to hear me tell her that."

"Liar," Taurus regarded his friend with a definite chill in his light eyes. "Have you already forgotten how hard it was for her to take you at your word when you claimed you loved her enough to move heaven and earth to have her?" Taurus walked around in front of Kraven when he turned his back.

"She told you how much she'd been hurt in the past and you told her you weren't like other men- blah, blah, blah..."

"Hell mate, I'm not!" Kraven looked venomous and slightly offended.

"Bullshit," Taurus appeared equally venomous. "If you let her go, you're no better than the rest. Worse maybe, since *unlike* the others *you* managed to take her heart."

Kraven blinked a defeated look shadowing his fierce features.

"Don't make the mistake *I* did, letting Nile leave when I had her here." Taurus closed the shallow distance between him and Kraven. "I was blessed that it turned out the way it did but we both know how easy it could have gone the other way." He squeezed Kraven's shoulder.

"Think about it," he said.

***

Far Rockaway, New York~

Gabriel Tesano's pale blue gaze was virtually unreadable. He looked down into the face of his lifeless son. Gabe's eyes repeatedly returned to the base of Brogue's neck where his throat had been cut.

"Russo did a good job, huh?" Gabriel cleared his throat. Grief had turned his voice to gravel as he commended the mortician he'd hired to work on his son.

Vale Tesano walked up to the gleaming Blackwood casket where his nephew would rest for an eternity. "He looks like Guiya, doesn't he?"

Gabriel rubbed his eyes at Vale's mention of his deceased lover- the mother of his only child. The reminder succeeded in shaking his stoic demeanor and he gave into the tears pressuring his eyes.

"We're going to get who did this."

"And where would you suggest we start?" Gabriel's back stiffened when he looked at his brother. "The list is chocked full of enemies itching to come after us."

"Us?" Vale frowned. "No one's got the balls, Gabe."

"Don't be overconfident, little brother."

"Are you forgetting the boy had a list of enemies all his own?"

"That, I remember all too well." Tentatively, Gabriel reached out to stroke a lock of Brogue's light hair. "I also remember that our enemies often intersected at the most obvious levels."

Vale smothered laughter just barely. "Please don't tell me you're talkin' about our brothers and nephews?" He gave into laughter but then stopped abruptly. "Let me repeat- with emphasis this time- they don't have the balls to fuck with us and definitely not like this." He waved a bejeweled hand toward Brogue.

Gabriel rolled his eyes. "I won't waste my time explaining why you're a damned idiot to think that, but in this case I'm referring to another."

Vale's expression cleared. His body tensed however, adding another two inches to his 5'6" height. "He'd have no reason to- we all parted as friends, Grekka."

"Friends," Gabriel spoke the word like it was poison. "No such thing. We were never friends. He always despised what we were doing." He focused on the onyx cufflinks glinting at his wrists and sighed. "He told me himself that our collaboration produced a mutual benefit and nothing more."

"Mutual benefit or the obsessions of two mad men?" Vale challenged.

Gabe towered over him easily. "That's our brother you're talking about."

"Gabriel, Humphrey was insane and he's dead now. Our business is too lucrative to risk anymore damage because of this bullshit."

"What's got you so scared now, V?" Gabriel fixed his younger brother with a sneer that ran the length of his scant stature. "There was a time when you were just as interested in the results of this as Hump was." He moved a step closer. "Or maybe you're just more paranoid about the reach of our brothers and nephews than you're willing to admit."

***

Queens, New York~

"Thanks, Rena," Aaron Tesano watched his housekeeper leave the tray of water and sodas she brought into the room for he and his brothers.

"She still being a mama hen?" Pitch asked when the short, round Greek woman left the bedroom suite.

"You shouldn't complain," Aaron watched longingly as his brother uncapped a bottle of soda. "At least you get something besides water."

"I hope Rena keeps up the good work," Roman waved his soda bottle. "You're lookin' good."

"That may be," Aaron grimaced, peering dismally into his water glass. "But I'd give anything for one stiff drink."

Laughter broke out among the brothers.

"How's Immi?" Aaron asked.

"Beautiful."

Roman's response brought smiles to his brother's faces.

"Like you're newlyweds again, huh?" Aaron chuckled.

"God yes," Roman savored the response and leaned back in the armchair he claimed near the floor to ceiling windows along the entire second floor of Aaron's brownstone.

"So when's she comin' to see me?" Aaron finally took a long swallow of the water.

Roman dragged both hands through his thick dark hair and laced his fingers behind his head. "I remember you telling her that you'd take her dancing when she got out of that chair. She said to tell you she'd see you when you get out of that bed."

"Any word on how long that'll be?" Pitch asked once more laughter had silenced between them.

"That I'm home says a lot," Aaron shifted on the pillows behind his back. "If they're confident that my blood pressure's stable after my next heart exam, then I'll be back to my old tricks."

"Ah hell!" Roman doubled over to bellow through his laughter.

"So how long before you two talk to me about what happened in Vegas with Brogue?"

Roman and Pitch exchanged smiles, not bothering to ask how their big brother knew about that.

"We took care of the body- untraceable to us." Pitch said.

Aaron turned the water glass on the napkin beneath it. "Good thing our nephew and his father have an endless supply of enemies."

"Yeah Ari um…" Pitch massaged his square jaw and sat up straighter in the arm chair that matched Roman's. "It's the enemies we want to talk about."

"We told the guys about shutting down whatever Hump and the others were caught up in." Roman explained, noticing Aaron's confusion. "We want 'em to take over with that."

"But they need more to go on than what you've been able to tell them." Aaron guessed.

Roman nodded. "Help us point them in the right direction."

Aaron's expression was unreadable. "What do you think I can tell them?"

"Anything Ari," Pitch whispered insistently. "Anything that can help us shed light on what those fools were involved in."

"We weren't close, fellas." Aaron smoothed his hands across his angular face and sighed. "Definitely not close enough to share clubhouse secrets." He laughed. "Funny how things change. We were once very close, had some years between us but we were the first two... we had a bond until-"

Roman and Pitch traded another glance when they spied the look that ghosted over Aaron's face.

"What Ari?"

Aaron blinked and looked to Pitch. "We were close until Papa brought *you* home."

Pitch's handsome, grizzled face softened when he smiled and nodded as though Aaron's words hadn't stirred surprise. "Be glad you were too young to remember *those* good old early days." He told Roman.

"Ma was fit to be tied." Aaron shook his head. "And that wouldn't have done any good. It helped even less that Pop told her you were coming and that was that."

"Did they argue a lot over it?" Roman asked.

"Hell yes they did." Aaron downed more of his water. "But Hump found out about it first. It was another month after he heard their first fight over it before Pitch came to live with us. Things were rough. They already had four of us counting Gabe and Stone. Then Pitch came to make five." His grin was a mix of sorrow and mild humor.

"It was a stretch- very hard times 'til Pop made his first stash playin' the market."

Pitch grinned on the memory. "People worshipped him when they found out he had a gift for that Wall Street shit."

"But that made things easier- the money had to help ease the tension." Roman said.

"Hmph," Aaron gestured. "Pop could've been a millionaire right out the gate and Ma would've still been pissed over Pitch bein' there," he winced. "Sorry man."

Pitch waved a hand to silently douse his brother's apology. "I never blamed Miss Athie for how she felt," he said.

"It wasn't your fault." Roman's smile was grim. "You didn't ask to be born."

"That may be little brother, but think how Immi would take it if you'd brought home your child from another woman for *her* to raise."

Roman massaged the bridge of his nose. "I probably wouldn't be living right now."

Pitch chuckled. "Then add that to the fact that your folks were already strugglin' to make ends meet."

"And add to *that* the fact that Pitch's mother was a black woman." Aaron said.

Silence dropped in heavy among the men then.

"I think things were uglier because of that. Lines were drawn but they weren't as visible 'til we all got older." Aaron pulled a thread at the cuff of his robe's sleeve. "I wasn't asked to take part in whatever Hump had goin' on with Stone and Gabe."

"Probably because they knew you couldn't have stomached it."

"Sounds like you've got most of the puzzle figured." Aaron smiled solemnly at Roman. "What else are you after?"

"There's still a lot unanswered Ari," Roman spread his hands resignedly. "We have no idea where else to start looking. What?" Roman noticed Aaron silence what he was about to say.

Aaron studied his fingertips bracing against one another. "I was going to ask about Hill." Aaron recalled that his brother's oldest son had exiled himself from his immediate family following Imani's accident.

Roman leaned back in his chair and shook his head woefully. "He's been a good source but that guilt of his... it's a powerful thing."

"And Caiphus? He and Hill travel in the same circles, don't they?"

Roman laughed. "My youngest son is as secretive as my eldest."

"It'll be alright Ro," Pitch reached over to squeeze his brother's shoulder. "We've got two of 'em straightened out," he referred to Pike and Smoak. "We'll get the other two on track soon enough."

Roman nodded, silently admitting how hard it was to believe that.

***

"I'm sorry, baby."

Darby wore a shadowed expression while crossing the sun-drenched field toward the stables. She'd called her mother seeking news on getting information about her father's family in Ireland. Unfortunately, Sean Ellis was still against it.

"Well I'd still love it if you guys came to the party anyway."

"Darby Olivia Ellis!" Lisa laughed. "You won't sweet talk your father into *that* in person any better than you will over the phone."

"Mommy I swear I'm not gonna try that."

"Right."

"Right." Darby could only quell her chuckle a second longer. "I won't try it *too* much. I miss you guys," her voice softened. "This'll be the perfect chance to see how the business is thriving and I'll have the chance to introduce you guys to everybody."

"We'll see, baby. I'll work on your father."

"Mmm hmm…" Darby tucked a hand into the back pocket of her riding jeans. "Why don't you make that sound like a chore?"

"Honey…working on my husband is one of life's sweet pleasures."

Darby threw back her head. "Walked right into that one didn't I?" her heart suddenly thudded to her throat at the sight of Kraven arriving around one side of the large, multilevel stable. He was riding his Clydesdale Hadrian. Perched in front of Kraven and giggling madly was Quincee.

"Keep working on Daddy about his family, Mommy. I need this." She said and ended the call shortly afterwards. She eased the cell into a side pocket on her burgundy linen blazer and headed over to Kraven and the baby. She approached in time to see Michaela arriving from inside the stables.

"Does Quest even mind a little bit that his best girl is wrapping all these men around her finger?"

"Nah…" Mick's bright stare, like Darby's, was fixed on Kraven who commanded Hadrian's reins with one hand while the other pressed securely against Quincee's middle to keep her steady. "He takes some kind of sick pleasure in reminding them that she's going home with him."

The ladies were still laughing as Kraven brought Hadrian to a stop. He gave the large animal an affectionate

187

A Lover's Sin

rub and then; cradling Quincee against him, expertly eased off Hadrian's back. The little girl was breathless from laughter as Kraven nuzzled her ear and let her pet Hadrian's thick, shimmering champagne colored mane.

The sight caused Darby's thudding heart to make a graceful swan dive from her throat to her stomach. Kraven DeBurgh was a natural with kids. It was no wonder that he'd want one- *many* of his own.

"Mama!" Quincee saw Mick and pointed. "Horsie!" She produced a relative pronunciation of the word and pointed to indicate that she wanted Mick to come pet Hadrian too. Of course, the precocious child wasn't satisfied until Darby came to pet the horse as well.

"She's gonna be a smart one," Darby voiced the compliment to her husband once Michaela had gone to take Quincee to a late afternoon picnic that Yohan and Melina had asked to have with the child.

Kraven watched Mick strolling off with the baby as well. "She's an absolute dream," his lilting tone was hushed.

Darby curled both hands around a muscular arm and drew him closer. "It's very sexy to see a man doting on a child that way, you know?"

The declaration captured Kraven's full attention and he turned to his wife. "Is it now?" he asked.

Darby gave a curt nod. "Uh-huh."

Kraven tugged her closer and upward until he had her at eye level. "How sexy?"

Without shame, Darby wrapped her legs around his back and lavished him with a hungry kiss. Kraven released her arms to slip his about her waist. Darby let her fingers get lost in his hair and added more heat to her kiss. She was so involved in the act that she didn't realize Kraven was carrying her into the stable. Not until she felt them ascending a stairway did she try to break the kiss. Kraven merely cupped her chin firmly, silently insisting on her cooperation.

"Kraven we shouldn't- not here."

"Hands are gone for the day," he assured her, his lips and tongue suckling her earlobe. "Besides, we're the Lord and Lady we can do whatever we bloody well please."

Darby would've laughed, but her mouth was again thoroughly engaged in their kiss. Surrendering most willingly, she pulled her hands from Kraven's hair and slipped off her blazer. It had barely hit the hay dusted ground when she was tugging her shirt from the waistband of her jeans.

Kraven took the steps of the narrow wooden stairway with the confidence of having climbed them many times before. Darby gave a yelp of surprise when she was suddenly flung into a mound of golden hay. Exasperated yet laughing mindlessly, she tossed fistfuls of the stuff at her husband. He went to his knees amidst the showering of hay that clung to his clothes and hair as it did Darby's.

She was still laughing, happiness having fully blossomed inside her. Her laughter quieted as she took stock of the intensity in his vibrant emerald eyes. She cleared her throat to douse the last of the laughter, accepting that he was bent on being serious instead of playful. She silenced, though earlier exertions kept her abundant bust line heaving, easily drawing her husband's gaze.

Kraven put his head against the cleavage visible above the straining top button of her cream colored shirt. He took the button between his teeth and made quick work of un-securing it.

Darby's resulting gasp mingled with a cry when she heard her shirt rip as the button came undone. Kraven made no apologies for destroying her clothes and continued to subject the shirt and the rest of its buttons to the same fate.

Tugging her up without ceremony, he pulled the tattered garment from her back and then relieved her of boots, jeans and underthings. Darby's chest continued to heave furiously. The determination on Kraven's darkly alluring face had her heart thudding yet again.

Once he had her naked- had her clothing strewn all over the hay covered loft, he merely studied her. The intensity of his expression transitioned from hunger to something more ravenous.

His eyes clashed with hers and in that moment, Darby didn't dare move.

"Do I frighten you, Lass?"

The question was the last she could have predicted. Immediately, she shook her head sending hay strewn honey blonde curls into her brown face. Kraven brought his face closer to hers. He frowned, turning his features fiercer and infinitely more provocative.

"Even after what I told you? Even after that?"

Her head shaking took on a stubborn element. "No Kraven."

"Don't lie to me."

"I swear it." She swallowed with effort. "You don't frighten me. You never will."

He smiled but the gesture did little to soften his expression. He dipped his head subtly, taking a slow possessive survey of her curvy frame. "I want my babies inside you." The smile he wore intensified when he caught her blink and her eyes widen a fraction.

"Ahh… I think I've done it. There's that fear…"

"Kraven-"

"I want my babies inside you and I won't apologize for that. I know you're uncertain, but you should know that I plan to wear you down on that, love. I know I promised that I wouldn't but... well...I lied."

Darby felt her lashes fluttering. Her reaction had nothing to do with fear or uncertainty.

"I won't pass on every opportunity to make that happen," he said. "I want to put myself here," his hand smoothed across her belly. He gave her a light shove deeper into the hay and kept his eyes fixed on hers while freeing himself from the confines of his jeans.

Darby's heart returned to its thudding state as she watched his sex emerge from the button fly of the loose fitting denims he wore with a lightweight cobalt blue sweatshirt. He removed none of his clothing however. One hand imprisoned her bare thigh and he pulled her down. He was feasting then-insatiable for the feel of her nipple against his tongue. He alternated between the full cinnamon brown globes while claiming her with his erection.

Darby was too weak, too aroused by his words, his manner and the granite length that filled her almost to overflowing. Her hands rested in the soft hay as her hips bucked and twisted to meet his thrusts in a fashion that was both needy and demanding.

Late afternoon sunlight streamed between the loose planks in the stable roof. It cascaded over the lovers and made Darby ache with the desire to see the golden tint drenching Kraven's powerful torso as his muscles bunches and flexed amidst his movements.

Insistently, she pushed at the sweatshirt until Kraven obliged and dragged it over his head. Darby nuzzled her head back into the hay and felt orgasmic shudders slam her when his upper body was bared.

A Lover's Sin

Clenching fists, she pounded them lightly against the wall of flesh that practically blocked all else from view. She raked her rounded nails down his back until they connected with the waistband of his unfastened jeans. She shoved down denims and boxers until she was cupping his bare ass in her hands.

Kraven settled himself fully to cover Darby's quivering body. His perfect teeth grazed her earlobe while one hand cupped her breast to manipulate the nipple beneath his thumb. Darby's resulting whimpers stroked Kraven's ego as deliciously as her sex gloved and released his width.

"No..." she moaned, feeling him coming inside her and realizing they'd be done soon.

Kraven knew it wouldn't be long before he was ready again. The pleasure of filling her with his seed was an act that aroused him like no other. He took her thighs and spread her further thus deepening the penetration and flow of his release.

Once they were spent, Kraven trembled as strongly as Darby. Together, they drifted into a nap that lasted just shy of fifteen minutes before they woke to make love all over again.

FIFTEEN

When Darby woke again she was decidedly disoriented
and had trouble determining when she'd left the stables.
Not until one of the housemaids came to check on her at
Kraven's request did Darby begin to make sense of things.

Apparently her husband had carried her in from the
stables following their fourth round of…stimulation. Darby
smiled and hid her face in the down pillows lining the
headboard. The double king bed sat on a platform and
provided a dreamlike view of the hills and mountains far in
the distance. Darby recalled how the housemaid blushed
upon telling her the story. The young auburn haired maid
went on to inform Darby that she'd been asleep for the
better part of the day- another factor in her present
disorientation.

The sleep was needed and had done her body good. Not surprising, she was in no hurry to pull herself from beneath the heavy quilts especially when she realized the chill of the day had warranted the use of the fireplaces. The infrequent pop and crackle of the heavy logs possessed the power to lull her back into sleep. Darby was giving into that very indulgence when the sound of knocking rose above the hissing flames.

Nile stuck her head inside the room seconds later. In her hands, she carried a tray of hot tea and biscuits.

Laughing, Darby extended her hands toward her best friend.

"Is everything alright?" Nile was asking once she'd set down the tray and hugged Darby.

"Apparently my husband made a big show of carrying me in over his shoulder once he was done with me in the cave."

Laughter abounded between the friends for a while. Then, they took a survey of what the tray held.

"That'll certainly give the lady staff more material for their daydreams- as if they need any." Nile licked a smidge of wild berry jam from her finger. "Kraven's looks alone probably have their thoughts in X-rated mode for most of the day anyway."

"Hmph, for certain," Darby scooted up in bed and poured the tea.

"This is good," Nile pressed a hand against Darby's cheek. "You seem happier than you have."

"Kraven wants me pregnant- all the time if he has his way."

Nile's very dark lovely face was a picture of elation. "He should, this place is too big not to be filled with at least two kids."

"Two?!" Darby looked horrified.

194

A Lover's Sin

"You're right," Nile however had misread her friend's expression. "The *clan* wouldn't be complete without at least four."

"I'm gonna be sick," Darby buried her face in her hands.

"Hey…" Nile tilted her head and blinked as if she were realizing that her friend's emotions weren't running along the same happy vein as her own. Setting the tea cup back to the tray, Nile folded her legs beneath her and waited.

"I'm sorry," Darby's miserable look was reflected in the tone of her voice.

"For…?" Nile appeared even more bewildered.

Darby drew her hands back through her hair and rested her elbows to her raised knees. "Here I am acting this way over having kids when…"

Nile blinked suddenly understanding her friend's concern. "Hey?" She tugged the frilly cuff of the sleeve that covered Darby's wrist. "We've always been there for one another and we always will be. Your feelings about kids-whatever they are- don't make me love you any less." She tugged one of Darby's curls. "And they don't make me look down in judgment over whatever opinions you've got about the path your life should take. Now," she retrieved her tea cup. "Talk to me."

"You know I love kids but you also know that I've never thought that *having* them was best for me." Darby waited for Nile's nod, her voluminous green stare holding trace amounts of expectancy and uncertainty.

"Having kids has been on my mind more lately than it's ever been."

"Oh Cherì," Nile reached out to squeeze Darby's foot beneath the covers. "That's because you're in love and your husband wants so much to share that with you."

"I've been working myself to death trying to keep it off my mind."

Nile shook her head. "Why?"

"Daddy went crazy when I asked him about finding his family." Darby leaned over to pinch a corner from one of the flaky scratch-made biscuits.

Nile studied the contents of her cup. "Do you think that's necessary-still? After all this time?"

"You're right I know." Darby reached for the biscuit and took a bigger bite. "It's stupid to set myself up for that kind of drama but I'm obsessed with needing to know...how they'll react to me."

"You know, Cheri there *is* a chance that they won't slam the door in your face when they discover who you are."

"But if they do, Ny..." Darby considered the possibility while finishing off the large biscuit. "I feel like I should be armed with knowing what that'd feel like."

"Mon Dieu..." Nile downed some of the flavorful chamomile blend. "I won't pretend to understand *why* you're letting this rattle you so. You know you're going to have a massively difficult time convincing Kraven to even let you put yourself in that situation."

"Which is exactly why I probably won't tell him."

"Now listen, that-"

"Nothing's set in stone," Darby waved her hands defensively. "I don't even know if Daddy's family is still in Ireland and if they are I don't know which part. I don't even know my grandparent's full names. Daddy's like the CIA with hiding this information."

"Good for Mr. Sean," Nile spoke the words softly following up with a quick sip of tea.

Darby rolled her eyes and scooted back down a bit in the bed. "Kraven probably won't even let me set foot outside the house once he finds out…"

Nile gave pause at the odd tone in Darby's voice. "Finds out…"

Smiling then, Darby looked over at her friend. "Finds out I'm pregnant."

Nile swallowed and then slowly she returned her tea cup to the tray. Once that was done, she let out a yelp and began to bounce up and down on the bed as she clapped wildly.

Darby dissolved into laughter and found herself wrapped in a hug moments later.

"How long have you known?" Nile's dark eyes sparkled as brilliantly as the small row of sequins along the scooping neckline of the gold sweater she wore. "Why didn't you tell me before? Why haven't you told Kraven?"

"I've suspected for a couple of weeks, but I wouldn't let myself think about it and then all hell broke loose and I…I only confirmed it day before yesterday." She recalled how hard it was not to tell Kraven during their time in the stable. "I haven't even been to see my doctor yet." She squeezed Nile's hands. "I was working so hard while I was in Edinburgh, I forgot my pills more than a few times and then when Kraven came…I don't believe I thought about them once. I didn't tell you Nile, because I didn't want to upset you. A child was always *your* dream."

"I'm living my dream, Cherì. Taurus is…to die for."

"Mon Dieu!" Darby agreed in her best faux French accent and let her lashes flutter.

"And now my very best friend is bringing a new life into the world- a life that I get to be a part of. No Cherì 'upset' is the last thing I feel."

The friends held each other in a tight clutch and lost track of time.

***

Darby considered it a sign when; just two days later, her parents arrived in Scotland. Kraven sent a car to collect them from the airport. Sean and Lisa Ellis were in time for a late lunch with the rest of the guests.

The dinner that evening was a fun, bawdy affair complete with dynamic food, drink, laughter, music and dancing. Kraven let the staff off for the night and he and the guys took over kitchen responsibilities. The ladies recalled a similar cooking experience at Michaela's newly sold Chicago home before Fernando's and County's wedding.

Sean and Lisa couldn't keep their eyes dry for laughing so hard over the stories that were relayed at the dinner table.

Darby took part in all the excitement but she declined drink. She hoped no one- most of all Kraven- noticed. She had yet to share the news with him due in part to her parent's arrival. She hoped the visit might signal her father's readiness to give in to her demands for information about his family.

"I just don't know."

Her mother's words had Darby caught between hope and disappointment. Mother and daughter shared a few private moments on a balcony off from the sitting room where everyone was gathering for after dinner drinks.

"I just don't know if it's wise for you to keep obsessing over this, sweetie. Kraven's bound to notice how agitated it makes you," Lisa leaned over to tuck a curl behind Darby's ear. "Do you even realize how hard a time he has keeping his eyes off you once you walk into a room?"

Darby bowed her head and smiled.

"Fernando seems better." Lisa decided to change the subject then.

"Being here's done him a lot of good," Darby noted, becoming fixated on a lone star twinkling in the distance.

Lisa was more fixated on her daughter. Her chestnut gaze was soft as it studied Darby's profile. "I think this place is good for more than just Fernando."

Darby gave an exaggerated shrug. "It's good to be home with family and friends." She moved to kiss Lisa's smooth mahogany brown cheek. "It's all cause for celebration." She added.

The long, delicate arch of Lisa's brows rose to relay skepticism. "Since when is ginger ale a celebration drink?"

Darby's frown was playful. "Depends on what's in the ginger ale."

The women laughed but when Darby suddenly cleared her throat and took a quick, nervous sip of the drink, Lisa blinked.

"Darby?" She breathed on the verge of realization. Leaning in, she cupped her daughter's face to search her gaze. "Honey?" her tone was a gasp.

Darby pressed her lips together while nodding her confirmation. "Yes," she responded in the same gasping tone.

Lisa's mouth formed a perfect O. She put a hand to Darby's stomach and held it there. "Kraven must be so happy?"

"I haven't told him yet, Mama."

"But why-" Lisa closed her eyes as if she had answered her own question. "Baby are you really serious about this?" Easily, Lisa read her daughter's expression recognizing it as one she knew so well.

"The more we say 'no' the more you're gonna want this, huh?" Lisa rolled her eyes. "And don't give me that pitiful smile."

Darby tucked her hands into the long bell sleeves of her rust colored swing dress and tried to wipe her face of emotion. She only succeeded in blinking owlishly.

"Fine." Lisa gave a sudden toss of her curly bobbed hair.

Amazed, Darby watched her mother pull out a mobile from the front pocket of her pin-striped burgundy trousers. She sent a text.

"Their names and the town they're in. It's all I have."

Darby lunged over and kissed her mother's cheek again.

"Spoiled rotten," Lisa grumbled yet squeezed her child tight. "You be careful, you hear?"

***

The guys grudgingly agreed to the girls going into town shopping the next afternoon. The men knew they had little say in the matter since chances were strong that their wives would venture off with or without their approval. Kraven eased everyone's minds when he reminded them that Caiphus, Hill and Smoak were staying at the inn and could keep an eye out. With everyone satisfied the shopping trip commenced.

In town, Sabra and Sybilla joined in for the simple outing that only consisted of lunch at Seamus Wallace's café and shopping at his wife's boutique.

It was no surprise that Sabra commanded the bulk of the attention from Elena Wallace's staff. She'd only attended the jaunt to have time with her family, but she was nicely surprised by the selection of attire on the racks of Elena's Dress.

While Johari, Sybilla and County entertained themselves by browsing the extensive selection of scarves, belts and hats, Melina, Nile and Michaela got stuck with the job of complimenting Sabra's choices as she tried on one outfit after another.

Darby had ventured off to have a little business chat with Elena's nieces regarding the website and other marketing issues she'd been unable to discuss during the last several days. After the talk, the girls left Darby to make final notes in the privacy of Elena's office. She was there when a knock sounded on the open door.

"Come on in. I'm just finishing up." Darby called. When there was no sound of movement, she glanced up. Her welcome smile froze before it had the chance to broaden.

The woman in the doorway had skin the color of rich, golden brown- like black coffee with just a hint of cream. Her eyes were a remarkable shade of silver. She was tall and moved with a gracefulness that proved she wasn't in the habit of rushing.

"I'm sorry," Darby stood behind the dainty white Chippendale desk. "I don't think I have much wall space available just now in case you've come bearing more donations."

Persephone James cast a cool quick look across her shoulder. "You're a hard woman to find alone." Her boots made the faintest tap as she stepped into the office.

"You're a hard woman to find at all." Darby tossed her pen to the desk. "To what do I owe the pleasure?"

Persephone's easy look sharpened with sudden urgency. "Is he alright?" She asked.

"Who?" Darby shook her head but only received Persephone's pointed look in reply. "You're asking about Fernando?" She moved from behind the desk then. "Why?"

Persephone pushed the office door shut without looking back at it. "I only plan to tell this story once so you'd better get the agent in here."

"Bill." Darby breathed.

"I'm actually here to talk to *her* but the chance to speak with both of you is even better."

"What's this all about?" Darby folded her arms across her black turtleneck.

"First you answer *my* question. Is he alright?"

"He's going to be fine. The bullet only grazed him."

Persephone blinked, the silvery orbs of her eyes glinting like twin strikes of lightning. "The news made it sound serious."

"They were concerned about some extensive bleeding." Darby lifted her chin. "Now I'll ask again. What are you doing here?"

Moving deeper into the office, Persephone found a perch on the corner of the desk. "Haven't you figured it out yet Lady DeBurgh? I'm the one who shot him."

SIXTEEN

There was no way for Persephone to speak privately with Darby and Sybilla without rousing the suspicion of everyone in the boutique. Persephone wasn't too keen on the idea of facing a crowd, but she realized she had little say in the matter. Her reluctance gave way when she discovered Contessa was there. As she couldn't pose explanation (or apology) to Fernando Ramsey, posing one to his wife was both necessary and overdue.

So as not to arouse suspicion, Elena Wallace instructed her staff not to show the CLOSED sign. They were to merely monitor the door and inform any new customers that they were working on an unexpected shipment. Unofficially, the shop was then a meeting place.

"I didn't do this to Fernando for the reason you're thinking but please know that I deeply regret the pain I forced on you both. I *am* sorry."

County's face was without emotion. "Maybe you should just tell me why you did it bitch and the reason had better be damn good." She was rigid beneath the hold Michaela kept on her arm. It helped. County ached to claw the woman's face.

Sighing then, Persephone moved to the chair behind the desk that Darby had earlier suggested she take. "If I hadn't shot him, someone else would have and I can promise you it wouldn't have been a flesh wound."

"What?" Mick, Darby and Johari blurted at once.

"I've been trying to warn you forever and a day," Persephone said.

"Really? Ever heard of a phone, idiot?"

"Sabra..." Sybilla moved closer to the desk. "Go on Persephone."

Persephone braced her elbows to the desk and raked her fingers through the close-cropped waves of onyx hair which held natural streaks of walnut brown. "I couldn't take a chance on anyone knowing it was me." She looked up at Darby. "I took a chance on giving you that painting but when *you*," she looked to Nile, "started seeing Taurus Ramsey, I figured that was as close as I dared to get." She focused her eyes on the desk again. "I certainly couldn't talk to any of the Tesanos."

"Why? Because of your drama-fest with Hill?"

"Sabra!" Sybilla gave a fast, firm wave to silence her cousin.

"My original plan was to talk to you Nile at your event in Montenegro a couple of years ago." Persephone gave a wan smile. "I second guessed that when I saw Taurus there. I was going to give you the painting then but I just decided to wait until you were back at the gallery." She looked toward Darby again.

Sybilla claimed a high-backed chair near the row of white oak file cabinets. "What was so special about that painting?" She asked.

"The piece was done by a man named Austin Chappell. You recognize the name." Persephone took note of the telling looks that went around the room.

"He's dead, you know?" Melina's gaze was hard.

Persephone nodded. "The piece was done from memory- it's a place at the northern tip of Madagascar- in a place called Sambava. We all used to call the place itself an island."

"And island?" County recalled Fernando's story about the area.

"You were there?" Darby asked.

Again, Persephone nodded. "That painting was my abstract attempt at warning you all about what was coming. It was stupid," she grimaced at herself. "I have a habit of sharing info the second I find it- I don't think. I don't even bother to confirm that it'll *mean* anything for the intended party." She looked to Nile again.

"Cufi Muhammad was your father. I thought maybe he'd brought you there and you'd recognize it." Sadness shadowed her striking gaze. "So many other fathers brought their daughters…"

"We know about the ovaries." Nile said.

Persephone shrugged from the black linen jacket she wore. "I couldn't think of how best to tell you what was coming so I just left the picture along with the rest of Austin's work."

"How'd you get it?" Mick's voice was hushed.

"I bought it." Persephone shrugged. "All but the one piece. Austin gave it to me when I went to warn *him*. I asked him to get word to… Hill," she coughed and pressed her thumb into the corner of her eye. "I even sent you a note," she told Mick. "It had all the names I thought might be on the list."

Sybilla leaned closer. "What list?"

"My sister's list. She's been waiting on this for years and it looks like her waiting is at its end."

In his study, seated before the fire with brandy and the chill of late afternoon setting in, Kraven tapped his fingers to his brow in a show of concentration. Seated across from his son-in-law, Sean Ellis smiled a smile of triumph.

The men had taken a few hours to indulge in a game of Chess while Darby shopped and Lisa Ellis took a long, jet-lag induced nap.

"Bloody hell," frustrated, Kraven made his move.

Sean chuckled an evil chuckle and made his move. "Check mate, Boy-o."

"Next time, Sir," Kraven issued his usual promise. He had yet to best his father-in-law in the game.

"Anything else I can beat you at, Son?"

Kraven had already forgotten his defeat. "Sir, was there ever a time that you questioned your... orders?"

Sean smoothed his hands across the khakis where they covered his thighs. The easy tinge slowly faded from his tanned, ruggedly attractive face. Long, auburn brows tugged close at the start of a frown. "Son?" Was all that he could manage in response.

Kraven tapped his fingers to one corner of the centuries old chess table with its rich mix of maple, cherry and black woods. "I was active in the service for a long time. I opted for that life instead of college." He nudged one of Sean Ellis' captured pawns.

"I did well taking orders... so well, that I was selected from the ranks to handle more... specialized services."

Sean's expression changed as he comprehended the underlying meaning of the words.

"The things I did..." Kraven smirked and kept his eyes downcast. "I suppose I could attribute them to certain aspects of my upbringing." The smirk became more defined while he recalled the time spent in Sambava- the time that forged him into the man he would just as soon forget.

"Darby doesn't know what I was. She doesn't have all the details about that part of my life."

"You make it sound like a disease, boy." Sean leaned close to grate out the words. "You were a soldier," his tone was laced with pride.

"It was nothing like what you were a part of, Sir." Kraven bumped the toe of his boot against one of the chess table's massive claw feet. "There was no pride, no happy homecoming celebrations and medal ceremonies. There were only orders and blood..." He folded his hands into the hem of the green crew shirt which was the same vivid hue as his eyes.

"*You* were the true soldier, Sir. You made an honest career of it, but was there ever a time when you wondered what 'for the greater good' meant? Did you ever discover that it was a load of crap because there *is* no such thing?"

Sean bridged his fingers before his jaw and maintained his stoic demeanor. "Kraven, whatever those days involved, they're over for you now."

"Over, but not forgotten. Doing the wrong things for the right reasons...they're still the wrong things, Sir. Sinful things."

"So, it means nothing that my daughter loves you?"

"It means everything." Kraven's voice was hushed, yet strong.

"I'm not sure that you understand how tightly her heart was bound." Sean's face appeared gaunt. "She's always been afraid of falling in love and being hurt by it or worse- someone falling in love with her and she... disappointing them." He leaned back to regard Kraven thoughtfully.

"These things... these things you're doing your damndest to smother, will tear you up inside. Kraven, a soldier is at his best, his mind most sound, his heart set when he's in the shit because he knows he must depend on all of his faculties if he hopes to survive. But it's later, lad... Later when he's alone in the dark with only his thoughts- his memories for company, that's when the madness thrives.

"I know all too well about doing the wrong things for the right reasons," Sean set his mouth into a grim line. "There were times I believed I stayed in and made a career of it because I was afraid of what I'd see in the dark with only those memories interrupting the silence."

"But you... don't believe that, Sir?" Kraven sounded wary.

"I was saved." Sean settled back more comfortably in the deep armchair. "A soldier is supposed to be a dauntless order-taker, no questions asked and; above all, no uncertainty or fear displayed."

"Ever," Kraven and Sean spoke the word in unison.

Sean chuckled, studying his hands while rubbing them one inside the other. "None of that comes into play with my wife. You see lad, every soldier needs his weapon. Lisa's mine. Those dark memories don't stand a chance against her."

"So you're saying I should talk to my wife."

"I'm saying you should have done so a long time ago. But yes, now would be good."

Kraven set his elbows to the table and pushed both hands through his hair. "I think I'll die if she leaves me, Sir. I know that sounds flowery and dramatic, but I fear it. I was near to a walking corpse when I met her. She doesn't know how she pulled me back from that."

"I think she does, but it wouldn't hurt for you to mention something along those lines when you talk to her."

"I'm afraid of what she might do, Sir."

"Ha! You should be! My girl has one hell of a temper!"

Robust laughter livened the lamp-lit room.

Kraven nodded, still wearing a grin. "Thank you, Sir." He leaned across the table and shook hands with his father-in-law.

"Your sisters?" Sybilla breathed in a soft, stunned tone. She'd done well to speak the words. The other women had been struck silent rapt with interest over the story.

Persephone nodded. "Maeva's not my sister, though. She came to live with us after her father was killed-even changed her last name to match Evangela's."

"Sounds like a crazy wench," Sabra sneered. "She was lucky to have a friend, let alone one with a family willin' to take her in."

"That wasn't luck," Persephone's full lips curved into a grimace. "That was my sister protecting her accomplice. Maeva's father's death remains an unsolved murder. From what I understand, he wasn't the most beloved man in town so the cops didn't waste many man hours on solving the crime. They finally wrote it off as him meeting up with some out-of-towner who wasn't taking his crap.

"But it was no out-of-towner," Persephone watched her hands splayed before her on the desk. "Eva and Mae butchered him and bragged about it to the only audience they trusted at the time- me. *I* certainly wasn't going to betray their confidence especially when they'd already threatened to kill me and had the blood on their hands to prove they'd already done it once.

"They told me it was because Cleon Raymond; Maeva's father, had touched Eva. Mae went crazy which is saying a lot- but she's obsessive about protecting her which is a good thing I guess, since Eva's the only one who can control her. They're killers, you see?" She shrugged as though it were a matter of fact. "It comes natural to them and I've never seen anything like it."

"Jesus..." Sabra watched Persephone in horror.

"It's how they make their money and they're very successful. Dangerous yet beautiful- they're both older than any of us, but can pass for ten...fifteen years younger that their actual ages. The men their crew goes after never see them coming. Hmph," her expression softened. "At least they never see them *coming* the way they should."

Persephone spotted the doubt on the faces of her audience. "How else do you think they were able to take out a man like Brogue Tesano?"

"Why'd you pick Fernando to shoot when Kraven was there too?" Darby asked.

"I'm sorry," Again Persephone fixed on Contessa. "I'm so very sorry. I had the clearest shot of Fernando. I also knew it'd shake things up the most in Eva's camp- buy you guys time to figure a way to track them. They're following the list in the...order of events from that night."

County closed her eyes, massaging the lump of emotion at the base of her throat. "You mean, the order they took turns with your sister."

A Lover's Sin

"They told you?" Persephone gave County a measured look. "According to Eva, Fernando didn't... take a turn." She smiled wanly when Contessa exhaled in relief.

"He set it up and was there though which earned him a spot on the list. Their plans were to go after the ones responsible for the island's existence."

"How do you know all this?"

Persephone smiled at Bill. "It was supposed to be our 'greatest mission'." She curved her index and middle fingers to quote the phrase. "We'd been planning it for years. I knew everything- down to the little calling cards they planned to leave with each body." She fidgeted with the silver links on her wrist watch.

"I didn't know what impact my...intervention might have but something had to be done."

"Why won't you talk to Hill?" Nile asked.

"I can't do that."

"Hey?" Darby tapped her fingers to the desk until Persephone looked up at her. "You *are* trying to save his life, you know? I'm pretty sure he'd listen to you."

"I'll say," Sabra blurted, hooking a finger in the pocket of her skin-tight denims. "And why the fuck would you want to help the man who raped your sister?"

"Sabi..."

"It's okay," Persephone told Bill before looking back at Sabra. "What happened that night wasn't rape. Things like that happened all the time on the island. Consensually. Girls gained status- gifts, some had their own apartments. Some got excused from all the weird testing that went on there... they greatly benefitted by being popular among the guys."

"I'm sure half of them didn't *want* to be there." Mick championed.

"True," Persephone shrugged the delicate arch of her brows, "but way more than half accepted it, especially when they were being paid. For a little extra money, guys got a little extra from the girls- beyond what was required. There were things some girls did that others didn't or didn't know *how* to do as well. My sister and her crew made a name for themselves, but when the Captain's best soldiers drugged her, they made a mistake. They changed the rules without her permission."

"The Captain?" Johari inquired from the loveseat she shared with Melina.

"There were instructors all over the place," Persephone explained, "each had his own squad to train. There was a captain in charge of the instructors, the squads, the testing-everything. Perjas...something, I don't know- he was rarely seen. I never met him but if your performance on the island caught his attention in a favorable light you earned a place among his best."

"But Persephone, all this still doesn't explain why you're helping us." Melina challenged.

Persephone closed her eyes to massage her neck as she spoke. "I loved Eva *and* Mae once. I tracked them to that island foolishly hoping to save them-how I even got there is a story all its own...but I had to try, gave into my habit for acting on the first bit of info I could find..."

She studied the recessed lighting in the office ceiling. "They didn't want my help," she remembered, "didn't want to be saved- not by me... when I told them I wasn't there to join up, Eva had Mae beat me until I agreed to play along. That's how I met Hill." She looked to Nile.

"At the time I didn't realize how lucky I was that it was him who... broke me in and then I fell in love with him and *then* I chose him over them. After that, things got...messier. I got away the first chance I had- snuck onto

A Lover's Sin

your dad's ship when he came to drop off new girls." She smiled sadly at Nile that time. "It was years before I saw my sisters again. When I did, they threatened to kill me- they don't forgive betrayal but I didn't care."

She covered her face with her hands and inhaled as though it pained her to do so. "When they realized I wouldn't fall in line because of their threats- they threatened to take my girls."

Darby blinked and looked to Sybilla.

"Hill's girls." Persephone confirmed and gave her audience a few quiet moments to accept the news.

"I um...Hill and me it was...*drama* from the jump." She sent Sabra a look. "We'd broken up- *again* before I even knew I was pregnant. Eva and Mae... I don't know how they found out but they were waiting to *congratulate* me the day I walked out of the OB's office. They made their threats and told me they'd keep in touch. I ran. I never told Hill. The twins are five now. They were three when Eva found us." She shivered as though a chill had skimmed her spine.

"I knew they'd take them. They didn't plan to kill them but to raise them. Eva wants to turn them into what she is. Mae... well she's only brawn but Evangela...Eva's the real monster."

"Persephone," Bill walked over to squeeze the woman's shaking hands. "I can protect you and the girls. You don't have to worry- not anymore."

Persephone's captivating golden brown face wore an incredulous look. "You think I plan to stick around? I'm taking a chance now with Hill being just a few doors down from this place. And you can best bet Eva's got eyes here too. You're all being watched Sybilla- you'd do better to make sure every member of your own family's protected."

She looked to Contessa and shook her head. "I had to know how he was. I'm an excellent shot. I was taught by the best, my sister doesn't surround herself with mediocre assistants. My intent wasn't to put his life in danger, but to save it."

Bill squeezed Persephone's hands again until Persephone looked her way. "Let me help you," she pleaded.

Persephone produced a pitiable smile. "When you catch them, don't worry, I'll be there to help you put them away. Hopefully, my capacity will only be as an attendant at their funerals, but I'll happily testify if you choose to take the high road and bring them in to be tried in a court of law. Until then, forget you ever saw me."

SEVENTEEN

The next morning brought with it, the sights and sounds of a party in preparation. The gathering for Darby's clients was set to take place that night. She hadn't had much to do other than make up the guest list. Kraven had hired people to handle the rest.

A good thing too. Following the unexpected meeting with Persephone James and the revelations she'd brought with her, Darby had been in no frame of mind to do much else. Sybilla had been last to speak with Persephone but she'd remained unsuccessful in changing the woman's mind.

The girls returned to the estate in time for a late supper and early bedtime. Thankfully, their husbands took their resigned moods as exhaustion after the outing.

Darby gathered the folds of her peach lounging robe and took a seat in the big hideous-looking plaid chair that

Kraven had insisted on keeping in their bedroom. She settled into the chair and turned her face into the back. She inhaled Kraven's scent, drawing comfort from the fragrance. Turning her attention to the picture window beside the chair, she absently observed the party planners and caterers at work.

In spite of all the shocking tidbits that Persephone James had shared, Darby was only impressed by the bottom line: Persephone was a mother doing what she thought was right for her kids.

"Oh baby," Darby smoothed a hand across her as yet non-existent belly. "Am I crazy?" She asked her unborn child. After all, easing her curiosity about her father's family was a far cry from protecting her child from crazed psychopaths.

The door opened and Kraven walked in. The black T-shirt clung to his chest and back thanks to the rivulets of sweat pouring from his skin. He'd taken a break from the grueling hours of usual morning work at the castle which now had the look and feel of a hunting lodge. He stood just inside the bed chamber looking decidedly weary while massaging his neck and grunting as the pressure soothed the bunched muscles there. A good portion of the weariness faded however when he noticed Darby in the deep chair across the room.

"Lass! Ha! The chair is finally workin' its magic on you, eh? Told you, didn't I?"

"Don't be so sure it's the chair," she cautioned maneuvering herself to face him. "You're all over it and I like the smell."

"Ouch. Guess I should stay away just now, huh?" He gave a tug to the tail of the sweaty shirt hanging past the waistband of his equally grimy gray sweats.

Pushing to her knees, Darby untied her robe's belt. "Now why would you think that?"

"Well then," Kraven's heavy brows rose as understanding claimed his face. "As I did say I'd pass on no opportunity…" He made sure the door was shut and locked and then crossed the room. He eased the robe from her shoulders and slipped into the chair where he pulled her down to his lap. For a time, he took comfort in the feel of her bottom. The plump cheeks caressed his shaft as he held her back against him.

Darby whimpered once his hands came up and around in front of her to cup her breasts. Languidly, he weighed the honey brown mounds while fondling the hardening nipples in the center. She wanted to face him but he wouldn't let her. Instead, he kept her back toward him and leaned closer to apply wet, open mouthed kisses between her shoulder blades.

Shuddering, Darby cried out yet again when he spread her legs further so that they draped either side of his thighs. He subjected her to a delicious fingering that sent Darby's head falling back to his shoulder while sensation stoked fire inside her. She moved up and down along the three calloused fingers he thrust into her. Shameless and wickedly, she moved, folding her hands over the arms of the chair. Nothing mattered except what he was doing and that he not stop.

Kraven did not stop, though he did change tactics. His unexpectedly vivid eyes darkened to a hunter green as he studied the graceful line of her neck. Baby fine tendrils clung to her nape when she dragged her fingers through her curls. Kraven watched her gather up a mound while feverishly circling her hips to the deep relentless plundering of his fingers.

Darby tensed like a bow string when she was suddenly filled by Kraven's thick erection. She was on the threshold of orgasm soon after.

"Don't you dare."

His words; growled against her ear, had Darby laughing and crying out at once. Her cries merged into mewling pleas when his fingertips worked her clit. As her breasts were left unattended, Darby cupped them herself.

The sight of her actions sent his sex stiffening anew and even lengthening inside her body. His hormones hummed insistently and then demanded more. He kept one hand at her belly; the other cupped her thigh subsequently driving himself deeper.

Complete satisfaction visited them moments later. They were then panting, depleted as they lay sprawled in the chair.

***

Michaela was like a dog with a bone. But what else was new? She asked herself while shuffling through the notebooks and folders she'd brought with her to get a little work done during the course of the trip.

Quincee was doing her best to smother Quest under the pillows that lined the rugged-looking maple headboard of the king bed. Mick meanwhile conducted a determined search for the note Persephone James had alluded to in her revealing conversation the day before.

Mick remembered the note. She'd gotten it shortly after returning from California with Nile when they'd gone to visit family and introduce them to Quinn. Mick recalled scanning said note and seeing the names. She figured it belonged to Quest and had been sent to her by mistake… or something. She hadn't really had the time to dwell on it. She didn't remember giving it to Quest so she figured she must have shoved it into some of her work papers. She hoped she'd brought it with her. Grimly, she realized that most of the people on the list had probably been *dealt* with already.

Success arrived following that acknowledgement. Mick found the list tucked between the last few pages of one of her notebooks. It was still attached to the envelope it had arrived in.

Quincee shrieked when her father launched a playful retaliation to her pillow attack. Mick smiled, looking on at the sight before refocusing on the list of names.

Austin Chappell, Gram Walters, Brogue Tesano, Hilliam Tesano, Kraven DeBurgh, Fernando Ramsey, Vale Tesano, Gabriel Tesano, Eston Perjas.

"Quest..." Mick called.

"Stay..." Darby begged, nibbling Kraven's earlobe.

They lay cuddled in bed following their time spent in the old chair for which Darby had finally found appreciation.

"I shouldn't... things still need to be done before the party."

She pushed the hair from his forehead and smiled when it returned in a lazy fall of lush onyx. "Are you okay?" She asked.

"Hmph," Kraven pushed himself up on one sinewy shoulder and treated his eyes to a peek at her bare form beneath the covers. "I'm quite excellent, thank you." He drawled.

"But there's something else?" Darby guessed tentatively.

Kraven let the covers fall and pressed his forehead to hers. "It can wait."

"So there *is* something?"

"Lass? It can wait."

Darby nodded, knowing she'd get no more out of him than that.

"You've got a big night ahead," he kissed her forehead that time. "Get another nap, why don't you? I know I took a lot out of you earlier."

"Show off," she accused while her cheeks burned.

"I'm off for a shower," his kiss was full across her mouth then. "I love you." He added and then left the bed.

Darby watched until he'd disappeared inside the bathroom.

***

"...and they have a highly developed sense of smell. They'll definitely not shy away from the scent of blood."

"They're gorgeous." Kraven remarked from where he stooped between the two massively built Belgian Shepherds. "When's the next litter due?" He looked up at the trainer and breeder who'd brought the dogs to the estate for showing that afternoon.

"We're expecting a new one in about two weeks," the shorter and stockier of the two Irishmen said. "It'll be an additional six to eight weeks 'fore they're ready to leave their dame. We estimate your being able to take ownership in about two to two and a half months."

Kraven nodded at the two male dogs he petted. Of the Groenendael and Malinoi variant, the animals were indeed breathtaking.

"I want a mix of both variants," Kraven stood, but still observed the dogs, "fully grown males *and* females to observe before I make a final decision." He extended a hand for shaking. "See my man Seamus to discuss delivery and payment."

The men each shook Kraven's hand with utmost enthusiasm. "You won't be disappointed Lord DeBurgh." The trainer said.

"I don't expect I'll be." Kraven followed along as the two men led the animals across a high grown field at the northern end of the castle.

"Are they trained to kill?" He asked, watching the dogs walk ahead of the men.

They stopped and faced Kraven. The partners traded glances before nodding as one.

"If the need arose," said the breeder, "they won't hesitate to *spill* blood in addition to sniffing it out."

***

"Good party planner is worth their weight, I'm tellin' you." Sabra tossed her hair over the one shoulder bared by the cut of the poppy red dress that draped gracefully from the shoulder it covered to just past the back of her knee. The airy satin garment showed off her very long legs and the strappy platform sandals of the same color as the dress. She had been discussing the outcome of the party and how quickly and wonderfully it had been put together.

Darby's client appreciation party began in the lower level of the manor house and spilled out across the rear of the estate between house and castle. It was certainly a sight with the outdoors sparkling of golden lighting and the acoustic mixes that enticed many guests to make use of the dance floors in the ballroom and on the terrace.

PR by Ellis customers fully supported the event. Some traveled from as far as South America for the gathering. With such an extensive list, the guests had been encouraged to stay and celebrate the grand opening of the DeBurgh Hunting Lodge to take place the following weekend.

The clients were all too excited by the chance to take residence inside the castle and boast of being among the first guests inside the highly anticipated establishment.

"So how long are we gonna pretend we didn't hear what we did?" Sabra inquired once she and her peers were situated with canapés and drinks.

"Moses says that Bill's been hitting a brick wall for years trying to clean up what Marc and Houston did." Johari brushed her hands free of crumbs from the goat cheese topped cracker she'd just popped into her mouth. "He said she'd found out so much before any of us even started digging around in it all." A lock of red hair brushed her arm through the slitted sleeve of her tan smock dress when she shrugged. "I think she deserves time to find a way to handle it- legally."

Melina fidgeted with the draping silver necklace that complimented the lilac tone of her tunic dress. "So we're just gonna keep this from them?"

The women looked across the yard to where the guys sat huddled in conversation.

"I agree with Jo." Mick said. "I think they've got enough to keep 'em talking."

"She thought it was hers at first and then when she paid attention to the names..." Quest used his fist as prop for his jaw while he slouched back on a cushioned chair as he watched the list being passed around.

"Why are Gabe's and Vale's names on it?" Smoak wondered.

Fernando was shaking his head. "I can't recall ever seeing them there."

"Did you ever hear their names mentioned?" Moses was scanning the list then.

"Never." Fernando said.

"Hill never mentioned them either. Or this Eston Perjas." Caiphus chimed in. "Kraven?" He called.

"Aye..." Kraven was grim his gaze fixed on the list Moses held. "His name I know." He looked to Fern. "We both do."

Fernando took the sheet from his brother and studied it. "The shit they shoveled into our systems was made by him."

"So how long do you plan on working with Caiphus and not telling him what you know?" Sabra asked her cousin when they had a moment alone.

Sybilla watched the clear spiked heel of her pump as her foot swung back and forth. "Persephone's got nothing to do with that."

"How can you say that?" Sabra's voice was uncharacteristically soft.

"Hill doesn't know about them- that's best for now."

"Bill-"

"Think about it." Bill leaned forward, trapping Sabra's brown gaze in the line of her gray one. "The first thing he'll do is try to find her and if he does, who do you think will be hot on his heels?" She sat back in the padded deck chair and re-crossed her short, shapely legs. "I know Hill Tesano is damn good at *not* being found if he doesn't want to be, but I won't take that chance- not with those babies in the middle of all this."

Sabra blinked and finally nodded, coming down off her anxiety as logic intervened.

Sybilla closed her eyes to inhale deeply before she looked over to where Caiphus sat.

***

The party was an unquestionable success but Darby couldn't get her husband off her mind. His mood from earlier that day had stuck with her. She knew he had a lot on his mind. Who among them, didn't? Nevertheless, his manner nagged at her too much not to question it. He'd made such a discreet exit from the party; she hadn't even noticed him leaving. She found Seamus in the dining room speaking to the caterers and picked his brain about her husband's whereabouts.

"That boy's a working fool," Seamus rolled his eyes. "They've been constructing a new addition to the stables for the dogs. He mentioned going out there to give it another look earlier."

Darby stood on her toes to kiss Seamus' cheek. She ran into her father in the hall past the den. Sean Ellis pulled his daughter into a squeeze.

"This is my fifth time saying this tonight, but I really am proud of you, you know?" He said.

Darby closed her eyes to savor her father's embrace. "Thank you for being here Daddy."

"It was worth that long ass flight just to see how happy you are."

Darby was still laughing over her father's words, when a waiter came by with a tray of champagne. She declined.

"Nonsense," Sean scoffed, "it's a celebration."

"Daddy I can't."

"What do you mean?" He moved to take a second glass. "Come on."

"Daddy," Darby folded both hands across his forearm and squeezed. "I can't. I um, I'm not sure it's good for your grandchild."

Sean blinked, and then slowly set down both glasses. "You have my grandbaby in there?" He asked once the waiter had moved on. He let out a yelp and lifted Darby high once she'd bit her lip and nodded. Whirling her around, Sean planted a kiss to her mouth.

"Where's Kraven?" He asked.

"Oh Daddy he- he doesn't know yet," She clutched her father's upper arms beneath his black sport coat. "But I think it's time I took care of that. Don't um, don't say anything to anybody else yet. Nile already knows…so does Mommy."

"That woman…" Sean sighed, then kissed his daughter's cheek. "Go and find your husband," he cupped her chin, "I love you."

Darby threw herself into his arms again. "I love you too, Daddy." She laughed again when the man sprinted off. Then, following her father's example, she sprinted off to continue her search for Kraven.

She ran all the way to the stables, bursting through a side door and calling out to her husband. She was heading toward the back of the structure, when he grabbed her. She knew within a second that it wasn't Kraven.

"He's not here yet, *Lassie*," A man with an American accent poorly mocked Kraven's Scottish brogue. "We're all just gonna wait for him to make an appearance."

Darby ceased her struggles when she saw a second man come into view. He clutched what looked like a sawed off shotgun.

"Shouldn't be long," the man holding Darby said, "He's never more than a foot away from you, is he?" his arm tightened beneath her breasts and he turned his face into her hair and inhaled.

"Can't say I blame him," the man murmured. "You know, I've dabbled in a little chocolate over the years, myself. Never had the nerve to marry one."

The man clutching the shot gun grinned. "Too hard to handle, huh Lee?"

"Ahh…" *Lee* chuckled. "They do keep a man on his toes, but they're well worth the work once you get one in the sack." He inhaled Darby's hair again and squeezed her tighter when she renewed her struggles. "This one must be somethin' else for the man to give her his name and title. Let's see, shall we?"

"I'm next if she's as good as she looks," the shotgun wielder's leer slid from Darby's face to her chest.

The instant her captor released her, Darby hauled off and smashed her fist into his jaw. The man howled at the force of the blow but then recovered and back-handed Darby in retaliation. She landed in a mound of hay but got to her feet quickly. The man wielding the shot gun was already coming to the rescue.

"Get back, Rafe!" Lee ordered his approaching friend. "I got this!" Blood and spittle flew from the wound opened by the unexpected blow he'd just endured.

Darby had already torn away the scalloped hem of her black off shoulder dress. She wound the edges of the strip around each fist.

Lee's grin was lecherous. "I see you're ready for me, bitch."

Darby's grin was equally lecherous. "Very." She used the tip of her pump to kick a slew of hay and sand into his face.

She only managed to disorient him briefly but it was long enough to give her time to get in back of him. She moved in closer to rope the fabric of the dress and tighten the noose.

Darby's attacker tried to buck her off, but she held fast until it looked like success was imminent.

"Lee!" *Rafe* called out to his friend.

"I said…get…back!" Lee's breath was fast failing him but the desire to maintain his dignity was strong. Somehow, he got a second wind and was able to shake Darby's hold.

She landed in the hay but didn't get to her feet before her opponent had gained the advantage.

"Let's see how you like *me* on your back, bitch." He stood over her and hissed the words while undoing his belt.

Darby looked around the stall where he'd cornered her. *Anything can be a weapon, Lass.* She heard Kraven's voice in her head seconds before her eyes landed on a pitchfork- the handle laid nearest her peeking out of the hay. Lightning quick, she grabbed hold and shoved the tool forward as her attacker closed in.

Her thrust imbedded the prongs of the pitchfork deeply into the man's thigh. He released an inhuman howl and fell to his knees. Rafe; still holding the shotgun, moved forward in earnest but gained little distance once Kraven's fist landed in his midsection. The gun slid across the dusty flooring and landed in a far corner. The blow left the man writhing in pain in a ball on the floor.

Kraven's focus had already turned to Darby and the man still howling in fury and torture next to her. Disbelief mingled with something more savage in the darkened green of his gaze.

Darby was breathless and only able to stare as she measured the fierceness and menacing intent on his face. He looked on the man who was then whimpering from the damage done by the pitchfork still lodged deep in his thigh.

"You touched her." Kraven's voice was quiet. It wasn't a question.

The injured man barely had the time to say he was sorry before Kraven broke his neck. Darby's hands flew to her mouth when she heard the bone snap.

The second perpetrator was attempting to crawl toward the gun in the corner. Rafe stilled at the sound of Kraven's footfalls and shadow emerging between him and the weapon he sought.

"She paid us!" he broke down into sobs as his body trembled.

Kraven's smile was like a slash across his darkly magnificent features. He stooped close to the trembling man. "Well then let's make sure she gets her money's worth, eh?"

From the stall, Darby watched in horror and fascination as Kraven's scarred fists pounded the man's face and body. Whatever blows the other man managed to land, only widened Kraven's gruesome smile. Darby knew her attacker's fate was sealed and that he would soon be as dead as his partner. Kraven was merely toying with him at that point anyway. She watched him tire of the pitiful fight eventually. He pummeled the man's face, gradually turning it into a jellied mess.

"Kraven!"

Fists poised in mid-air when he heard her, he took a few moments to catch his breath. He then snapped the man's neck with effortless, efficient skill. When he left the body and turned back to Darby, his killing machine persona had faded into one that was humble, uncertain and afraid. Tentatively, he wiped bloodied palms on his trousers.

"Are you okay, love?"

She nodded fast.

"He touched you."

Darby looked toward the man sprawled a few feet away. The pitchfork still protruded from his thigh.

"And I touched him," she said.

Kraven took a few steps toward his wife and lost the strength to stand. He dropped to his knees and Darby scrambled toward him. She then broke into an awkward run and hurled herself against his chest. When his arms came around her like steel bands, she gave into the relief she never thought she'd feel again.

Kraven cupped her neck, setting his thumb beneath her chin to tilt her head up to meet his hard kiss.

"Are you alright?" He shuddered, gripping her impossibly tight.

Nodding on his chest, Darby kept her eyes closed. "I am now."

Without another word, Kraven pulled her up high against him and carried her from the stable.

EIGHTEEN

Darby indulged in a long stretch and yawn before opening her eyes the next morning. She smiled and snuggled her head back into a pillow when she saw Kraven. He'd pulled the old plaid chair close to the bed and sat there dozing. She could have watched him that way forever but he began to stir and was soon going through the waking rituals of yawning and rubbing sleep from his eyes.

When his gaze set upon her, it was at once a vivid emerald instead of the rage-darkened hunter green.

"There's my girl," he moved to push her hair out of her face. "Are you okay?"

Darby only nodded, still watching him with dreaminess in her eyes.

Kraven traced the line of her nose and full mouth with his index finger. "Everyone's talking about what a bad ass you are." His deep laughter mingled in when she giggled.

She turned her face into his palm and kissed it. "I think they're mixing me up with you." She scooted closer and nuzzled her cheek against his. "Thank you," she said.

"Don't." Kraven shook his head when he pulled back.

"You saved my life."

"By doing something I swore I'd never do again. Something I once took a sick pleasure in Darby."

"Once," she shook her head, "but not now. I know you didn't do that because you wanted to."

"Oh, but you'd be wrong there, Lass." His smiled was sad. "I very much wanted to." His lashes fluttered as memories of the night stirred anger. "They touched you." The back of his hand brushed her jaw where a faint bruise blemished her brown skin.

Darby took his hand and squeezed. "You did what any man would."

A hint of apology and danger mingled into his smile. "I'm not *any* man, Love. I'm one of those men you look away from fast when you see them coming your way."

It was Darby who smiled apologetically then. "I can't think of a woman alive who'd look away fast if she saw you."

Kraven bowed his head and Darby could see that he was a smidge embarrassed by her observation. The reaction only lasted a moment unfortunately.

"I'm afraid there are women who'd disagree with you, there."

"What happened on that island was a long time ago." Darby reminded him.

"Not so long ago," Kraven sat back in the chair and rubbed his jaw thoughtfully.

"What?" Darby sat up amidst the bed covers.

"What happened that night…" he pulled his hand from his face and watched his fingers form a fist. "We were stupid then, hyped up and high… it was like smokin' pot and then wanting to see what a cocaine rush feels like on top of it. We were all a bunch of idiotic punks but I'm not talking about that night. I'm talking about things I've done when I'm as lucid as I am now. The connections I made on that island got me noticed for plumb assignments later when I opted for a life in the military instead of going to college. It nearly killed my parents-my Ma died shortly after that actually." He inhaled sharply and blinked as if to dissuade tears from appearing.

"But they'd given up on *saving me* long before I ever left for that bloody place. I didn't realize at the time that those assignments were related to the very people I'd turned my back on there." He rested his head back on the chair and fixed her with an easy look.

"You see, killing machines aren't easy to create. Our superiors wanted to hold onto us for as long as they could. But on the island, we weren't the most prized commodity."

"The girls…" Darby's voice was hushed.

"And not because they provided us with pleasure. We never knew what it was all about then. *Now* we know that it had something to do with ovaries and given what we know about the drugs they were pumping into us, it only lends more sickening overtones to what they were really up to. It also explains, in part, why some of the girls were allowed to leave."

Understanding crept into Darby's face.

"That's right, Lass. If what happened to them was the same as what happened to Nile and Dena then perhaps they'd lost their usefulness."

"So they just let them leave?" Darby couldn't believe that.

Kraven nodded. "For a while, but they were in no way *free*. They were sold to some... not very nice people but the customers were pleased with their acquisitions and all was well until someone sniffed a little too deeply into the shit. We're pretty sure it was Roman Tesano who sent them running for cover given what we now know of his brothers being linked to the island thanks to that list Mick found." Kraven leaned forward resting his elbows to his knees and studying the scars on his hands.

"All that running for cover initiated what we came to call clean-up projects. We were told that we were going after these 'not so nice people' because they were a cancer to the world order and like idiots we believed it." He grinned ill-humoredly.

"We were told to wipe them out and everything associated with them-*everyone*." He looked at his wife then. "I've taken lives, Darby. Lives that I now know were innocent, that I probably knew were innocent when they begged for mercy and I chose not to hear because they were part of a cancer and it was all for the *greater good*, you see?

"No." He said when she opened her mouth to speak. "There's no way that I can ever make this right- nothing I can say or even do."

He left the chair then. "I thought this place would help," he was staring out over the land from their bedroom window.

The party staff had made quick work of returning things to normal. There was no sign that a grand event had been held there the night before.

"I thought what I planned to do here would help wash away the rest of what I'd been," he turned back to

Darby. "And you as well. I was in the process of redeeming myself when I met you. I thought… maybe you were my gift- a sign from God that He was pleased." Kraven went to sit next to her on the bed.

"It doesn't work that way though." He brushed his thumb across the base of her throat and followed the move with his eyes. "Demons like that don't just linger in the past. They're with you every step of the way- right into the future."

"You're forgetting that *I'm* here too," Darby squeezed her hand around his wrist. "I'm not interested in sharing you with any demons."

Kraven let his hand drop along with his gaze. "I should've told you this before I went after you the way that I did."

Darby smiled, remembering. "Yeah you did sort of sweep me off my feet."

"I was afraid you'd vanish if I waited." One shoulder rose beneath his blue heather chamois shirt. "I knew very quickly that you were everything I wanted. When you went back to California after being here with me… I couldn't rest, couldn't sleep, my mood was… let's just say that Seamus threatened some very nasty things if I didn't find you and tell you how I felt and not to give up 'til you were all mine.

"When I came to your place that day," he squeezed his eyes shut briefly, "I should've told you everything about the kind of man I was."

She scooted closer, taking his face in her hands. "I keep trying to tell you that I know what kind of man you are Kraven Skyelar DeBurgh." She kissed him when his cheeks flushed.

"You're a man who treats his friends like gold. Who loves them like they're his very own blood. A man who takes little girls on horseback rides and whose made a very lucky woman feel a love she never let herself even daydream of finding."

They indulged in a sweeter, lengthier kiss but then Kraven shook his head. "I want you to step back from this, Lass." He pulled her hands from his face. "Think about what I've told you. I'm very sorry for keeping such secrets but now that you know them," he cleared his throat, the sleek line of his brows drawing close when he frowned at a sudden pressure behind his eyes. "I'll understand if you um- if you feel that- that you need to leave-"

"I'm pregnant." She shrugged simply, her shoulders appearing most delicate beneath the cotton straps of the mauve nightie she wore. She fixed him with a playfully challenging smile when his brilliant eyes widened and fell to her nonexistent waist.

Darby settled back comfortably against the headboard and clasped her hands. "Your baby is inside me, Lord DeBurgh so I'm afraid you're stuck with me- us." She pressed her lips together and awaited his reaction.

Disbelief held his expression captive as he faced her fully on the bed before sliding toward her. He braced a hand on either side of her hips and studied her in awe. All traces of uncertainty, regret and self-loathing had lifted like mist.

"I'm in there? You mean that?"

"I mean that."

He blinked several times and then uttered a short, quick sound akin to laughter. He was kissing her mouth hard in the next instant. She laughed as their tongues collided in a melding of desire and devotion. Darby touched Kraven's face and felt the moisture of tears sprinkling his long dark lashes. Laughter claimed her again as her own happy tears revealed.

***

While Darby's client party ushered in a wave of guests, it was nothing compared to the slew of new arrivals to the estate over the next several days. The place became more alive with the arrival of family and DeBurgh acquaintances to Near Invernesshire to celebrate the opening of the hunting lodge. Kraven's uncles and their wives all made an especially grand impression. Loud and gregarious, the group put the rest of the guests in even higher spirits.

The pride they all felt over their nephew's accomplishments was more than obvious. Although Kraven had said he needed no one to validate his decision to move forward with the lodge, the support from his relatives clearly meant a lot to him.

Of special importance, was the approval from his uncle Skyelar MacDonough DeBurgh from whom Kraven had received his middle name. The man was as boisterous as he was massive. No one believed he was the youngest of Kraven's four uncles. Smoak and Caiphus took a special liking to the man as he reminded them of their uncle Pitch.

Darby had been understandably surprised by the welcome she'd received when Kraven introduced her as his wife back when they were first married. Everyone treated her with utmost respect and actually seemed elated by the sudden union. To that date, Darby had met no one who'd made her feel anything other than welcome. Still, she couldn't help but to wonder how long that would last once she and Kraven made their latest announcement.

"Where is she?!"

A hush fell over the sitting room where all the women had gathered to become better acquainted over tea and sweet cakes.

Skyelar DeBurgh looked as out of place there as a pig in a bridal shop. The man lost none of his confidence however as he barreled into the room in search of his niece-in-law. When Skyelar found Darby seated with her mother and his wife Breanna, he sat on the coffee table before Darby could move.

"Is this boy serious, lamb?" He queried, expression set in a big sun-kissed face framed in a bushy black beard and thick unruly salt and pepper waves of hair atop his head.

Darby looked up at Kraven who had come to stand behind where his uncle sat on the table. "Serious about what, uncle Skye?" She asked.

Skyelar gave the clarification to his wife instead. "Seems the DeBurgh clan is about to be blessed with a new addition."

Breanna gasped and brought both hands to her round cheeks.

Darby's smile was bright. "He is, uncle." She'd barely gotten the words out before Skyelar and Breanna tugged her into a fierce hug and kissed her cheeks.

The entire room was loud with applause. Some had already been made aware of Darby's delicate condition while others were hearing it for the first time. Everyone was equally thrilled by the news. Pretty soon, the 'women's only' event had become a mixed gathering as everyone joined in on the getting acquainted mixer turned baby shower.

***

A Lover's Sin

Vilanculos, Mozambique~

After years of unrest, horrifically dramatic events and the discovery of the child they shared, Jasper Stone wed his long-time and only love Carmen Ramsey. The ceremony was as unique and achingly beautiful as their star-crossed affair had always been.

Jasper had insisted on very little pomp and circumstance for the event. The last thing he wanted was a big Ramsey-caliber shindig. Carmen however worked very well with what she had. The locale; needless to say, was exquisite. The sky was an endless cascade of blue dotted by puffs of white above a sea so clear and beckoning that it could have mirrored the sky above.

There was no shortage of wedding attendants. The entire village had been invited. All were eager to wish long lives and endless joy to the newly wedded couple.

Jasper and Carmen both agreed that there was no way they could have married without the presence of their girl. It didn't take much persuasion for Pike to agree that this was one event where his wife's attendance was most important. Though Sabella understood her husband's reasons for not wanting her in Scotland, she was still a bit agitated with him. The chance to watch her parents finally become husband and wife more than made up for it.

"Are you really mine after all this time?" Jasper asked his bride as they swayed to Louis Armstrong's *"We Have All The Time In The World"*.

Carmen cuddled closer to her husband. Her light eyes harbored a loving tint that was as captivating as the peach chiffon of her gown. "All yours. All yours forever. Does that scare you?"

"It terrifies me," he grinned. "I hope I can live up to your expectations."

She tugged on the lapel of his gray suit coat. "I only expect you to love me."

"Well then..." Effortlessly, he pulled her off her feet until they were eye to eye and sharing a very thorough kiss.

***

Although Quincee wouldn't be two for another few months, Kraven insisted on giving her a party after things calmed down following the lodge opening but before the Ramseys left Scotland. There would be no need for party planners or caterers. Everyone agreed that a good, old-fashioned barbeque would suffice.

No one argued when Kraven insisted on being the head chef. The knowledge that he was about to become a father, had shed a different light on his concerns. He still harbored much regret and sorrow over the things he had been a part of. He now accepted the fact that they had played their part in shaping the man who had won Darby's heart- the man whose child she was going to have.

The demons of his past stood no chance against such a love. Of that, he was sure and, at last, content.

Darby was checking the cinch as she tightened the belt on the gray wrap dress she'd selected following her appointment. Kraven had flown in her doctor from Edinburgh to give her a thorough check-up. As she had not yet set a date with the man to actually confirm the pregnancy, Darby was overly relieved to have the doctor not only confirm the results of the over-the-counter test but to also assure that all the excitement as of late had not adversely affected her condition. All the same, Dr. Webster

Dennison had the expectant parents set a time for Darby to come into the office for a follow-up exam.

"Dr. Dennison expects us next week." Kraven informed his wife once he'd returned to the bedroom and eased both hands about her waist.

"Was it really necessary to fly him all the way out here, Kraven?" Darby studied her reflection in the full length mirror.

"Mmm hmm..." He busied himself with nibbling her earlobe. "It was really necessary."

Darby fingered her curls while Kraven carried out his assault on the skin beneath her ear. "Are you gonna be one of those annoying, overprotective, overindulgent fathers-to-be, jumping every time I sneeze?"

"Hmm...I thought I already was that." He switched his 'assault' to the other ear. "But since you asked, I'm obviously not living all the way up to it." He cupped her hips and drew her back more snug into him. "Guess I need to do more, huh?"

Darby groaned when her head fell back to his chest.

"This should go a ways in sealing my fate as an overindulgent father-to-be." He dropped a quick kiss to her neck.

Turning in the loose circle of his embrace, Darby fixed him with an overtly suspicious glare. "What have you done?"

He straightened to his full height and grinned down at her wickedly. "Come with me and find out," he offered his arm.

Reluctant at first, Darby finally slipped her hands around his elbow and curved her fingers into the soft fabric of the golden cream V-neck sweater which accentuated the healthy glow of his copper-toned skin. They left the room

with Darby subjecting Kraven to an endless barrage of
questions regarding their destination.

"Have I told you how much I like the way the light
up here catches in your hair?" He pulled her hand from his
arm and eased around in back of her to push her hair from
her neck thus providing him with the chance to brush his
mouth across her nape.

Darby could have swooned over his handling but
she resisted. "I'm not making another move until you tell
me where we're going?"

Kraven retaliated by tugging her into a secluded
area in the corridor between the wall and a broad stone
column. "Even though I enjoy the way you fill out this
dress, I'm gonna have the best time taking you out of it
later."

Darby believed she was panting by the time he
released her from his kiss.

"Maybe we should just stay up here, then?" he
made a move as if to sling her over his shoulder.

"Alright, dammit!" Darby hissed, glancing round to
see if they were still alone in the hall. "No more questions,"
she promised.

Kraven nodded satisfactorily and offered his arm
again. Darby's compliance however didn't cease his
naughty compliments and boasts regarding his plans upon
the return to their bedroom. Darby's cheeks were burning
by the time they stepped into his study. The two people
waiting in the room stood slowly from the sofa they shared
before the fire.

"Oh," Darby chirped, figuring her husband had
more of his relatives for her to meet.

The woman near the sofa suddenly gasped. She was
of average height with expressive eyes that tilted just
slightly at the corners. Her hair was a thick, silvery blonde

mass that framed her face in a mass of thick ringlets. The man at her side was tall and broad with rugged, sun-kissed features proving he spent much time outdoors. The lower half of his handsome face was hidden behind a heavy, reddish-gold beard. Hair covered his head in a hoard of waves the same striking color as his whiskers.

The woman attempted to whisper then, but her words carried across the room. "Gear, she has Seanie's eyes."

"And your hair, Aeni." The man's voice held a gruffer sound but it was soft when he spoke the words.

Darby gasped then and stumbled back a bit on her pearl gray pumps. Her retreat was broken by Kraven's chest. Squeezing her arms, he nudged her across the room.

"Geary and Aenid Ellis, this is your granddaughter Darby." He said.

Darby wanted to succumb to the desire to wilt but Kraven's support prevented that. At last, she expelled a tuft of breath and shook her head in wonder.

"How?" She shuddered.

He kissed her cheek. "Your Ma worried that you might do something silly and bull-headed like run off to Ireland without telling me."

"I wanted to do it alone," her eyes were blurry with tears. "I didn't want you there when… to see them…when they slammed the door in my face."

"No love, no." Aenid whispered, shaking her head defiantly. "Seanie never told us, he-"

"Had good reason not to," Geary Ellis intervened. "Many in the family took issue when he married your mother, sweetness. It wasn't the most pleasant situation and we-" he looked down suddenly reaching out for his wife's trembling hand and folding it within his own.

"We were perhaps the worst of all," he confessed, "we said nothing-*did* nothing. We let them go- believing we were in agreement with the idiots who gave them such worry. We are sorry, dearest."

Darby blinked away tears while she looked into her grandfather's face as he smiled sadly.

"This is all we have of them," Aenid had stepped closer to Darby. In her hands, she held a worn wedding photo of a younger Sean and Lisa Ellis.

"I kept it in my bible," Aenid sniffled while studying the picture. "Every night, I pray they are safe and happy wherever they are." She offered the photo to her granddaughter.

"Kraven's promised us a more recent picture. I thought you might like to have this one."

Darby accepted the photo and her hands brushed Aenid's as she did so. Suddenly, Aenid closed her hand over Darby's and squeezed as if she were trying to memorize the feel. Growing bolder, Aenid touched Darby's hair.

"Oh lovely," she sobbed, "They never told us about you. We never knew…" Aenid's fingers brushed Darby's brow and then she pulled her into a crushing hug.

Darby returned the hug in a manner just as fierce. There was crying and not just on the part of grandmother and granddaughter. Kraven blinked water from his eyes while Geary turned his head away and brushed at the tears that had dropped to his cheeks.

The men caught each other's gazes and were soon chuckling in spite of themselves. Again, they shook hands before their wives drew them close for a group embrace.

NINETEEN

"**S**o am I a completely overindulgent father-to-be now?"

"You are *the* most exceptionally wonderful father-to-be in the history of fathers-to-be." Darby planted a hard, smacking kiss to her husband's jaw. "Thank you," she searched his emerald gaze with her own.

Kraven maintained eye contact even as he pressed a kiss to the back of Darby's hand. "You know I'd give you anything if it's in my power, Lass."

"Thank you for giving me this." She shuddered on a sob when they hugged.

"Did you think I couldn't understand how much this meant to you?" He squeezed her tighter.

Darby kept her fingers curled in the neckline of Kraven's sweater as they embraced on the other side of the study. They watched Darby's grandparents in soft conversation with her parents. Darby believed that it would be one of the most beautiful memories she would ever have.

"What do you think will happen next?" She asked.

Kraven rested his chin atop Darby's head. "More talking," he said, "they have a lot of catching up to do. A lot of things need to be said."

"Do you think my dad will ever forgive them?"

Kraven smoothed his hand over her back. "Oh I think he may," he said as he studied the two couples.

Sean Ellis had taken his mother's hand and squeezed it in much the same manner that Geary Ellis held onto Lisa's while she sat next to him on the sofa. The fire burning in the hearth seemed to blaze with new life.

***

"You're sure?" Evangela looked down at Saffron who sat frowning at one of the four monitors on the desk.

"According to the DeBurgh Hunting Lodge's very impressive website, the grand opening celebration will be held as scheduled."

"And still no word from Lee or Rafe?" Evangela referred to the men who had been put in place to serve as special engravers to the DeBurgh Castle's woodwork while plotting to fulfill their true business which was to kill Kraven DeBurgh.

"Zip," Saffron confirmed.

Evangela shoved her hands into the pockets of her camouflage capris and paced once back and forth in front of the desk. Then, suddenly she gripped the beveled edge of the finely crafted oak furnishing and shook it. A harsh roar erupted. The other women in the room tensed more than they already were. Maeva simply grinned.

"Sons of cunt-rotted bitches…" Eva seethed, smoothing hair away from her face and winding it into a loose ponytail as she paced and then stopped. "Put on your party dresses, girls."

"E. No." Casper left her perch on the edge of the coffee table. "This is a bad idea. Those grounds will be teeming with people that night."

"Shut it, Cas," Evangela had started to pace before Saffron's desk again. "I already said the next time we were doing it my way."

"Listen to me, E," Undaunted, Casper closed the distance between them. "The place was already like a fortress if what Lee and Rafe told us is true," she said. "Now you can best believe it'll be crawling with even more security for that event. We shouldn't risk-"

The warning silenced when Evangela's hand closed around Casper's throat. "What was that?" She squeezed the woman's windpipe. Only the sound of Casper's struggled breathing served as reply.

"Thought so," Evangela released Casper's throat and walked past without a second thought when the woman fell to her knees.

"E!"

"Not now Saf! I can't take anymore shit!"

"Oh this shit is some of the good stuff." Saffron kept her eyes on a monitor while waving to beckon Evangela. Everyone else followed suit as well.

"Years of waiting for a hit on this bastard's alias and voila."

"Saf..." Evangela peered at the screen more closely. "Am I reading this right?"

"Mmm hmm...ain't it sweet?"

"Jesus..." Lula breathed.

"What are we gonna do with this?" Rain asked.

Evangela smiled gleefully. "Well now... all kinds of stuff."

***

The inaugural hunt was set to take place at dawn the morning after the lodge's grand opening. The morning of the opening, the men in attendance decided an inaugural *tour* was also in order. The ladies were welcomed to attend but most opted for the warmer choice of remaining in their cozy beds when dawn came knocking.

Darby and Contessa were the only two women who rose at dawn to see the men off. Once the rowdy group was armed with thermoses of coffee and hot cider and had rode off on horseback, peacefulness returned to the immediate area. Darby was enjoying the briskness of the overcast morning when Contessa came to join her.

"Our girls are gonna call us a couple of saps for seeing off our brave men like the doting wives we are." Darby's voice carried on a lazy current as she relaxed on a cushioned lounge chair along the edge of the stone terrace.

"I'll take it," County's voice held the same laziness as she relaxed on a matching chair next to Darby. "Anyway, I had to at least *try* to convince my sexy yet sometimes stupid husband not to put his butt on a horse so soon after being shot. Oh well..." she wrapped herself tighter in the long mocha-colored sweater she wore. "A wife does what she can..."

"And is happy to have the opportunity, right?" Darby asked.

Contessa smiled and closed her eyes. "Amen."

Darby laughed then pushed herself up on the lounge. "So will it be tea or coffee? I can have Seamus get us something. He was up to see off everyone when they left for the tour."

"I'm good right now, girl." County sighed.

For a time, the two observed the castle far across the grounds. The rain-washed structure was just visible as it was shrouded in mist. The fine cloud wasn't so thick however that it totally shielded the golden lighting that illuminated the centuries-old construction.

"Damn...does this ever get old?" County asked her hostess.

Darby flexed her toes inside her slippers and shivered in contentment. "Ask me in about fifty years."

County laughed. "Amen again."

"I'll tell you the truth though," Darby folded her arms across the long, cotton lounging robe she wore. "All these events and parties... you know the one I can't wait for?"

"Hmm...?"

"Quincee's barbeque."

County's laughter was louder that time. "Amen a third time. Back to simple things."

"Mmm...they're what make it all worth the craziness." Darby said.

Silence returned as the women settled back into enjoying the view and the natural melody of rustling brush and birdsong. Twenty minutes had passed before another sign of life appeared.

"Good morning Seamus," Darby's smile widened when she saw the man emerge around the heavy dangle of vines that claimed a far wall that sheltered the sides of terrace.

"We were thinking it'd be nice to have breakfast set out on the terrace when the guys get back..." Darby's suggestion trailed off into silence when she noticed the women accompanying Seamus...and the guns they carried.

"Well, well isn't this cozy?" Evangela Leer inquired as she slowed her stroll and observed her surroundings in a manner that was mockingly admiring. Then, she gasped laying a hand alongside her face as though she'd remembered something.

"Apologies for neglecting my manners, I'm Evangela Leer and these are my associates," she threw out a general wave but didn't glance back.

"Bitch," County moved off the lounge chair.

"Ah, ah, ah Mrs. Ramsey. Don't move. You wouldn't want us to use these," she tapped a German model .9mm to the leg of the skin tight white pantsuit she sported. The gun was fixed with a silencer.

Evangela smiled, tilting her head as if to follow the line of County's gaze where it drifted toward the weapon. "I mean, you wouldn't want us to use them *just yet*, would you?" She giggled when County's eyes snapped back to hers. Evangela ceased her grinning a second later. "But just in case you think I'm bluffing," she said and whirled round to put a bullet in Seamus' leg.

Darby and County shrieked in unison while Seamus grunted loudly and staggered between Lula and Santi who held onto each of his arms. Evangela made a show with the gun, blowing on the tip of the muzzle.

"Now that we've got that out of the way," she sighed, caressing the shaft of the gun as if it were a lover. "Hubbies gone hunting, have they? How manly of them."

"What do you want?" Darby asked, uncertain if her words carried sound as she could barely hear them over her heart beating in her ears.

Evangela appeared stunned. "Why, to see the brides up close for one," She stepped closer and County went to clutch Darby's hand.

"Lovely," Evangela breathed when she and Darby were almost nose to nose. Then she looked to Contessa. "Both of you are. I expected nothing less of my friends though. They always claim the top shelf bitches. But *you*," she studied County a split second before backhanding her with a gloved fist. "You don't listen. I said 'don't move'," she whispered.

Darby kept a tight hold to County whose lip then oozed blood. "What do you want?" She asked again.

"Ah Lady DeBurgh, Lady DeBurgh I'm hurt. I wanted to get acquainted." Evangela batted her long lashes in an innocent fashion. "Have a little girl talk, share stories of our experiences, yada, yada…" She straightened and smirked back at her associates.

"They've got no idea what I'm talking about." Her expression was mockingly crestfallen when she looked back to Darby and County. "Guess this chat will be quite revealing. May be a bit hard to take," She laughed and tapped the muzzle of the gun to Darby's cheek.

"Speaking of hard to take…what a magnificent cock your husband has." Evangela sighed the words, moving closer so that her cheek just grazed Darby's then. "Guess that's why he likes his bed partners on the chocolate side." She stepped back a space to scan the length of Darby's body. "White girls like to think they can handle that kind of power but… well they're wimps." She grinned and threw a wink across her shoulder.

"Sorry Santi," she told her only white accomplice, and then turned back to Darby.

"Kraven was really sweet, letting his friends get inside first." She smirked. "He might've killed me with that thing, coming at me the way he did- all that power." Her lashes fluttered as if she were savoring the memory. "I wonder if he's grown any since then? It's been a while since I've had him."

"Missing it, are we?" Darby smiled when her words stirred a growl from Maeva.

"It's alright, Mae..." Evangela shook her head, though a bit of the confidence had dimmed in her expressive eyes. "They told you?"

It was Darby's turn to smirk. "Mmm hmm..."

"And what did they say? That I begged for it and more after they were done? Tsk, tsk... guess you guys didn't get the full story after all."

"From what we understand, such things were commonplace if the price was right." Darby's glee broadened when she saw Evangela blink. Emboldened, she moved closer to her captor. "Or maybe it wasn't the *price* but the party favors they brought to the event."

The curious light in Evangela's eyes gave way to discovery. "Now how would you know that pissed me off? Not from the hubbies... that little insight wouldn't have come from them."

"The little twat." Maeva's rough voice grated.

"Ahh...baby sis is closer than I thought." Evangela tapped the gun muzzle to her jaw then. "What else did she share? Did she tell you that she was the one who shot your man?" She sneered at Contessa. "Funny... he didn't even have the chance to try me."

Contessa shrugged. "He's always been lucky that way."

"Could have been interesting, though." Evangela didn't seem agitated. "A little brother sister action. Oh!" She saw the devastation flash in County's stare. "That's right- sweet Persephone didn't know that part. There's lots she doesn't know. But yes, the late Marcus Ramsey was my father. Seems dear old dad had his sick interests for a long time. My mother was easy pickins back then being a live in maid and all." Evangela raked a hand through her straight locks. "She should've considered herself a lucky one- he was a gorgeous son of a bitch, I know *I'm* thankful for such good genes if I do say so myself. So what else did my sister have to tell?"

"That you're all a bunch of twisted freaks!" County blurted, barely managing to press her lips together when Darby squeezed her hand.

"Ah honey," Evangela sauntered close. "No need to take little sis's word on that. We'd love to show you how twisted we *really* are. Gotta have *some* way to pass time 'til the menfolk return."

"Don't you touch em!" Seamus had gotten to his knees between Lula and Santi where they'd dropped him. His pant leg was soaked with blood.

Evangela responded by giving the man a bullet to the arm for his trouble. Darby and Contessa cried out while Seamus gurgled in pain.

"What a disappointment," Evangela sighed and then came close to County and cupped her breast. "I hope *you're* a screamer."

Darby wanted to close her eyes and pray, but she knew that wasn't in the best interest of things. She needed a weapon, but didn't think she'd be lucky enough to find any pitchforks lying around the terrace. Again, there was the sound of growling from the gargantuan-sized woman that stood just behind them. Hearing the sound then, Darby did close her eyes to pray.

"What the fuck?" Santi Dumont hissed.

Darby eyes flew open and she saw the shock and curiosity on the faces of the women in her line of sight. She whirled around expecting to see the men returned, heroic and on horseback. Nothing prepared her for the sight standing some twenty feet across the yard- A row of the large and fiercely beautiful animals. Their features could have passed for wolf or wild dog. Their coats were heavy and ranged in color from stark white to pitch black.

AlTonya Washington

Growls; ones that far outmatched the ones of Maeva Leer's resonated across the lightly fogged landscape. Fanglike teeth seemed to glint when they bared and dripped with saliva.

"Jesus- Darby," County gasped.

Darby didn't think twice. She grabbed County's arm. "Run!"

The order galvanized everyone-every*thing* into action. The moment was nothing short of pandemonium. County and Darby broke into their run before their captors moved. When the dogs advanced, so did Evangela and her crew. Guns were aimed and firing. A bullet found the shin of one dog, but it didn't take long for the rest of the pack to close in and begin its attack.

Darby and Contessa looked back to see three of the women facing the brunt of the siege. In disbelief they watched as Maeva Leer boldly faced one of the dogs. The face-off between woman and beast was grotesquely captivating. They went to ground in a flurry of fists, claws, teeth and fangs. Somehow, Maeva emerged the victor when she broke her opponent's neck.

Two of Evangela Leer's associates, broke away and scattered bolting for the heavy shelter of the forest with the dogs in pursuit. One crew member wasn't so lucky. The woman was mauled in a vicious onslaught. Darby barely had time to place a hand over her mouth when a bloodied Seamus managed to drag himself up to clutch a fistful of her robe.

"Go!" He roared to the women in his charge.

They ran, turning their backs on the sounds of ravenous barks, growling and a woman's screams as she met her death.

"Feel free to bake pies with the women while we go catch supper in the morn!" Skyelar DeBurgh's heavy timbre roared above the laughter and conversation of his tour mates as he teased his older brother Rixey. The man had just stated his preference to playing a few rounds of golf instead of taking part in the next morning's hunt.

Kraven, Quest and Yohan opted for walking back to the castle as opposed to returning on horseback. Reins in hand, the guys led their horses back toward the stable while the rest of their party trotted close behind.

"Quay's gonna be jealous that he missed out on all this male bonding."

Quest chuckled over Kraven's tease. "Quay Ramsey doesn't even roll over to scratch his ass 'til ten in the morning. Rest assured he wouldn't be offended by being left out." The dimple emerged when Quest smirked at the thought of his twin. "Fool's gonna have a helluva initiation when that baby comes."

"Looks like Quincee's got the manor house jumpin'." Yohan noted amidst the laughter surrounding him.

"Whole place is lit," Quest noted, tilting his head while looking toward the house. "Guess there're more early risers among us than we thought."

Kraven eyed the excessive lighting with a mix of amusement and suspicion. The fog had lifted but the day promised to be overcast and there was still a slight layer of mist all around. He bowed his head a fraction, closing his eyes to rely on his ears. He caught the sound of engines a second before he looked up and saw Jeeps heading toward them.

"No…" he whispered and broke into a run across the land.

Quest and Yohan followed suit. Fernando and the others diverted their horses from the direction of the stables and headed toward the scene in the distance.

It was no exaggeration to say that every man in the tour party felt his heart sink when he realized why the house was alive at such an early hour. The entire lower level was filled with guests and staff from the manor and castle. Kraven's male employees had assumed their roles as security and had locked down the grounds following the morning's fireworks.

Fireworks resumed when the husbands burst in to find their wives. The volume of conversation became almost deafening as explanations abounded.

Thanks to Seamus' quick thinking, Darby and Contessa had been secured in the house while the dogs tended to the intruders. The man had been taken to his bed chamber and treated for his injuries. The gunshot wounds had provided the needed stimuli to rouse the dogs into action. The blood in the air had all but drawn them a map to the terrace.

Sadly, the intruder casualties had been small in number. It would take time to make a positive identification on the woman who had been killed in the mauling. Smoak was all but certain that it was Rain Su lying amidst the debris of torn clothing, hair and fur.

Caiphus and Sybilla; realizing the questions sure to be raised once local law enforcement was involved, set aside their differences. They made quick work of getting their own people to the scene to help keep up appearances. The guests and members of the DeBurgh family on hand for the lodge opening were comforted by the arrival of the official looking personnel.

***

"Look at this," Fernando grimaced when he pulled away the icepack Contessa held to her mouth. Gingerly, he brushed his thumb across the ugly cut on her lip.

"It's nothing," County wriggled back on the thick pillows crowding the headboard of their guestroom bed. "Every woman should have a honeymoon this exciting. Besides, that bitch couldn't hit worth a damn-ow!" She braced against the pain the words sent shooting through her jaw.

Fernando had to smile. His translucent stare narrowed as he focused on the path his thumb traced from her temple to her cheek. He set the ice pack in place and put her hand to it. Next, he was settling against the headboard and gathering her close, keeping her snug in his lap.

"There's only one remedy for this, you know?"

"Mmm?" County was already being lulled by his cologne and the depth of his voice.

"Strict bed rest."

"Really?" She sounded intrigued but looked a tad suspicions when she eased back to study at him. "Alone?"

"Well hell no, someone's gotta watch out and make sure you keep your butt in here."

"You're right," County snuggled back into place. "I need constant supervision."

"Agreed," Fernando murmured moments before he dropped the softest kiss to her bruised mouth.

County tingled from sensation but she wasn't totally numbed from the pain. "Ow." She said one more time.

"Are there anymore sociopath, psychotic wenches I need to be on the lookout for?" Darby asked while she and Kraven shared one of the cushioned lounges that dotted the terrace.

The DeBurghs had enjoyed a bit of alone time on the terrace that finally cleared of all the madness that had occurred there earlier. Quietly they observed the rolling greenery surrounding their home. The sound of conversation drifting in from the indoors had an unexpectedly soothing affect. Lounging close to where Kraven and Darby relaxed were some of the Belgian Shepherds. The dogs had earned their places as the newest residents of the DeBurgh estate.

"Psychotic wenches…" Kraven's hair lifted on the wind when he turned his face toward the breeze. "Let me think…there *is* my aunt Dehli. You've not as yet had the pleasure. Socio-psycho of the highest order."

Darby's laughter held a lazy element as she cuddled close to Kraven. She gave into the exhaustion brought on by the excitement of the morning and the contentment stirred by her husband's heart beating under her ear.

"I've told you the lot of it, Darby," he sounded serious then. "But if I find that there's any more to be told, I won't waste time bringing it to your doorstep."

"You better," she squeezed him tighter. "I'm pretty good with a pitchfork."

"I remember," he chuckled before they kissed languidly.

"Tell me," she ordered when they drew apart and she noticed his expression.

"What happened this morning was just the beginning. They have to be dealt with or they'll never stop."

Darby nodded and watched her fingertips brushing the pulse pounding strongly at his throat. "Does this mean you're leaving to help?"

"It means I'll do whatever I can so long as it doesn't require me to be away from you." He rested a hand to her tummy. "From you both. I'm afraid you're stuck with me too."

"I like the sound of that." She murmured into his neck.

"Know what I like the sound of?" He waited for her to look at him. "Hearing you say you love me."

Darby trailed her kiss to his jaw. "I love you."

"And I love you. Beyond always," he kissed her. "We're gonna be parents," he said against her mouth.

"Mmm..." Darby shivered in her happiness. "I hope this kid's ready for us."

Kisses resumed and were interrupted only by brief instances of laughter that warmed the crisp, misty air.

EPILOGUE

Seattle, Washington~ Two Weeks Later...

"You're sure?"

"I wish I wasn't but I checked five times just to be certain I hadn't tracked it wrong. The money's been funneling out of your uncle's accounts since before he was killed."

Quest reared back in the chair behind his desk and groaned before slamming down a fist. "Why the hell did I have to pick at this?"

Drake Reinard's laughter came through the phone line. "You always were a tad anal."

"Thanks," Quest managed only mild laughter before frustration reclaimed his mood. "How could that kind of money have been taken from Houston's accounts without him knowing?"

"That's the part I can't figure." Drake's smoothly accented voice held a strained tone. "Do you think maybe he *did* know about it?"

"Makes no sense," Quest tapped his fingers to his forehead and tried to comprehend what he'd just been told by his Chief Operating Officer. "He would've given her anything. He *did* give her anything."

"Well I'll have the report sent out to you tomorrow, alright?" Drake cleared his throat. "Q? What's your next move?"

"To talk to her husband and brother first, I guess. Maybe they can help me figure out what the hell to do."

"I'm sorry I had to bring this to you Quest."

"I asked you to remember?"

"Talk to you soon, man."

The connection broke and then Quest turned his chair to study the rainy scene from the windows behind the desk in his home office. His disquiet was interrupted by a quick knock and he saw Michaela rushing into the room.

The dark hue to his gaze cleared to be replaced by the natural gray haze of his stare. Seeing his wife sparked the left dimpled smile when she came around behind the desk and sat on the corner.

"Thank you," he murmured, sliding his hand beneath her thin robe to stroke one of her lush, bare thighs.

"Quest," she took his seeking hand and squeezed it. "The list. The list of names."

"Yeah," he nodded once. "It's around here somewhere."

"Did anything about it seem weird to you?"

Quest grinned and rested his head back on the leather swivel. "You mean besides my cousin's name being on it and somebody wanting him dead?"

Mick rolled her eyes and reached across the desk for a sticky pad. "It's Spanish, Quest." She grumbled.

"What's Spanish?" His query was absent. He was far more intrigued by the delights hidden beneath Michaela's robe.

"The name," she grabbed a pen. "It's his name."

Lines began to mar the flawless skin of Quest's brow. "Whose name?" Gradually, he was tuning into what she was saying.

Mick finished her furious scribbling on the pad and used the pen to point.

"Eston Perjas." She slid the pen downward. "The name is Spanish for Jasper Stone."

***

Dena sent a quick text to the florist who had requested that their appointment be pushed back an extra half hour. Dena had responded by requesting a *full* hour as she had not too long ago left the shower. She had yet to finish her hair or select an outfit for the meeting. The florist was happy to accommodate the change.

Dena admitted she was decidedly giddy about the meeting. Boredom had slowly, yet consistently been driving her insane. Taking over the planning of her aunt's wedding had given her the sense of purpose she'd been craving.

"And now the doorbell's ringing," she whispered, wondering if she should ask the florist to move the meeting to a different day altogether.

Dena hurried down the back staircase and was reaching the front door by the visitor's fourth insistent ring.

She flung open the door and reacted a split second too late to close it in Evangela Leer's face.

"Hello cousin," Evangela greeted with a cunning smile.

The last thing Dena remembered was feeling Maeva Leer's fist hitting her cheek before everything went black.

Dear Reader,

I truly hope you enjoyed this latest installment. Next to the Elder's book, this story was by far, the most complex to date. So many elements and characters were essential to the progression of the story. Your patience throughout the creative process was most appreciated although I realize that the wait was difficult for many of you. I do hope that this book was worth waiting for.

I also hope that you see some method to my madness. Kraven's and Darby's characters roused several questions back when the couple was first introduced. Many of you have been interested in what role they had to play amidst the Ramseys and Tesanos. You also wondered about the brevity of their initial story "Lover's Allure". I hope that you now understand my reasoning behind their whirlwind romance and Kraven's cryptic story of his ill-fated boyhood adventure.

I hope you were pleased by our beloved Fernando's recovery (told you I love him too). No way was I going to allow us to lose him.

The story of the island has been shared, but only in part. There is still much more to be revealed and everyone still has more of a role to play. The stage has been set and the characters are in motion. I hope you're prepared for where this leads. As always, I'm eager for your thoughts and reactions. I've said it before, but it's always worth repeating: Your support is the fuel that feeds my motivation.

Blessings and Thanks,
Love, AlTonya
altonya@lovealtonya.com

www.lovealtonya.com

ALTONYA'S TITLE LIST

Remember Love
Guarded Love
Finding Love Again
Love Scheme
Wild Ravens (Historical)
In The Midst of Passion
A Lover's Dream (Ramsey I)
A Lover's Pretense (Ramsey II)
Pride and Consequence
A Lover's Mask (Ramsey III)
A Lover's Regret (Ramsey IV)
A Lover's Worth (Ramsey V)
Soul's Desire (Ebook/Short Story)
Through It All (Ebook/Novella)
Rival's Desire
Hudson's Crossing
Passion's Furies (Historical)
A Lover's Beauty (Ramsey VI)
A Lover's Soul (Ramsey VII)
Lover's Allure (Ramsey Romance Novella)
A Ramsey Wedding (Novella)
Book of Scandal- The Ramsey Elders
Layers
Another Love
Expectation of Beauty (YA Romance)
Truth In Sensuality (Erotica)
Ruler of Perfection (Erotica)
Pleasure's Powerhouse (Erotica)
The Doctor's Private Visit
As Good As The First Time
Lover's Origin (Ramsey/Tesano Novella)
A Lover's Shame (Ramsey/Tesano I)
Every Chance I Get
What the Heart Wants
Private Melody
Pleasure After Hours
A Lover's Hate (Ramsey/Tesano II)
Texas Love Song
His Texas Touch

FIND ALTONYA ON THE WEB

www.lovealtonya.com
www.facebook.com/altonyaw
www.shelfari.com/novelgurl
www.goodreads.com
www.twitter.com/#!/ramseysgirl

An AlTonya Exclusive

16342145R00155

Made in the USA
Lexington, KY
18 July 2012